THE
CAPTIVE'S
CROWN

A story of inclusion, diversity and redemption

Eliana was a slave to prostitution—with no hope of deliverance.
Will her dreams remain impossible?

Olusola Sophia Anyanwu

ISBN: 978-1-91539-804-8 (paperback)

Other books by Olusola Sophia Anyanwu

1. Stories for Younger Generations

2. Stories from the Heart [published by Austin Macaulay]

3. The Confession

4. The Crown

5. Turning the Clock Hands backwards

6. Their Journey from Earth to Heaven

7. The Captive's Crown

8. The New Creatures [a sequel to The Captive's Crown]

9. The Robe

www.olusolasophiaanyanwuauthor.com

January 2019

Contents

Dedication

For the blessed memory of the woman in Luke 7:36-40; 47-48; 50 in the New Testament of the Bible—*Jesus anointed by a sinful woman:*

"A Pharisee invited Jesus to have dinner with him and Jesus went to his house and sat down to eat. In that town was a woman who lived a sinful life. She heard that Jesus was eating in the Pharisee's house, so she brought an alabaster jar full of perfume and stood behind Jesus at His feet crying and wetting his feet with her tears. Then she dried His feet with her hair, kissed them and poured the perfume on them. When the Pharisee saw this, he said to himself, "if this man were really a prophet, he would know who this woman is who is touching him; he would know what kind of sinful life she lives!"

47-48: "I tell you then, the great love she has shown proves that her many sins have been forgiven. But whoever has been forgiven little shows only a little love.' Then Jesus said to the woman, "Your sins are forgiven..."

50: "Your faith has saved you; go in peace."

MANTRA

Jesus did many other miraculous signs in the presence of his disciples *which are not recorded...'* (John 20:30)

Acknowledgements

I give the glory and honour to Abba God, the Father Almighty; the Lord Jesus Christ our Saviour, and the Holy Spirit, who is the Power of God, for translating me from the Kingdom of Darkness to the Kingdom of Light. I say a special THANK YOU to the Lord Jesus for loving me still, despite my imperfections.

A big THANKS to all true Saints of Christ: partners, friends, and ministering servants of God who work in His vineyard to demonstrate true love.

Introduction

Have you wondered about the woman who dried Jesus' feet with her hair as her tears fell fast in torrents? Here is her full story in fantasy!

Eliana unfolds the fantasied story of the prostitute who finds salvation at the feet of Jesus in a party—Luke 7:36-50 of the New Testament Bible. Here, she uses many names to hide her identity.

She is also Miriam, the beautiful and wealthy woman who has engaged in prostitution all her life. To different people, she is a mysterious woman with many personalities. Her few associates are outcasts like her. Miriam hides in the huge wealth she has amassed through years of prostitution and believes she has no family nor hope of ever being integrated into normal society or living a normal life outside prostitution. So, she dreams of another life in another world she thinks is utterly impossible.

Miriam has made many attempts to get herself out of this perilous lifestyle, which all failed. Through her efforts, she has created costly mistakes. Her trade as a prostitute helps her drown her sorrows and live a life of illusion. She believes she has no escape from her fears and insecurities, the reason she lives only for her business and does not believe in love. People she meets are viewed through her faulty lens of distrust, making her lack confidence in people. She has experienced betrayal, deception, and treachery.

Miriam uses a business strategy to personally engage with one of her clients—Jocheb Kazi—to grant him emotional therapy. She develops the idea that engaging with Jocheb might ignite her desire to find true love, peace, and security. Through him, she meets new associates who talk about Jesus, but she is terrified to step out of the world where she feels secure. Eventually, she experiences hope as she hears stories of an extraordinary man who embraces and welcomes every outcast. His name is JESUS! He believes in love, peace, restoration, and family.

What finally convinces Miriam to meet with the Lord Jesus and be so brazenly bold to do what she did to Him before a whole gathering of guests at a party?

Find out!

Preface

Eliana's life-changing story will appeal to anyone needing encouragement and hope. It also gives readers a glimpse into the three years ministry of our Lord Jesus Christ when He was on earth, two thousand years ago, from a fictional perspective.

Lord Jesus Christ brought deliverance, enlightenment, wholeness, joy, healing, salvation, peace, unity, love, and myriads of blessings to the lives of the people and everyone who crossed His path. Some came to know Him directly; others heard of Him and came to hear Him, while some individuals witnessed or benefitted from His miraculous deeds.

Everyone who met Jesus had their lives transformed for the best. Even after His death, He still affects people's lives for the best.

The story also reassures us that our faith in Abba through the Lord Jesus Christ will help us overcome our challenges and open new doors no human can close. Finally, it reaffirms that Abba is the same yesterday, today, and forevermore.

We get to see how good God is if we believe He can change our old sinful ways by transforming our minds. We see how He restores hope, faith, and love. We see how Abba heals the broken-hearted from diseases, sicknesses, and demons. We see what happens when people are delivered from the bondage of sin: He came to set the captives free from whatever chains held them in bondage.

In the story, we meet people like Miriam, who feel alone, forgotten, and betrayed. We also have people like Zara, Jocheb, and Razilla, who were all raised in unhealthy environments defined by the poor choices of their parents. However, we are encouraged by the change in their life stories that meeting the Lord Jesus is the way to Abba God, through whom He turns our circumstances around for the best.

Through this story, my purpose is to bring awareness of Abba God and make the Lord Jesus Christ famous to all generations and across all faiths because He is the way to Abba.

ENDORSEMENTS

This was well written. It is a great story of Jesus bringing salvation through the forgiveness of sins and spiritual rebirth to Eliana. Having received these gifts, her relationship with God is restored, and consequently, her relationships with others too are restored. She is now empowered to forgive her abusers and all who have hurt her. Great story! Well done, author Sophia!! – Dr Femi Adebayo. Brethren Fellowship Pastor.

Sophia Anyanwu takes readers on a rollercoaster of a journey into the life of Eliana.

She was rejected by her family and then initiated into a life of prostitution to survive, changing her name at the same time to Reubena, to cover her shame.

Still trying to keep up with Eliana's state of mind, she changes her name again from Reubena to Safirah, then to Dinah as she moves to Sidon to become a servant girl. Finally, she changed her name to Miriam!

But for how long will Eliana be able to hide her past and the person she really is?

What happens when her husband finds out the truth? Or doesn't he?

Is it possible for Eliana to be completely healed by God? Is there actually a God? Where was God when Eliana was going through such turmoil?

A complete turnaround! Is it possible?

So many questions needing so many answers...

Read on to see how Eliana's story ends.

Dr Lydia Taiwo

Published Author

2019 Finalist – The Wishing Shelf Book awards

PROLOGUE -
The Enemy Strikes

For He shall give His angels charge over you
(Psalm 91:11).

Asher heard the loud, hoarse, and screechy wailing of Rachel, his wife, as he tended to the sheep in the neighbouring fields. He was sure the whole of Ramah had gotten tired of it! Her incessant mourning and wailing for over three months, day and night, were getting to him in a bad way. He knew he could no longer put up with it. She was not the only mother that lost her children to the sword of Herod. She had a baby daughter, yet she refused to be comforted. Their daughter— Eliana-Mary, almost four months, was not doing well at all. Rachel could no longer feed and care for her. Their once charming, healthy child with an unusual beauty of hair crown had become gaunt, light, and hardly had the strength to cry…

'Shalom, Father Asher!'

Asher welcomed the glad intrusion on his thoughts. 'Shalom, Father Omri. I hope you remain well?'

'Thank you, and I am so sorry again for the loss of your two sons.' He saw the sorrow cloud his listener's face as a deep sigh escaped his throat.

'Abba knows best,' Asher said, shrugging his shoulders and watching Omri's eyes scan the fields.

'I know I was not affected because my four children are girls. Still, the sons of my brothers and kinsmen like you are mine as well. Hear my heart today, Asher. I have come to advise you. You cannot continue like this. Listen well.'

'I will listen well,' Asher said, as the laments of his wife reached him again like claws clutching at his already sore heart.

'I have seen how your wife has taken to the disastrous tragedy that befell our land of Judea. If you do not heed my advice, you will lose your own sanity, and eventually, your life.'

'What can I do? My parents are dead. Her parents are elderly, my siblings and her siblings are mourning as well. The worse is that her mind is gone because she has refused to be comforted! She does not recognise me or even know her own child!! What can I do?'

'Start your life over again. You are still young. First, find a way to get rid of a burden you no longer can carry because...'

'How?'

'Sell your assets. Take her to a bigger city for treatment, though I doubt she will recover. As for the baby, give her out. She hasn't a chance.'

Father Asher looked at his adviser. A seed had been planted in his heart. It would germinate, bear fruits, and through cross-pollination, blossom in Miriam's personality in Jerusalem twenty-seven years later...

FIRST YEAR:
Night

Chapter One

Better is the end of a thing than the beginning (Ecclesiastes 7:8).

Miriam hurried the man out of her bed to prepare for the next customer.

'You should go to your home now. I have let you have almost double the time you are entitled to,' she coaxed in a mildly irritated tone.

Josef was one of her regular customers. When she first met him two years ago, he was Jocheb. Ever since the beginning of this year, he had been telling her truths about himself. He was more regular and generous in his payments for his pleasures. Jocheb did not stir till she repeated herself. Then he protested.

'Why are you rushing me out? Don't I pay you generously?'

Immediately he said that, he regretted it. He didn't mean it that way. His fears were confirmed as Miriam had taken it the way he feared she would. A silent veil of melancholy clouded her eyes. Her tone subtly became harsh.

'So, you were paying for extra time and not giving from the appreciation of your heart?' she asked in a low tone.

Jocheb got up from the comfortable mattress filled with refined hay, only affordable by wealthy people, and hugged her. She didn't resist him, but he broke off anyway. He gave a stretch and unconsciously swept the luxurious room with a few glances. He was familiar with her silk, satin, and velvet choices for rugs, curtains, towels, and feminine wear. His senses soaked in the exotic fragrance, which never failed to excite and arouse his sexual emotions. She was evidently good in her business and prospering. He seemed to stall.

'If you can pay for more time, you would not need to go.'

'I am going to...Galilee to see and listen to the Prophet.'

'Oh yes, you went last month,' she suddenly piped up. 'The same Prophet you said does all sorts of wonderful things. Is this going to be your second time?'

'No. I have gone twice. There is always a huge crowd listening to the Prophet, and yet, no matter how far away I am from Him, I can distinctly hear and see Him.' He dressed as he spoke and saw that she was interested in what he was saying and not just for conversation's sake. She kept her head poised in the listening mode...waiting.

'I didn't understand what He said, but I experienced peace and something else I can't put into words. Also, I noticed He allowed people like Razilla to stay near Him. Zara, too, tells me a lot about Him. So, I really want to go again.'

He was fully draped in light striped cotton, with his sash tied across his belly like a belt. He saw she was watching him. She was still interested in what he was saying with rapt attention.

'Who is Razilla?'

'She was who introduced Zara to the Prophet. Zara has told me that Razilla used to be a whore on the outskirts of Jerusalem. I met her once when Zara needed helpers to pack stuff for her. We could go together to see the prophet next time if you like.'

He waited just a few seconds for her response, and when none was forthcoming, he saw that she just stood up to tidy up the bed. Next, she would attend to herself in readiness for the next customer. It was a ritual. He embraced her again and left. The queue for her bed was getting lengthier.

Chapter Two

The time has come to have mercy on her
(Psalm 102:13b).

The next customer came into Miriam's bed, and like a seasoned professional tycoon, she assessed her next customer expertly. She gave the appropriate actions that would suit his needs perfectly. So versed was she at this that she kept her heart and mind to herself while her body was at work.

She thought of Jocheb. He, like some others—her rich clients, was generous, but she sensed a difference. She enjoyed his talking to her because his response was not artificial. His embraces were meaningful. She knew her heart wanted to get involved, cross its business barriers, and flow out of its boundary to the emotional threshold, where it was forbidden. She had noted that he cared to talk to her conversationally and not chat shop. He was that kind of man everyone loathed, even worse than a leper. His trade was in secrecy. He attended to perverts at night. During the daytime, according to him, he mended shoes, bags, leather products, and other trivial odd jobs. She never questioned how such jobs gave him the luxurious lifestyle he indulged in. It was not her concern. He sought her attention once in a blue moon because he wanted to probably still feel human, as a man. She was conscious that she was aware of his neediness. Maybe one day, he might tell her his full story. The other month, he had asked her for her real name. She felt he had asked that in exchange for revealing his own name to her. Before waiting for her to supply her real name, he had asked her if she was happy. Even now, it still hurts. Tears stung in her eyes. A lump of pain forced its way down her throat. Her customer was looking at her as she groaned at the pain deep in her heart, which was bathed with feelings of sorrow, regret, shame, bitterness, humiliation, and defeat. It seemed relocating and changing her name had not really helped. That question he asked regarding her welfare had aroused the image of a beautiful newborn infant. It seemed what she thought was buried in fathoms of layers in the bottomless abyss of her heart was just surface deep. A simple question about her well-being from Jocheb had exposed her vulnerability.

This customer would go away, feeling that she was responding to the throes and heat of sex. His turn was over, and she got her reward. He was obviously impressed and had given a large tip on top of her flat rate. Kazim was a polygamist and belonged to the aristocratic class. She knew he was a gentile, probably a Roman because he was not as tanned as the Jews, but he wore his beard and hair long and was circumcised like the Jewish men. She could tell from the quality of his mantel that he was very wealthy.

Suddenly, it occurred to her that the calibre of men who visited her did so because of the very high pedestal she had placed herself. She had her own water stored in a cistern in her house and not just the courtyard cistern used by everyone else. Most importantly, unlike others in her trade, she had no inhibition and always went the extra mile to ensure the satisfaction of her customers. She made them feel it was not business. This alone attracted customers who paid in gold and silver. Her earthenware carrying oil lamps was silver plaited.

Chapter Three

The thief comes only to steal and kill and destroy; I have come that they may have life and have it to the full (John 10:10).

Her dwelling in Jerusalem had been deliberate. Jerusalem was both a political and commercial centre. Foreign traders from Sidon, Tyre, India and Arabia, even as far as Babylon, passed through Jerusalem. These were the men who had enriched her over the years. Her clothes and house were scented with spices from Arabia, and she wore on herself expensive perfume. She had jars of expensive and exquisite perfume; some were worth a year's wages, like the Nard. Also, she had invested in property in Jerusalem and beyond.

She was 27 that year, and she thought about her age and herself as she often did in her mind while her customers were occupied with her body. As she saw it, her body was a complex and complicated living organism. It was part of her and yet not really with her. Her only devotion to her body, she mused to herself, was to feed, adorn, and protect it. For this service, her body brought in wealthy customers like Kazim, Jocheb, Tobiah, Sheik Omar, and countless others. Tobiah had not come for a long while now. Her mind went to Jocheb again. If she ever wanted the chance to live a normal life again, Jocheb would be her gateway. That is, if he just wanted Miriam. Nobody would want to know or ever want to have Safirah or Reubena or Eliana. *Why did she go there?* She had spoiled her own mood. With the intoxicating drop from Kazim, she had ended her night business and was closed to all other customers. It was night-time, but not too late to be seen around. She could pay calls to her business associates who managed her estates for her. Or she could go and just gaze on her wealth in property acquisition. No. She wanted to pay Zara another visit. She didn't usually visit people except for commercial purposes. Even at that, it was very rare. People she had business and commercial links, even in other towns, came to see her here in Jerusalem. They were paid in cash or kind for overseeing the taverns, hotels, and flats she had acquired over the years in Judea.

She had a purpose for this visit to Zara. She just wanted to glean some information from her. In all their 12 years of acquaintanceship, this visit would be the second time. The first time had not been a bad idea, she thought. Zara had two places of abode: business and residential. She had visited the business home. It had looked bare, and then she had learnt that Zara had been transferring stuff from there to her residential abode and would eventually let out the business house situated near the Northern Gate. It occurred to her that Zara was very much business-minded like herself, as briefly reflected on her personal investment. She felt she had not done badly investment-wise in commercial property: five properties in Jerusalem and one in Sidon. *Sidon*...She sighed heavily. *Sidon*...the image of a newborn infant sprung up. She shook her head and subdued the bitter bile rising in her throat.

'I mustn't let the ghost of Dinah disturb me and ruin my evening,' she spoke out softly to herself. 'I must see Zara.'

She had realised that speaking out to herself like this often helped her fight the ghosts of Eliana, Reubena, Safirah, and Dinah. She so much longed to talk to someone about her past without fear and shame, but she lacked the courage, and therefore, remained desolate in her heart. The questions in her life remained unanswered: *why was she in Jerusalem doing what she was doing? Who and where were her family? Who was she? How could she change her life? How could she be rid of sexual addiction for good? How could she be rid of the ghosts? They* followed her everywhere when she moved destination. Hurriedly, she carried her money purse, always hidden in the pouch under her sarong. This she tied tightly to her body. Her long hair would cover up her entire body down to below her hips. Uncovering her head was the logo of her trade. As soon as her money became too much to be kept on her, she invested in commercial property, expensive perfumes, gold, costly and delicate pottery, and silk materials.

She suddenly realised that her thoughts were visiting Sidon. *Sidon…*She was inviting the ghosts. She stepped out quickly before they could prevent her from visiting Zara. She left her house by the back door. Her clients would then know that she was closed for business…

Chapter Four

I focus all my energies on this one thing; forgetting
what lies behind and reaching forward to what is
ahead (Philippians 3:13).

Jocheb was overwhelmed. He had lost the desire to please this customer completely. What had come over him?

'What is weighing on your mind and stealing your attention from me? I am not naive. You don't have to pretend and feign affection. I cannot feel the heat of your passion, Jocheb, and this is not the first time.'

Jocheb was silent before replying. He had listened in utter silence. He had not been taken by surprise. 'You are right. Something is weighing on my mind but not stealing my attention,' he confirmed after being silent for a while. How could he own up to Yosey, son of Ziha, that his sexuality was changing? *Had changed.* During the past two months, he had given up some time to follow the Prophet and his throng. He came away from each meeting feeling different. Yosey was staring him in the face and using his eyes to mock at his lack of an erection.

'Please, don't lie to me. I said I am not naive.'

Yosey looked at Jocheb closely. It would be his own loss to lose this strong, hard-bodied, tall, and energetic young man. *How old was he? 29? 30?* He couldn't tell. He had never asked. Biliah, the prostitute at East Gate, recommended him when he had complained about his former lover. And now this! Biliah herself was no longer available for such service. He could not afford to lose Jocheb.

'Jocheb, come. Please, I am pleading. Is it anything about me?'

Jocheb shook his head.

'I pay you well, don't I?' Jocheb nodded.

Yosey suddenly felt confident in his status. He was a respected elder of the Sadducees' Council. He had a comfortable home with a posh business as a building contractor. He had two offices attached to his home. The second was the room where he met clients like Jocheb behind locked doors.

He tried to resume intimacy, but Jocheb's passion was cold. Jocheb was an unwilling lover. This was how it had happened with Nebo, who said the Master was calling him to some other vocation. And that was it. He could not bear changing his lovers. It was difficult to find the right one that clicked. Nebo had been more eager, with the eagerness of a woman. Still, he preferred Jocheb. There was much stronger chemistry between them. He actually loved him.

'Can you honestly tell me what is weighing on your mind? Jocheb, can you tell me?' He felt desperate. His masculinity would not receive a second blow in the space of six months.

'Will you believe me, Yosey? I still love you.' He sat up on the bed, his back leaning on the carved wooden bedboard.

'Then how is it then that my touch is dead on your body and my advances do not arouse you? I don't understand. Jocheb, what is on your mind? You have not told me.'

Jocheb let out a deep sigh and held Yosey's left hand in both his palms. He gave it a firm squeeze and then released it. He looked down at him as he lay on his side and could not understand how he had developed a sudden lack of sexual interest. He now had an aversion towards this forty-or-so-year-old handsome fellow Jew. They had both experienced an amazing, intense relationship for five months running.

'Yosey, I first went to Galilee three months ago. Since then, each month, I have been going to Galilee. I was by Galilee Lake three weeks ago, and just last week, I was in Capernaum. Why am I telling you this?' he asked, not waiting for a response but continuing, 'gradually, my life has not been the same from listening to the Prophet.' His listener remained unmoving on the bed and passive.

As he spoke, he nodded his head slowly and severally and wore a grave look on his face. It was as if he could picture his experiences on an invisible screen in front of his eyes. He continued whilst Yosey listened in fear.

'Three weeks ago, by the Lake of Galilee, all of us who were there saw the Prophet bless a meal of five loaves of bread. I saw Him hold each one high above and pray over it. He did the same with the fish—just two. The lakeside was so quiet, and only His voice could be heard clearly. I heard Him as if He was speaking to just me alone. We were asked to sit down in groups of hundreds with the help of His disciples and some helpers. Soon, I felt this powerfully charged vibes of a silent echo in the atmosphere. It came from the crowds of thousands of people! At last, I saw. I would not have believed what I saw, too, until I heard what those closest to me said: *"The bread does not decrease but increases!"* We all saw the Prophet sharing each of those loaves and fish in several hundred pieces! Yet, this meal continued to multiply as He broke it, and it had gone round all of us in more than sufficient quantity!!'

He paused. He had seen Yosey raise his eyebrows, maybe in surprise or disbelief.

'Yosey, that experience was so life-changing for me. I ate the bread and did not feel hungry for three days after that!! Strange, I know!!' he said, seeing Yosey's mocking expression. Suddenly feeling bolder, he carried on.

'I had this strong desire to follow the Prophet and his followers after that. It was as if eating that bread bewitched me! If I were a man with normal inclinations, I would have had the courage to follow Him.' Jocheb did not want to voice out to Yosey that he felt unclean to be around people like the Prophet!

Chapter Five

*Jesus did not need man's testimony about man, for He
knew what was in a man (John 2:25).*

'What are you implying that you cannot say directly to me?'

'That bread I ate changed my system. Please, follow me next week on Wednesday. I go on a Wednesday if chanced. There is this woman who used to be a lady of red. Her name is Razilla. She always knows where the Prophet is. Will you come with me?'

'Does he always share bread?' he asked, not looking credulous but with disbelief.

'From what I heard, I think so. Sometimes too, He heals people of all manner of illnesses and diseases. Other times, He prays for the crowd or children and their mothers. Other times, too, He does what all other prophets do—talk.'

'I understand he heals and talks. But you said He prays for the crowd, women, and children? What do you mean? Is this praying different from how it is done in the synagogue from the Siddur, our prayer book?' He then changed from lying sideways and sat up with Jocheb on the bed.

'He blesses people.'

'What's his name?'

'You mean you have not heard about the Rabbi Jesus?' he questioned in utter disbelief. A moment's pause later, his listener just stared at him with something looking like pity in his eyes. Ignoring the hint, he continued, 'He is the Son of Joseph, from the line of David and the tribe of Judah. A Nazarene by birth.'

'You mean he is the brother of James, one of my masons? I know that family! Is he the son of that carpenter from Galilee?' he asked with a loud, demeaning tone.

'Shh. People might hear you.'

'Well, everyone knows! It may have happened about 30 years ago. Still, the rumour and stigma are still there. I heard it first from my father. His blood is tainted. *Your prophet* was not *sired by the carpenter he calls his father*,' he whispered mockingly, with his mouth close to Jocheb's right ear. 'He may not even be a Jew! Of course, I have heard of him!! What do you think we discuss at the market and city square these days? He is definitely not famous with the Pharisees, scribes, and teachers of the law.'

'How do you mean?'

'Are you not aware that he claims equality with God? Wait, I listened patiently to you. Your Prophet Jesus is also reputed to be a destroyer of the Law and Jewish traditions. He is introducing a new covenant different from Moses. The crowds who follow him are those who are curious like you or cynical, dispossessed, hungry, and physically needy.'

'I don't care. All I know is that Jesus is a Prophet, and He is not like any man I have ever known. He is a most extraordinary teacher who talks about the Kingdom of God...'

'Seeking recognition, status, or some position of authority in his new kingdom, Josef? Is that it?'

'I desire to know Him personally and understand His way of life from His perspective.'

'Is that the issue here, Jocheb?' he asked, feeling jealous. 'Perhaps you are consumed with...'

'No, you are very wrong! Not in that way.'

'Then why have you come here to taunt me?'

'Yosey, you know I loved you, at least from our past relationship. But now, I love you as a brother. I want you to meet the Prophet. I am sure the same thing will happen to you.'

'I am a true Pharisee. You should know better. No doctrine other than the one handed down to us by our forefathers should be accepted and practised.'

'Yes. But this man does not claim to change the laws and the prophets. He says He has come to fulfil them. To prove this, He does good to all people. Hundreds. To mention a few, do you know He is responsible for Zadok receiving his sight? Zadok is a member of the Sanhedrin. What about Aham? He is of Greek origin, but is he not a Pharisee like you? It is not just our own people. He raised Jairus' daughter, who is a Roman centurion, from the dead! I know you, too, have heard about Rabbi Jesus and all that He does in Judea, but you keep resisting. Look, I have decided I will no longer be under the yoke of Satan. I want to enjoy the freedom, liberty, and new life Abba offers me through Rabbi Jesus. Not only will you receive physical healing, but you will also receive spiritual healing. Come with me; I implore you to meet the Prophet. We can go together if you like. The devil will do everything he can to stop you from seeing the Prophet. It happened to me too. My sister spoke to me and urged me the way I am urging you now until I was persuaded to hear the Prophet speak.'

He saw Yosey shake his head, but he was not discouraged and continued, 'I went, and I was so mesmerised that I did not think of food or anything else but to hear Him speak and witness miracles first-hand as He healed all who came to Him. But then, the greatest miracle of all...I will never forget it as long as I live! He fed all those people up to 5,000 with bread and fish. That bread has changed me completely. I feel it physically and spiritually. Now, Yosey, I want to become one of His followers.'

'Jocheb, now that you have made your point, you are free to leave my house. But remember, my heart and door are always open to you. Return to me once you have satisfied your curiosity about this prophet.'

As Jocheb shrugged his shoulders and got up from Yosey's bed, his ex-lover made one last attempt to rekindle the embers of what they had shared in the past. Jocheb remained unflinching. Yosey saw he didn't weaken. Jocheb got up and dressed his nakedness.

'I may not have to go with you, but where do you go to meet this Jesus? You think he is a prophet?'

'It is easy to find him. There is always a crowd of people following him, like how bees swarm around honey. He is not resident in one place, but he will come to the synagogue in whichever town he is at on the Sabbath. Just ask at any of the city gates, and you will get the right information about His whereabouts.' Jocheb left.

After he had shut his door after Jocheb's departure, he swore he was going to spy on his activities. He should have done the same with Nebo, as he reasoned with regret. He, too, might have been using the prophet's story as an excuse. But yet, as he pondered deeply, he had seen the naked sincerity and conviction in Jocheb as he spoke passionately about what he had seen, heard, and felt. Everyone knew Zadok in Bethany. He was rich but blind and always depended on others to move around. He received his sight amongst many others who had always sat at the synagogue entrance!!! He knew he was no longer cynical about Jesus, but now merely curious. He would see things for himself...

SECOND YEAR:
Twilight

Chapter Six

*Consequently, **Faith** comes from hearing the message
and the message is heard through the word about
Christ (Romans 10:17).*

'Josef?'

Jocheb was so startled by that *name* that he coughed out food from his mouth and spluttered some apologies in utter embarrassment.

'What is wrong? Did you just see a ghost?' Miriam asked, totally stupefied and looking behind her at the same time. She had seen real naked fear in his eyes. She felt a sense of alarm and stopped eating.

'What is the matter? Please say something.'

She truly has no idea, he thought. He was not about to admit to her that it was the effect of hearing his real name which invoked the sudden memories of his past.

'Miriam. I was taken unawares when you called me *Josef* and not Jocheb. I did not think you would remember. It is a shocking revelation to me.'

'Shocking revelation? But why?'

'That you listen. You are perceptive, and I have underestimated you. I never thought you listened that day. Six months ago.'

'Do you then regret telling me your real name?'

'My real name? No! No, no,' then after a pause, 'I wanted you to know. But then, I remember you didn't tell me yours.'

He looked at her, and there was admiration and something else Miriam saw and read in his eyes. She recognised instantly that it was something that had become partly alien to her: meddling and merging the heart with the mind together. This she considered unprofessional. It was never real. Had she not tried involving her heart with her mind when she was Dinah?

'What makes you think I have another name?' she asked with a blank, icy stare.

'Okay, let us enjoy this meal together. You are a good cook.' He waited for the affirmation of his compliment. It did not come.

He is trying to side-track me, she thought. 'I called your name for a reason. How can I take your money for no services delivered? I feel like a cheat. I feel guilty, in fact.'

'But you have offered me this lovely meal and served me like a very special guest of worth! Miriam, what better hospitality can the likes of me expect? I, too, am very grateful.'

She decided on the spur-of-the-moment that she was not going to let him know that she would still have offered him hospitality without him paying for it. Instead, she was itching to ask him a question.

'Your listening to the Rabbi these past few months has indeed changed you! So, I have a question for you.'

Before she could expatiate, Jocheb was hasty. He was bursting to tell her about Jesus of Nazareth—The Prophet.

'Miriam, please feel free to ask me your question. I will enlighten you as much as I can.'

'Okay, but don't lose your appetite on my account. As soon as we are finished eating, I promise my rapt attention as you answer my question.'

He nodded as he put a forkful of vegetable lentils wrapped in wheat bread into his mouth. He had already eaten half of his red meat and locusts. He decided to relax and enjoy his meal. It had just dawned on him that Miriam would not be having any customers this night. This day, he was all hers; he would eat well and please her. So, he threw more locusts into his mouth and chewed it satisfactorily, savouring the taste. What a rare delicacy at this time of the year! She was remarkable. His heart grew fonder towards her as he gave it free rein.

Chapter Seven

God is able to do exceedingly more than all we ask or imagine, according to His power that is at work within us (Ephesians 3:20).

'Josef, what is your story?' Miriam lunged at him as soon as she saw that he had done justice to his food. Again, she knew her heart was prodding into forbidden territory. She persisted because such stolen moments like this made her feel human.

It was a test. To what extent had being with the Prophet influenced Josef? Would he lie or tell the truth? She wanted to know. She would be the best judge because she had spoken with Zara. Josef did not know the extent of intimacy between Zara and herself. As far as Josef thought, Zara was just a business associate and a knowledgeable woman who was good at directing clients to the right service…

Jocheb needed comfort, but he did not want to visit Yosey for that. Where could he go? He felt raw. Naked. Exposed. Why had he told her the truth about who he was and his past? At least he had been honest, and she had remained dishonest. She still refused to say her real name despite his disclosure. Maybe she would never, now that she knew about his real past, even though she had shown no surprise or asked questions. Thanks to Abba!! He had held his pain and did not break down before her. She now knew how he made his living. She had never known he was a prostitute. The difference was that she plied her trade openly while his was in secrecy. He thought of his previous four clients. There was a time he used to visit each of them in one week until he met the wealthy Yosey, who bought him off from his other clients. His memory took him back to the meeting when his relationship with Yosey had started.

It had been here in Jerusalem. There was a crowd of important people at the city square, arguing heatedly about something. It was the place to get news about what was happening in Jerusalem and elsewhere. He had moved towards the crowd. Other times they gossiped. They were mostly Jewish leaders of the various religious sects and those in political authority. He was not interested in politics or religion. However, he drew near to them out of curiosity. What were they arguing about so heatedly? But as soon as he drew nearer, he received the usual glance from fellow men perusing his unusual height. It happened all the time, even though they had seen him on a couple of occasions now and again. He returned the head nods in greeting by nodding his in return. He was two heads taller than the average man. Yosey's stare had been subtle. That was enough. He went towards him.

'Jocheb, son of Kazi. House of Dan.'

He stretched out his hand in greeting. Yosey would understand his smile.

'Yosey, son of Uriah. House of Naphtali,' he returned the greeting, stretching out his hand for the handshake.

In that handshake that looked like the normal brotherly clasp of palms, Yosey had used one of his fingers to tickle his palm. Later, they both moved to the sidelines away from the din.

'I see there is some heated talk. Is it from the quarters of the Romans, the scribes, or just some debate?'

'Just some debate about Prophet John. The Baptist. You know him, of course?'

'Yes. What about him?'

'Well, he has been calling out to the whole city to repent and come for baptism at the River Jordan.'

'Yes, I know. I heard,' he replied, giving Yosey a fond look that left no doubts where his sexual inclinations lay.

'Some of us did that yesterday, and he threw insults at us. A genuine prophet wouldn't do that. Some people think he was right to chide us, while others believe it is wrong not to give the leaders and elders their deserved respect. What do you think, Jocheb?' The tone had become gentler. It was hushed and almost intimate.

'I am not religious at all, but I would like to hear *your* opinion about the prophet. Then I could tell you what I think as well. Is that a fair deal?'

To anyone observing them, they could have been like any other pair, engaging in the latest gossip. Yosey gave his address and expected Jocheb later that night. Their love relationship had begun...

Chapter Eight

We refuse to wear masks and play games. We keep
everything out in the open; the whole truth is on
display (2 Corinthians 4:2).

Jocheb was convinced that he could not go to Yosey for comfort. He would not understand; he would rather go to Zara. She would understand, she always had. It made him remember how they had both become so close from years ago when he visited her at the inn she worked in Capernaum as a teenager.

'Jocheb Kaziiii, my little brother!! See how tall you have become! Did you come on your own?' Even now, she fondly called him by his first and last name, dragging the *zi* of their last name in a ring tone. He found himself crying without control as memories of the past flooded his thoughts.

He could still visualize clearly the shock he had seen registered on her face when her fears were confirmed.

'You mean Mama let a nine-year-old boy come all the way here on his own?'

'It is all right, don't be so mad. You just said I have grown so tall. Mama thinks everyone would think I am sixteen! She had given him a welcome embrace into her little room, where she invited men to her bed to pay for their pleasure.

'How is Mama?' she had asked.

'She is broke and sent me to get some money off you.'

'I guessed right. Three months ago, she sent someone to fetch money off me! She has never been here to see me since I came here about three years ago! She always sends people. Don't worry, my dear little brother. Mama, herself, will have to come here and fetch you because I will not send you back to her on your own...

She had kept true to her word. She was just fifteen then, and he never went back because Mama never came to fetch him or even check if he had arrived safely. Thinking about it all now as a man, he had changed his reasoning that Mama didn't just want money but wanted to get rid of him. Her priority was to enjoy the men who visited her without embarrassment or shame and take all the financial benefits alone. He would never look for his mother. He got to hear of the horrible betrayal done to Zara when she was only twelve. No normal mother would set up her own daughter for men to sleep with. He and Zara developed an intimate bond that became even closer as they moved from Capernaum to Jerusalem. Neither had heard from their mother and cared less. Hot tears brimmed up his eyes again, and he felt the taste of bitterness down his throat as he swallowed. Zara would understand; she would never let him down. She was always there for him. His sister was all he had in the world. If fate were kind to him, Miriam would be his, too. One day...

After all, it was she who had referred him to Miriam for his business dealings, but solely for her own profit and business. It was not too deep into dusk. There were a few people on the street, which was lit up with different sizes and stages of candles from the windows of the houses. There was also the musky scent of incense mixed with the Sabbath meal. The dry air whiffed about with the different kinds of stuff some evening traders had brought out to sell. Jocheb went through the street in a haze, as if in a daze. The Sabbath meal should have been over minutes ago. It took him 20 minutes to get to the side of Jerusalem by the East Gate, where Zara had her business house. Her neighbourhood was a cluster of low-roofed houses with yellow candle lights showing through doors and window frames. Her private residence was further away, and she was rarely there. Good, she was in. He knocked on her door. She opened it and gave a shout of surprise.

Chapter Nine

Can anyone by worrying add a single hour to his life?
(Matthew 6:27)

'Jocheb Kaziiiiiiiiii!! Come in! I am happy to see you.' He hardly noticed her beautiful face, which was beaming, and her evening gown that accentuated her curves and slimness.

He stooped low to get in. He did not want to bang his head on the door frame. The lantern glow exaggerated his 6-foot-seven-inches on the room's walls. Jocheb sat on the stool nearer to him as his sister peered closer at him. Something was wrong. She did not need to be a seer to see that he was troubled. His eyes were reddish from crying. She would let him unburden his mind. She had not seen him for over two months since she learnt about his miracle, but she secretly discovered from Miriam that he was doing well.

'Zara, how are you?'

'I am well. And you?'

He could not speak, so he shook his head instead. He willed the gloom away from his eyes as he looked around the room. There was lots of wool of different colours. She was knitting jumpers, scarves, shawls, shrouds and cardigans for men, women, and children.

'I wish I could cry, but I don't think I have any tears left.'

Zara got up from her high stool in front of a richly carved polished ebony wooden table with lots of spools and other materials and came to hug him, stroking his hair.

'Jocheb, I am here for you. I will listen. You know I will never judge you. I will understand. Whatever way I can help, I will help. I have bread and soup with lentils. Let me go and get you some.'

'I have no appetite. Not because my heart is burdened, but because I have just come from a feast at Miriam's end. Please, do not worry. Thank you, Zara.'

She nodded her head and waited. She would understand if it were just a bout of depression. She, too, used to suffer from it until she met her beloved friend and Master from Nazareth.

'Zara?'

'Hmm'

'If you want to help me, please tell me the truth.'

She hesitated for a second while adjusting her cotton shawl over her back.

'Okay. What do you want to know?'

'I know Miriam is an acquaintance of yours. Is this so, or are you two close? Like does she now know the true relationship between us?'

She hesitated again for half a second. The new life she was meant to live and commit to has no room for anything false.

'Yes, we are close. About you and me? Not as siblings, but as kinsmen.'

'Did you also tell her my secret?'

'Yes.'

'ZARA, WHY HAVE YOU BETRAYED ME?' He shouted at her and got up at the same time. 'I told you not to tell *anybody* at all.' He began pacing up and down the room. He looked shocked and suddenly paler in pallor.

'Jocheb, please sit down. Listen to me.' She saw that he meekly obeyed, but he already looked distant and uninterested.

Chapter Ten

He does what's best for those who fear Him—hears
them call out and saves them (Psalm 145:19)

'We come from the same family. I did not tell her about your past or the circumstances that led you to this city. I was just trying to match you up.'

'How was that to work?'

'You are both in the same trade.'

'So? Were you not the one who advised me to follow Prophet Jesus? Have we not been sharing the messages we hear and praising God for the testimonies and miracles we hear from people? Like you, I have stopped that kind of life, and you know. I was going to woo her eventually. Now, that will never happen because of what you have done.'

'Listen, Jocheb. You know Biliah was once married properly. Her husband had not touched her for two years because she hissed at him or something silly like that. He had, in fact, concluded the divorce proceedings. All that remained for them was to go to Rabbi Dodo to officialise it. Hezron, the meat seller, had been pestering for her hand in marriage. They agreed to get married as soon as she was informed that she was officially free. He asked her to come and see his house so that he could start furnishing it to her taste. She went, and as she was leaving, he embraced her. That was all she did.'

'That is as good as committing adultery, Zara! A married woman who goes into another man's house and is seen to be hugged publicly? You know better, Zara. That is adultery. Don't make excuses for our friend!'

'I know, but he had put her away for two years, Jocheb! She wanted Hezron in her heart. She said she had been consumed with lust for Hezron. Someone misconstrued the situation anyway and reported her to Perez, her husband. He and his friends accused her of adultery.'

'Why are you telling me all this?' he asked, wondering if she was trying to push Biliah back his way. He had once told her he felt no sexual gratification of any sort when he went to Biliah. He remembered it was just that once and nothing had happened sexually between them. Miriam remained the only woman he could have normal sexual relations with.

'So that you can understand why I told Miriam.'

'What did you actually tell Miriam?' he asked, ignoring the Biliah's story.

'Wait, I have almost finished my story. Biliah was about to be stoned to death for a crime she felt she didn't commit. Next, she was dragged to the next village where Prophet Jesus was. They wanted Him to condemn her to death because of the adultery accusation by her accusers and the crowd of people gathered there. That was when she met Prophet Jesus for the first time. He saved her life that day. This was during *Rosh Hashanah*, the beginning of the year. He told her to sin no more.'

She was quiet, and he had to ask her what that meant.

'Zara, you have just told me that Biliah did not do it with Hezron. So then, what did the Prophet mean?'

'Jocheb, do you remember Ana?'

'Biliah's bondwoman servant, isn't she? What about her?' *Where was all this leading to? Guilt.*

'Perez never knew that his wife, Biliah, had turned to Ana for affection and love. This was what the Prophet was referring to. She got the understanding of that knowledge when she looked into His eyes. Since then, she has followed Him. She came and told me everything and eventually led me to the Prophet. I have learnt not to bear false witness, to tell the truth at all times and live the life the Prophet advises. That was why I asked you to meet the Prophet.'

'How does *all* this connect me with Miriam?'

'You used to be so fond of Biliah before your sexuality changed. So, would you like Biliah less for what I just disclosed to you about Ana and her?'

'I am heartbroken at what you have revealed to Miriam, but no, I don't like Biliah less. I don't and never intend to marry her. So, I don't care less!'

'Then good. Because Miriam once asked me not too long ago if I was the person who recommended you as a client to her. I couldn't lie and admit that it was me. Then, I simply told her you were also in the same trade with your own sex. So, she has always known and does not judge you as well, Jocheb.'

'You really did?'

She nodded her head. 'She does not reject you, Jocheb. That means something.'

'Why should she? It is purely business, and I pay her well,' he sounded defeated. *Why had his own sister done this to him?*

'She wanted to know about my parentage and family, but I swayed our conversation from that direction. So, what is troubling you?'

'She asked me for my life story, and I told her. Now she knows who I really am and why I came to Jerusalem and why I do what I do.'

Chapter Eleven

*Will they find delight in the Almighty? Will they call on
God at all times? (Job 27:10)*

'So, why are you upset seeing you have already revealed more
of yourself to her than I did? More importantly, you are in the same
trade, and she likes you.'

'And wait, we are not in the same trade! She does not do
business with her own sex! And when did she tell you she likes
me?' he asked, not believing his sister.

'She implied it when she was here a month and a half ago. She
said you were different and that you and she could become friends.
She made this positive comment after I had told her about your
trade.'

'What perplexes me is that when I asked her to tell me her own
story, she said she had no story because her family all died in a fire
accident! Just like that. Even about the fire accident, she was not
willing to say anything about that.'

'Jocheb, be patient. You and I have met the Prophet. She has
not. She told me too that she was an orphan with no family, as they
all died in a fire accident. That is all lies. We are friends, but I did

not press her to elaborate or confide in me. Meanwhile, believe her own story.'

'Her story might be true, Zara. When she meets the Prophet, she will want people with a clean history.'

'You can befriend Razi. She lives the new life like us, and she will never condemn your past. She is a good woman, a year or maybe two years younger than Miriam. Both of you will be fine. What do you say to that?'

'She doesn't even attract me in any way. I hardly know her. I want to marry because I love.' After a pause, 'Zara, you should not have told Miriam before I did. Look at Hezron. He did not want to be associated with a woman like Biliah, whom the whole of Jerusalem sees as an adulterer.'

'Biliah doesn't care!' She raised her voice a little. 'She no longer lusts for him or Ana.'

'Well, Zara, you should not have betrayed my confidence and trust in you. You should not have told Miriam about my trade before I did.'

'I could not lie. I want to be far away from anything false. I am so sorry. Please, Jocheb, forgive me. I did it with good intentions. Please, try to understand. If you get more involved with Prophet Jesus, you will understand me better. Please. What are you going to do now that you have left that trade?'

'I might invest in tomb building or well-digging or timber transport, or I might decide to go into commercial trading and become a merchant. I have money now. I am no longer afraid to venture out like before. So, I guess I have to be going home now.'

'Wait, Jocheb! You have not told me how Miriam took your story.'

'She was not shocked or surprised. Then I knew she had known. I realised both of you were more than mere acquaintances. Also, I could sense by her refusal to let me into her own story as her own way to show that she disapproves of me.'

'Please, Jocheb; you are wrong. Nothing ever shocks or surprises Miriam. Give her time. Her own story might be worse than ours. Did you tell her *everything?*'

'Yes, I did. Zara, I like her too. I thought she would like me more for being open. I was being transparent and honest. I think it was a mistake to open up so soon. So, I will keep away from her until she tells me about herself.'

Chapter Twelve

Yes, I have loved you with an everlasting love;
therefore with kindness, I have drawn you
(Jeremiah 31:3).

Jocheb could see that Zara was so shocked. It showed in her beautiful eyes. She was just six years older than him in his 28 years old body, but she looked like an 18-year-old girl. Maybe it was also because she had not had a single baby. Jocheb was sure that was why Perez wanted to do away with Biliah, too. He kept this to himself for now.

'You mean she now knows that we are children of a fallen woman from different fathers, and your father died of leprosy?' She was shocked.

'Yes.'

'Then you cannot keep away. There should be no condition. She still accepts you, and you too should still accept her and wait patiently for the light of the Prophet to get her out of the darkness. Please, Jocheb!'

'I like your advice. I will give her time. I hope she meets the Prophet. Why don't you take her there?'

'I have tried. I have been more than surprised over her last two visits. She never used to visit. Jocheb, Miriam is melting. She listens to the testimonies, miracles, and ways of the new life I tell her. For now, she is just happy to listen to me about Prophet Jesus, but she is scared to meet Him or go near where He is.'

'Why?'

'She now knows that the Prophet can see through people. You know what I mean?'

'No.'

Everyone knows He can discern facts and other information about a person accurately without being told.'

Her brother shrugged. 'Ah, Zara. I have to go now. I will come back sometime to hear more about the Prophet. You must have learned a lot. I can see the effects of your being around His presence already. Thank you so much for introducing me to Him.'

'Jocheb, do you still think of our mother and others?'

'They are dead to me!' He parted with that after her hugging him. 'Don't stay away too long,' she had said as a repartee.

Zara thought of Jocheb immediately after he had left. He said he would try a different trade. How many times had he tried then his body would hunger for sex of his kind and could do nothing else? He was looking for a way out of his evil life. As soon as she mentioned the Prophet, he had quickly hearkened, following the Prophet at his chanced opportunity. He ate the Prophet's bread, and the seed of his transformation had been sown in him. He had felt purged and cleansed by that contact through the Prophet's holy hands and blessed bread. His faith in the Prophet had obviously healed him. It had happened to Nebo, Tobiah, and Biliah! She never ceased to marvel when she contemplated the manner of Jocheb's deliverance from male prostitution. It was a miracle, as it was for Biliah, Tobias, Nebo, and herself!

Chapter Thirteen

Satisfy us in the morning that we may rejoice all our
days (Psalm 90:14)

His confession had begun a train of thoughts in her mind. She felt so guilty, like a traitor. Her using Biliah's story to cover up! *Had she really betrayed him? Had she ruined his chances of experiencing true love? Should she have let the budding relationship between Miriam and Jocheb blossom naturally?*

'What have I done to Jocheb?' she whispered aloud, with pain etched in her heart. She was close to tears. She would ask her new mother if she had wronged her brother. Then she remembered she had confided in Mother Mary, the mother of the Prophet. She had hoped for her sympathy and understanding the reason for her old way of life: having a debased and fallen woman as a mother. But she had been disappointed. She recalled her conversation with Mother Mary:

'I was just twelve when Mama sent me to collect something from her lover. I left home as a virgin: a girl with bright hopes for the future; a girl with dreams of getting married to a decent man one day and settling down to the life of a good wife and mother; a girl with pure thoughts who shunned her mother's promiscuous life. Mother Mary, my drink was spiked the evening I got to my father's house. She said he was my father but had another family he lived with, so he could only visit and not live permanently with us. Well, you won't believe it, I did not meet any family. I really don't know the truth. Rather, I saw two men he said were his brothers passing through the town. His family were away to visit the wife's relations in Galilee. After he welcomed me with a drink and a good supper, I remember feeling this deep drowsiness. I remember him undressing me and doing things a father should never do to his daughter. Those brothers of his took me in turns, and I was helpless, broken—damaged inside and outside...'

When she had begun to cry, Mother Mary had responded in a way she never expected after patiently listening to her woes without once interrupting or even displaying any reaction. Even moving away from the Aramaic dialect to the Jerusalem one had offended her ears.

'It is all right now, Zara. Do not soak yourself in the past. That is just dangerous and not helpful to you. It will only embrace you with guilt, regret, and bitterness. The worst is self-pity. You do not belong there anymore. You have moved on from your past. You have the future before you. Always look ahead. Now that you have seen the Light of Jesus, you should extend it to your family members who are in still the dark. You will have to forgive your parents so that they can see the light of Jesus through you...'

Chapter Fourteen

*For I will be merciful to their unrighteousness, and
their sins and their lawless deeds, I will remember no
more (Hebrews 8:12).*

Then, she was very much a new follower of the Prophet the
way Jocheb was now. She had not understood a lot of the
Prophet's teachings, especially the concept of forgiveness,
but she realised His teachings were nuggets of wisdom that were
lodged deep down in her heart...

With her company of fellow women who all tended to the
Prophet and his disciples, Mother Mary was always happy to make
her understand what the Prophet had taught about the new way of
living life. Mother Mary told her that the Prophet said people were
not perfect, but if they dealt honestly with their issues of pride,
anger, unforgiveness, and sinful addictions, then Abba would help
them. She had advised that it was better not to hide behind a mask:
hiding and covering things one struggled with in the heart would
not help. *This is what Jocheb had done with Miriam.*

She recalled Mother Mary had told her the story of the
Prodigal Son—a squanderer of his father's wealth and a wayward
lad. Though the irresponsible lad had repented, he received his
father's pardon! The father forgave his son! Mother Mary had

explained it as the Prophet had. Zara knew that she had taken off the mask of shame so that God could move her into her destiny. She was no longer living in guilt about her past. This was what she wanted for Jocheb. He was meant to use his past as a testimony to lead people towards the light of the Lord Jesus. She made it her resolve to take Jocheb and Miriam to meet Prophet Jesus and his followers. What made her draw back now, as she told herself, in her mind was that she had been advised to go and make peace with her family at Nazareth! Peace!!!! Had the Prophet's mother really listened about her family? She didn't want to disobey, but she didn't want to do that now. She realised that this had become an obstacle that was preventing her from visiting Mother Mary, whom she regarded as her new mother. She determined in her heart to go first with Jocheb to meet Mother Mary. Could they both return home to make peace with their mother and her evil father? She shook her head and sighed. She felt it was impossible. She had an impossible box labelled *my impossible dreams* in her head, and this idea of forgiving her mother was thrown into that box. She reasoned it was unlikely. To Jocheb, their mother was dead. And to her? She was in denial.

She got up to tidy up the table. Jocheb had not eaten. He said he had just come from a feast. She had not queried that because she forgot to. His depression had momentarily distracted her. She questioned her motive. Why did she tell of her brother's secret? Was she gossiping? She knew it was not a case of her trying to diminish her brother's reputation. She may have been motivated by a desire to draw out Miriam's own story from her mouth. But that had not happened. Miriam was so beautiful. She had truly wanted her brother to be close to Miriam and eventually take her as his wife. She now saw people through the eyes of Jesus. She did not look down on Miriam. She truly believed that in time, Miriam would turn around.

Miriam's unique beauty was the source of her great wealth. She did not need to be told that. She knew Miriam had a story. Close as it seemed they were to each other, there was a barrier in their relationship. They were not jealous of each other or vying for competition as some business rivals would have done. They instinctively knew that they had been drawn to prostitution by their circumstances, which they had no control. It was not the age difference. *What was Miriam's story?* Was it similar to hers or worse? Zara thought of her own mother then, when 20 years ago, at the age of twelve, she had been sent on an errand that had changed the course of her life. It was a thought that kept reoccurring now and again, as if to explain why she found it beyond herself to forgive her mother—*she was totally evil.*

Chapter Fifteen

*But let justice flow like a river and let goodness flow
like a never-ending stream (Amos 5:24).*

'Johana?'

'Mama? Please, let me finish bathing Josef,' she had offered. The request had been turned down. Josef had tried to protest. They were both afraid of their mother. Their mother had come to where she was bathing her brother and hit him on the head several times. He yelled in pain.

'If you knew how to take care of yourself, would lice be crawling all over your head and hair? And all these rashes?' she hissed. 'Johana, you take the dates in the basket to Ram's house. He will put something in the basket for me.'

She remembered being downcast. Why had she not sent her during the day when she had finished the house chores of baking, shopping, and running other errands? Now she was a bit tired.

'Can I go with Josef? We could go together after his bath. It is just dates.'

'Can you not do as you are told, child!? It is urgent. Go now and don't return till he pays up for them! They come all the way from Egypt. Hurry now and make sure you are back before dusk. If it is too late, you can return in the morning. I need the money, and Ram will not be this way for the next six weeks.'

Johana knew she was scared when she went out without Josef, her six-year-old little brother. He was only six but could pass for a twelve-year-old because of his height. Josef had a way of punishing people who called them names or taunted them because they were children of a fallen woman.

'Please, Mama. Let Josef come.'

'No! Go now, before I get angry.'

Her mother's anger was terrible, more terrible than her own fear of going without Josef, and she hastily obeyed. She went to the man she had been told was her father—a man who lived with his own family.

Was it not this her 'father', who encouraged her when she was still a twelve-year-old virgin to give herself to a man from Tyre so that her family could live a better life? Did Queen Esther not do the same for her family, her 'father' had argued? Had she been wrong to obey this man who visited her mother's bed often and had sired her? What had been his motive then? That action with that man from Tyre and two others had made her a fallen woman. The Tyre man had recommended his two friends to visit his 'house' in the three days that followed, and they had her in turns. She felt despicable. When she returned home, her mother had not asked questions and was just interested in the basket that contained the money and gifts!

She had fallen into a deep depression. Since then, she had vowed never to be like her mother. She had harboured dreams of being a decent, virtuous maiden and married properly to whomever God would send her way, irrespective of her background. She had the hope because she knew she was gorgeous. Her 'father' came and advised her to change her name, leave Nazareth, and live elsewhere. Her mother had fought with her lover to desist from what he advised. Her mother had been so pained, shocked, and utterly disappointed that she, Johana, dared take her lover's advice against hers. She went to Capernaum because she was furious with Mama. She got employed in a tavern for prostitutes. Her mother's lover came after her there and continued with her what he had made her start with other men. How could she ever see him as a father or forgive him for what he had led her to do? Or her own mother? She shook her head. Surely, Mother Mary could not imagine what she had gone through at the age of twelve! *Forgive my mother indeed!!*

She had been lonely, frightened, and unsure then. Ram continued to take advantage of her. He had even encouraged her that her beauty would attract kings. She was not to return to Nazareth, but he and Mama would visit her. Mama never did because she was ashamed of her, but Ram, her lover, came like a thief at night, not wanting to be seen—not wanting to be associated with what she did. Yet, he was happy to take and share from her profits. At first, she was very proud that she was helping her family for the first three years, from age twelve to fifteen. She could pay her rent, take care of herself, and still help with whatever amount they demanded from her. It was not much after that, but she could manage. By sixteen, she became bitter, angry, disappointed, and hateful towards her family. Mama had sent her little brother, Josef, to come and live with her while continuing her sinful life! Her own mother had known all along what her lover was planning to do when she sent her twelve-year-old daughter to him—to get initiated. Then, when she was 19, she met Miriam. She cast her mind back to what had led to their meeting then.

She remembered the occasion when an Egyptian customer had come into her bed. He did something strange. Rather than hastily getting away when they were finished, he opened up a conversation with her!

'What is your name?' he had asked.

'Zara,' she lied.

'Well, Zara, I will advise you to go and visit Miriam in Jerusalem. Her house is called 'Miriam's House of Pleasures' by the Northern Gates. You can't miss it. She is younger, but she will teach you the tricks of this trade.'

She remembered how ashamed and utterly mortified she had felt. She was being compared to another prostitute and told to learn the trade properly!! She had developed a complex instantly and could not continue with any client until she had gone to meet this younger woman. She had gone the very next day. At least, she would have a 'friend'. That same year, she and her brother moved to Jerusalem. Jocheb had just turned 13. He was so tall that he looked over twenty in size and looks. His unusual height had been his undoing. It had attracted his first pervert, and he never looked at any woman except for Miriam. *I hope I have not destroyed his chances of settling down with a woman...*

Chapter Sixteen

*We give thanks for Your Name is near; men tell of
your wonderful deeds (Psalm 75:1).*

A client was busy with Miriam's body. He was not a stranger. He had once said his name was Kazim and that he had four wives. She had wondered that first time. If this was the truth, there were men like him who kept many wives or women who could not satisfy them and had to look outside for their pleasure. That was not her business. She confidently shifted the business to her body while her heart and mind resorted to a faraway place of safety. Her body would take care of Kazim. It knew what he wanted to hear. It knew what he wanted to have, which none of his wives could ever give. Her body was no novice ever since she had been a seven-year-old slave in the house of Jibril. She realised she was moaning and gasping in pain. Ouch!! Her heart and mind had not left!! She willed them to leave instantly, and she was successful.

Her mind and heart took her to the conversation between herself and Josef about twelve months ago.

'Miriam, I like you. This keeps me coming, not necessarily for your body but for you.'

Miriam was used to shop talk from her clients. They usually felt they should say something. For some others, it was their starters to make the ease of access into her body easier.

'Thank you.'

'Is that all you are going to say?'

'Yes.'

'Do you like me?'

'I appreciate your tips. You are my client.'

'Do you like me then? Surely, all your customers are not the same to you!'

She considered this. Yes, all her clients could not be jacketed together as *the same:* some were generous; some saw her as a business; some as a pleasure outlet and others came to vent their wounded pride, ego, or some other raw emotions on her body. There were some others too: the wild animals; the shy virgins looking to be initiated; the desperately lonely—not wanting her body, but her soul, her heart.

Within seconds, as she ran this through her mind, she tried to place Kazim, who was on top of her. Where did he belong? Lonely, yes. An animal, sometimes, but mostly to satisfy a raw pain she had discerned down in his soul. He was an ordinary man, and she had not taken any time to particularly note any worthy traits in him to classify him as appealing, handsome, or kind. Her heart was forbidden to cross that barrier. Her brain was so intelligent. It remembered names. It had never confused one for the other. No matter the disguises her clients put, her body never forgot another body once it had been associated with her for business. No matter the length of time, even if it were as long as five years or more, her body would throw out the name to her brain in the course of the business deal. So many of her clients had been enthralled. In the past, they had gone for cheaper services to Razilla, Zara, Biliah and others, but always returned to her. Many of her clients would address her in their wives' names in the process of business. Her brain picked it all up.

She knew Kazim's needs, and she pitied him. Her body was receiving a new level of osculation from Kazim: deliberate with intentional desires and longing. Her body had recorded that Jocheb had started this new level of sexual intimacy that Kazim was doing now. Where did she place people like Jocheb or Josef as he renamed himself? Many of her clients spoke out their real names as they saw their goal and triumph in sight during the business deal. Some others gave themselves appellations such as **Champion! Winner! Hero! Handsome! Wonderful! King!** The list was endless. She had noted that whatever the client called himself did not necessarily tag with him. That was not her body's concern.

Her body was capable of any task demanded of it, and it complied excellently with the client's needs. Her body was a slave. 'Command and Obey' was its business logo. Kazim was finished. He had been satisfied with her body. Her mind and heart were not yet through with their thoughts of assessing her different clients and their needs. She liked to entertain these thoughts. These kinds of thoughts did not invoke the ghosts of her past, but more importantly, she slept well with these thoughts deposited in her mind—*thoughts of Jocheb.*

Chapter Seventeen

For I know the thoughts that I think toward you,
sayeth Jehovah, thoughts of peace, and not of evil to
give you hope in your latter end (Jeremiah 29:11).

Mechanically going through the motions of business, she prepared for the next customer. He came. He was in his mid-seventies. She considered herself a physician. She recognised the age of clients through their private organs. Over the course of 22 years in her trade, she must have seen over a hundred types. Now, her expert body knew the exact age of a client through the look and need of their private bodies. For this customer, it had been a long, long while. Still, her body remembered him in the past. Then, he had wanted his organ massaged for several minutes. He had expected an instant miracle. He had treated her like a fancy toy he was delighted with, turning it around in his hands as he surveyed it from different angles. He had given childlike curiosity and wonder to every aspect of her body and eventually cried like a little boy.

This time around, her body tried a new technique for him. His wrinkled organ with aged skin and frail body had received genuine fascination, attention, and sexual love. He became confident and gave all the bottled-up commands he had in his huge sack of imagination. His member rose and gave a salute, and her body obeyed all the dictates of his command. He had muttered incoherently, *Thank you, Abba. Jacob is still able!!'* He wasn't wealthy at all. Who knew how he had managed his payment? It had not been her body's concern then. She also repeated the same treatment she gave him ten years ago, but she called his name this time. Her client achieved an amazing performance. Neither did he question the name she had named him.

Then her body broke its business protocol. She spoke. She initiated a passionate conversation with the client. It was not the shop-talk kind that she usually gave or responded to.

'Jacob, have you heard of Prophet Jesus?'

Her client became even more elated and relaxed.

'Yes! He is in Gadara. I hear he is good to all and has mercy on everyone. But most importantly, I hear that listening to him gives one strength, hope, and a renewed life. So, I wish to visit and listen to him soon.'

'Me too. I also hear he has divine powers to make people live godly lives. I want to eat his bread.'

'Which bread? Is he also a baker?'

'I don't know. Someone told me he miraculously fed a whole gathering of 5,000 people in the desert with bread and fish! Unbelievable, but it actually happened!! This person said that he did not think of food for three days as he followed him about before the miracle. He was not even hungry, even for days after eating that bread!! But best of all, this person was cured instantly of his sexual immorality.'

'Do you want to stop sinning in that way too?'

'Yes, but I can't stop my body hungering for it.'

'I was surprised to see that you are still in this business. I have never forgotten you. Really Miriam, if you truly want to stop sinning, just move away to another town, change your name, and start a different line of business. Nothing is stopping you. I see you are now very wealthy.'

'I have tried that more than three times. Doing all that did not give me joy, peace, or victory over my body. It is as if my happiness is dependent on the satisfaction and happiness I give to my clients. Their happiness is my happiness as well. This is why I give my best and all in what I do to please them. It kind of temporarily relieves me of my pain.'

'Then why have you not gone to Prophet Jesus to get some of that bread? You, too, will be cured of sexual immorality. I will go to Him soon; I am so lonely. I have spent all my life in abject poverty and misery. I have no family. I just want peace of mind and to be loved. I was happy with you just now, but it is short-lived. You don't know how hard I have saved and dreamt of being here, just to have that fleeting moment of happiness and love. As soon as I step out of your door, all that joy I achieved will dissipate and be lost. I cannot afford to pay for this kind of love as often as I want to. The pleasure is short-lived...'

The client continued to talk about his life and past, and she was none the worse for it. She instantly realised that her heart had not been involved. It was just a clever business strategy: being sensitive enough to know which of her clients wanted to talk for a while after business. She had to initiate passionate conversations. These types of clients regained their self-respect or energy, or the will to endure life. Perhaps something akin to friendship? She was not sure what it was. This gentleman, Jacob, had positively looked happier and at peace. She had accepted a tenth of the payment because of her from their business transaction. It was a way of encouraging him to come again. At least, he could come nine more times to feel happy and loved. They could talk like 'family' as they had done this night.

Zara had said being with Prophet Jesus made one aspire to be like Him and live His lifestyle. Razilla had confirmed this a few months ago. She had said the Prophet was 'gracious and full of compassion' in doing His wonderful works. She had felt good doing what she did to Jacob. They had tried to help each other, just like family. It was a lovely feeling, and she didn't feel so alone in the world.

Chapter Eighteen

*Surely then, you will delight yourself in the Almighty
and will lift up your face towards God (Job 22:26).*

Another client came, and she was reminded of Jocheb again. Clients like this one were enthralled and taken in by her natural beauty, like Jocheb. This one probably found her very different from others in her trade. She did not need to bother herself with artificial beautifiers. Kazim and a few others liked her to makeup, which she did for their sakes. Not this one. This one wanted her to pose nude. Her body knew his needs immediately. He would watch her dance or just get lost gazing at her as she gave different gymnastic moves. He would give some commands, and when he had reached the bursting point, he would next imagine he was a horse rider as he held her ankle-length hair and sat saddled on her back. Next, he would be transformed into a gardener, spraying water from his water can over the leaves, stem, flowers, and branches as if on a favourite plant in his imaginary garden.

She knew him. He never used his organ in proper coitus with her. They had never spoken to each other using words. She decided to have a little 'fun' with him: break his purpose and make him cross his own barrier; make him eat his own words and make him embrace his taboo. These types made mad haste as soon as their lust was pent up and released. They behaved like they had been possessed and woke up from an awful dream. All the guilt of their sin and crime spelt boldly in capital letters on their faces as they averted their eyes downwards. She read it all without a shock: ADULTERY, PERVERT, UNFAITHFULNESS, PRIDE, WICKEDNESS, REVENGE, HATRED, LUST, JEALOUSY, WANTONNESS, BISEXUALITY, INDULGENCE, PROMISCUITY, FORNICATION, IDOLATRY, HOMOSEXUALITY, POLLUTION, AVARICE...

The client was busy watching her lathing herself up in the mess he had made on her. It was exciting for him; he was a pervert. Her body had not been wrong in the assessment. She took her long, thick, glossy hair to towel herself and wrapped herself deliberately with it in a provoking way to tease his senses. Something in that gesture must have reminded him of something about someone. Maybe his wife. He instantly came to her crying and began the true motions of sexual love, murmuring and mixing up the names. 'Miriam, *I love you. I love you so much...Elizabeth, I really do love you!*' That was not her body's concern that he also knew her name. The whole of Judea knew. Her house was labelled, 'Miriam's House of Pleasures.' He was just a client. She thought about Jocheb again as her body did its work.

Had she been wrong with Jocheb? As soon as he told his little story, he looked pained, insecure, guilty, and something else she could not pinpoint. He didn't have to tell her his life story. He didn't have to say anything. Why did he do it? She had thought he was like the Jacob type, needing to unwind and unburden something in his chest. She was only trying to help him with his need. She had always assumed that she was aware of his need. Well, one could not have 100 percent success in business all the time. She had always had 100 percent, but this time, she had failed

Jocheb. How had that happened? It might have something to do with him meeting the Prophet. He did not want her sexually anymore. They had supper, and she wanted him to talk and be rid of whatever ghosts were bothering him. He got the opposite result. She was beginning to understand that meeting the Prophet meant being open. No secrets. Bringing out your past to the open? How did one achieve that without pain? See what happened to Jocheb!! No. She was not the cause of the pain she had discerned in him. Zara, too, had opened up to the Prophet's mother. Since then, she was aware that Zara avoided meeting her new mother.

What had Jocheb said as he poured out his heart? That was the never done thing in this trade. He, of all people, should know that. He had not lied. She had confirmed this from all that Zara had told her a while ago when she had visited Zara. She knew that nothing on earth would make her reveal her past personality to anyone living. Maybe if the Prophet asked her, but would she ever go? She wanted to meet the Prophet very much on one hand, but on the other hand, there were doubts. She had four lives. She had begun as Eliana. Over the years, in her search for true happiness, love and peace of mind, she had changed her true name to become, Reubena in Tyre. Reubena was too young, immature, and a complete novice. She had been badly burnt in Tyre. Reubena had been cheated by losing most of her wealth to her patrons. Then Safirah appeared mysteriously in Samaria, doing anything and everything to drown her past and regain her wealth. There was nothing she did not do as a whore. Safirah was not human, yet the ghosts of her previous lives and self-condemnation broke her. She sprang up as Dinah in Sidon, looking for healing and love at any cost. Dinah lost what was most precious to her: love and the gifts of life. Her heart became cold and lifeless.

77

Chapter Nineteen

He heals the broken hearted and binds up their
wounds (Psalm 147:3).

inah had resurfaced in Jerusalem as Miriam. Miriam was mature, very successful, wiser, professional, independent, shrewd, and extremely wealthy. She knew she had a stony heart only cut out for her trade and estate acquisition. She no longer believed in love, but Prophet Jesus did. It was time to visit Razilla and understand why the Prophet believed in love. She had never visited her. Yet, Razilla continued to visit her even though she had begun living the way of the new life. She had not forgotten something Razi had shared with her from the mouth of the Prophet, which she found very profound and provoked thoughts of reflection: *ask and it will be given to you; seek and you will find; knock and it will be opened to you.'*

She clung to those words with every fibre of her being, even deep in her soul, because it gave her hope and encouragement. Reflecting on those words grew her desire to meet the Prophet. *What a wise man!* A very wise man, and she liked wise people. Razi said the Prophet embraced everyone, and there were no third-class citizens or outcasts in his opinion of people. Everyone was equal; he saw the Jews and Gentiles the same. He saw the rich and poor the same, including the sinners and the righteous!! She was intrigued. For a while now, Razilla's visits had stopped. It must be discouraging to continue visiting without her showing any interest in returning the visit. So, she decided she would also visit Zara. It had been a long, long while. It was not wise to keep away from her only two 'friends' and discourage their continued friendship. Zara would tell her more about the Prophet Jesus. *And Jocheb too!* It was exactly a year since she last saw him. She knew that wherever he was, he would still think about her...

Her body voluntarily jerked itself in three strong spasms of sexual climax. Her body let out a huge sigh of deep satisfaction. It deserved to enjoy pleasure too, after all the hard work. It was a rare treat, and it felt so good to have 'Elizabeth's body.' Elizabeth's husband had finally shown her body respect, love, and genuine intimacy.

Elizabeth's husband was releasing himself in ejaculation. Even post-coitus had been remarkable for her body under the guise of 'Elizabeth'. She had won! She had made him break his oath. So, he had become the pig that bathed in its dirt or dog going back to its vomit. He jumped up after it all like a madman, backing away with his back facing her as he hurriedly wore his clothes. Still, she made him pay a fortune for the extra time. He would still be back. They were as addicted as she was. Her body was drawn to those who would treat it with respect, consideration, love, and genuine warm passion. At this point, her body did not care about the various names her clients were calling it. Right now, her body felt as human as Dinah had been, as human as Elizabeth was. Elizabeth's husband would return. She understood very well...

Chapter Twenty

For I am the Lord who heals you (Exodus 15:26).

Miriam felt sleepy and had no more customers for the night. She washed her hair and herself thoroughly, preparing for sleep, but it did not come even though it was about the first cock crow. It had been a hectic night. She thought about the seventy something-year-old Jacob. She wished she had asked him to come and pick her up when he was going to Gadara. People would think he was her own father. If she went alone, she did not want to ponder the horror or be treated like a leper!! People would recognise her, mock her, and make her regret for coming out to see a holy man. She remembered the advice she gave Jacob.

'Please, go and see the Prophet. If you do, eat his bread. You will end your life well.'

She might as well have been Zara. Those were the kind of words Zara had spoken to her then when she became a new follower of the Prophet and with a new mother.

Prophet Jesus. She thought about him. He was a good man. Everywhere he went, people said he was doing good: healing the blind, the leper, the lame, the deaf, the dumb, and the demon-possessed. And harlots like her? She knew of four: Razilla, Nebo, Zara, and Jocheb. Why will her case be different? She never liked to use that word—*harlot*. She must be ready to confront who she is now, bring out the past and bury it! Could she? *What about Dinah, the mother?* She pondered briefly about when she was Dinah for a few seconds.

'My lord, your bath water is ready.'

'Thank you, my beloved wife.

'After your bath, would you like me to massage your back?'

'No, Dinah, I just want to play with your hair while you sit on my lap. I want to get lost in the mystery of your eyes...'

She had worshipped her husband because she wanted to possess him forever and never let him go. Cling to an impossible dream she never thought would ever become possible in this lifetime until...

No! She knew what she wanted from the Prophet, even though it was too frightful to contemplate or mention. The ghosts might come back, and she did not want to cope with pushing them down. Suddenly, she was surprised at herself to have had those thoughts of Dinah running through her mind without feeling desolate, depraved, disgusted, downtrodden, and doomed. *So, thinking of Prophet Jesus had that powerful effect!!* The power to bar depression assailing her as it would have whenever she had thoughts of Dinah. She had not had this kind of thoughts of Dinah or her past for over two years!!

'Well, Prophet Jesus,' she suddenly spoke out, 'you know what I long for. You know the meanings of my every sigh. You know what my soul yearns for. Give me!! I will follow you. I want to.'

The angel who carried her request to Abba knew Eliana was unaware that she had just made a prayer request.

She fell into a very peaceful sleep. She might have dreamt, but when she woke up with the sun, she had the burning urge to visit Razilla and Zara.

THIRD YEAR:
Dawn

Chapter Twenty-One

Be doers and not hearers of the WORD only
(James 1:22).

Someone knocked on the door. Even in her dream, Zara heard the knock and woke up. She realised she had napped off as she was knitting. She had so many orders that she could not keep up. She would need to hire more helpers. She could afford to. As she put on her shawl and adjusted her clothing, she stood up and walked towards the door. She was also wondering who the caller was at that time of the day. Jocheb? Razilla? Miriam? When she opened the door, time froze. There was no speech from either the caller or Zara for thirty seconds. Zara rubbed her eyes to be sure she was not dreaming. What kind of New Year's gift was this? Finally, as the silence became suffocating, her visitor spoke.

'Shalom. Please, can I come in?'

'How much do you want?'

'I have not come for money.'

'What have you come for?'

The grudging silence resumed from where it had been interrupted.

'If you cannot tell me, I cannot let you in. Are you going to tell me?'

The caller turned off to go—worn out, weary, greatly disappointed, and at the same time not surprised. Just before turning completely away, another attempt at reconciliation was made.

'And Josef? Is he well?'

There was no verbal answer to this final attempted truce for peace, other than a nod of the head. So, the caller shifted back to the shadows of oblivion after greeting *Shalom.*

Seeing Johana again, after so many years, brought back her strength and toughened her resolve. Johana was still vibrant, beautiful, and was not wearing that look people like her type understood. There was no mask. She was at peace. She did not have that peculiar scent associated with prostitution, which only those familiar to the trade could not miss. Johana was happy? That was unmistakably obvious. What had happened all this while? Josef was all right, too. How could one have children and be so alone, starved, and probably dying like a chicken on the path? How ironic! She was not barren. She had two children, and they had turned their backs on her for good. They hated her. She saw that look in Johana's eyes. That look of distrust, suspicion, accusation, and a complete lack of sympathy. Not even a cup of water was offered! Not even the chance to rest her bleeding, dusty feet. Her throat was so parched that she was sure she would not make it back to Nazareth.

Everyone thought she had some terrible disease eating her away. They were correct, but sorrow, regret, and poverty were eating her. She had been out of business for over eight years and had become a beggar. Her dwelling had become so rundown and could no longer protect her from the elements. Where were all the men who had come to her bed when she was still youthful, beautiful, and healthy? She had relied on the charity of men. She was not exactly a prostitute in her own view, but her bed was free to those men who were happy to share her with their wives.

The last time she remembered visiting Johana in Capernaum was about 18 years ago. A big headache assailed her head, and a terrible heat wave like a whirlwind of dust enveloped her being. This always happened when she tried to think of her life, her children, and the past. It was one thing to turn one's back away from the past, but it was also a fact that one could not erase the memory of the past and its consequences: the evil she did her children and how she had lost their love and trust. She could not help blaming herself for her sins and the past. How could she when her children would not give her a chance to ask for their forgiveness? *Please, Abba, help me. Send your angels to give Johana a change of heart. I don't know what to do. Please, help me quickly.* She brought out her charity bowl, which had been hidden out of Johana's sight under her clothes.

'Please give me water,' she begged the first person who came across her way. No luck! Was today not supposed to be the last day of the year when people were generous and mindful of the poor? Where could she lie down and die? She felt death calling her. If only she could find Josef. He would not be as callous as his sister. But she had no strength to carry on, and she had no tears, which would have been a delightful treat to her tongue.

Chapter Twenty-Two

*May God be gracious to us and bless us and make His
face shine on us (Psalm 67:1).*

'Wait.'

She sat by the roadside, too tired to move on, and wondered if it were indeed Johana approaching her. *That was quick, Abba!! Thank you.* She saw Johana carried a bulgy, leather-skinned bag that had some stuff. She became apprehensive as well. She hastily splashed out her heart as Johana reached for her.

'Johana, please forgive me. Pity me. I am sorry. Did you bring water?'

Zara did. Her mother quenched her thirst and was handed some soft home-baked bread spiced with honey. Zara stood surveying the hilly terrains and hardly aware of the sunset breeze flirting with her skirt's hems, the evening's passers, or her mother hurriedly wolfing her food down. She clutched onto the leather bag.

'Are you ready to answer my question?' she asked when she saw that the woman had less food in her mouth.

'I have not come for money,' she repeated, but Zara said nothing.

She had never imagined she would be turned down. She did not come prepared for answering and giving responses of this nature. She was suddenly blank and did not know what was expected from her in terms of a response. Then like lightning, the answer came.

'Rabbi Jesus said people should make peace. So, I have come to make my peace with you and Josef.'

Zara, too, was tongue-tied. Mother Mary and her circle of close friends had urged her to make peace with this woman who allowed her lover's friend to disvirgin her and initiate her into prostitution. She had allowed her lover to profit from a twelve-year-old with other men. She had actually taken the money Ram gave her!! Also, she had never come to look for her all those years after they were separated, even when she persistently asked of her from Ram or whoever she had sent to collect money off her. What if she had died? Yet, she kept sending her lover to take money off her, and he had always managed to bed her. Ram made her see herself as a whore and not as his daughter. Once she had tried to resist, but she was weak against his charms and strength. This woman she was looking at right now must have known Ram abused her on top of taking her money for their own selfish benefit at her expense! Then another great evil—she had sent Josef as a child to travel unaccompanied all the way from Nazareth to Capernaum. She had not cared about his safety or whether he got kidnapped. All she wanted was to get money off her.

She had told Josef what Ram, their mother's lover, had done to her that evening since she did not come home for three days. Josef had never returned home, and yet, their mother had never come to find out if he was safe or not. However, she knew she was curious to learn how this hard-hearted evil woman had met Prophet Jesus and managed to know her whereabouts here in Jerusalem. Still, she was terrified of her. She would show kindness and hope their paths would never cross again.

Abigail waited while praying in her soul for Abba to soften Johana's heart towards her with sympathy. She could read her daughter's mind weighing the terrible evil she had done to them on the scales of her heart. Her sins were so heavy on that scale. Only Abba's divine intervention would put pure mercy on the other seat of the scale and give it a balance. Abigail waited in hope and anxiety…

Chapter Twenty-Three

*In all your ways acknowledge Him and He shall direct
your paths (Proverbs 3:6).*

Johana made up her mind. She already had a new mother, and this evil woman was no mother. They only had a biological connection, and she would send her away. Her evil deeds were too many and unforgivable. This surely was punishment for her mother's sins from Abba himself. So be it.

'Here is some money to help you. Here is some more food and water,' she said, handing the bag to her mother. 'Wear these shoes.' The woman received the bag and shoes but said nothing. 'There is an inn down the road by some large clusters of fig trees. I know the owner. Jephthah. Tell him that Zara sent you. It is only about 5 miles. You can rest for about three days. Then you can journey back home when you are restored to your strength. Bye and go well.'

'Thank you.'

She wanted to plead that she be allowed to stay with her till she had regained not only her strength but her health and sanity. The look on her daughter's face did not give her any encouragement. Her *daughter*? **Daughter!** MY OWN DAUGHTER!! *Her mind screamed!!!*

'My daughter, WAIT!!' she called out after her, standing up and running after her. 'Please, let me stay with you. Please, allow me. Don't reject me. Accept me as as...'

Choked with a lump of pain down her throat, she could not continue. She was prepared to become Johana's slave. It was better than being a beggar. Facing constant starvation and her guilt over how she had treated her children for the hope of gain was unbearable. She had never used the term 'daughter'. It kind of made her human.

'My house is not ready. I need to prepare it for your convenience. Stay at Jephthah's inn. He will take good care of you.'

'Please, let me sleep on the floor.'

'It is still daylight. There is no heat, and you have plenty of time to travel before darkness arrives. Now go!'

'I plead with you, please. You are my daughter. I have done as the Lord Jesus asked. Have you met Him? I have.'

Zara saw that the food and water had restored her mother's lost energy, and traits of her old stubborn nature were rearing their heads. She remembered that Mother Mary had prayed for her mother and herself to be reconciled. She looked at her mother properly and could not find the woman she used to call 'Mama'.

'What has happened to you?'

'Take me in, please.'

Zara was undecided. Was it possible? Where was Mama? That tall, beautiful woman with long dark silky hair; a flawless skin; expressive tiny eyes loaded with long thick lashes; dimpled cheeks; a long ringed neck; semi-full, shapely busts with a small waist; long slender legs carrying a shapely feminine torso, which was always adorned in lovely clothes.

Zara then realised that she had just described herself: she was the splitting image of the woman she once used to call 'Mama'. Now that woman looked shrunken, bent, had sunken eyes and the rest of her was flat, lifeless, and lustreless. In fact, she was ugly. She smelt dirty and looked unkempt. A week of good food and care should get her back to her health, looks, and spirit, and after that, she would have no excuse for wanting to linger in Jerusalem.

'Let us go.'

Chapter Twenty-Four

The woman she used to call 'Mama' suddenly knelt, sobbing profusely, as she clasped her arms around Zara's legs.

'I am sorry for my sins against you and Josef. I am a prodigal mother. I am returning to be a real mother. Tell me what to do to get you, my children, back.'

She bent over on Zara's feet and wept deep, body-racking sobs.

Zara said nothing; neither was she moved by the show of remorse from her mother. Helping her to her feet, they started off together towards home. She had made pleasing Prophet Jesus her highest priority. What was the point of being wealthy and having no purpose or true happiness in life? She would forgive Mama. Then she could resume without guilt or fear of remonstration the beautiful fellowship she had been enjoying with other followers of Prophet Jesus. She wanted to have pure motives without disguise or pretence. Prophet Jesus had said that the Pharisees were doing the right things for the wrong reasons. They worshipped God for people to praise them. She remembered when the Prophet said,

Blessed are the pure in heart. Her inner life should not be disguised, but open with no guile.

Mother Ahuva had explained it that way. On her own part, Johana realised she didn't want to pretend. That would be cheating Abba, who had ignored her sins and shown her His kindness when she needed mercy, help, and restoration. Prophet Jesus had forgiven her *everything, removing her mistakes, shame, and unworthiness.* What was her own mother's story? How dysfunctional had her own home and family been? She realised growing up that she had never really known her mother or her family background. Indeed, she did not know any extended family members. She had assumed she and Josef were outcasts because of their mother's lifestyle. She realised she felt light at heart, and there was now a purpose in her life. By Sabbath mealtime, they would be home.

'Mama, I forgive you *everything*,' she uttered in a tremulous voice.

Her mother was dumbstruck.

'Truly,' she reaffirmed in a firmer voice.

Johana knew she herself was now living a blessed life. Though she had no husband or children yet, there were changes in her health, relationships, and life. Since Abba had changed her heart, she was living a victorious life from where she had been a captive of the devil. Indeed, she was wearing the crown of victory on her head, and she would help her mother proudly wear hers as well. They were no longer captives.

She reckoned it was more important what God thought about her than people did. She would not be embarrassed to have Mama in her house—someone known as a fallen woman, slut, and awful mother, who had depended on men's charity for her survival and lustful pleasures in exchange for the treasures she had received from Abba.

Abigail's sobs had subsided, and her thoughts were rolling like waves over the shores of her mind—would Johana change her mind? Would Josef come and remember the past, persuade his sister to drive her away? How would Johana introduce her to friends—proudly, or with shame and regret? All she knew was that Abba had healed and forgiven her. He had just placed it in Johana's heart to forgive her. That was a huge mountain turned into a pebble! She would continue to trust Abba in faith and live the new life so that He would continue to show her His mercy and love.

Chapter Twenty-Five

Forget the past; do not dwell on former things
(Isaiah 43:18).

By the time Miriam became aware of time, she had spent virtually half the day with Razilla. What a wonderful way to spend the last day of this year! She promised herself that in the new coming year, she would visit more and probably stop sinning, *if she could.* She wished she had found time to spend with Zara as well. She had intended to split the time between the only two 'friends' she had. Maybe some other time, she would spend a day like this with Zara.

'Razi, did Zara tell you how she really got healed from prostitution?'

'You mean she has not told you yet? Razi asked, not hiding the great surprise her eyes expressed.' What has she told you about how Abba has saved her?'

'To be truthful, the two times I went to her, it was strictly very brief business. The few times she visited, I was not available or encouraging. On two occasions, she visited, and she was all about how the Prophet delivered fellow prostitutes. She told me about Nebo and Biliah and wanted to know my own story.'

'Testimony.'

'Is that what the old or new life story is called?'

'Miriam, you could put it that way, but my understanding of a testimony is a person's story of how Abba delivers them from their sin, afflictions, addictions, and anything else that holds them captive and prevents them from enjoying the blessings of Abba.'

'Abba? She always talks about Prophet Jesus.'

'Yes. That is because it is through the person of Lord Jesus that people can receive Abba's promise of salvation. Abba sent the Lord Jesus to set the captives free from their sins.'

'And salvation?'

'Ahh Miriam, that is the captive's crown—their goal and victory as they become one with Abba, the King of kings. Just try to imagine a life where all your impossible dreams become possible. Do you have such dreams, Miriam?'

'Dreams and unanswered questions. I told Zara that I am an orphan and all my family died in a fire. She did not believe me.'

'Abba's ways and thoughts are above ours, Miriam. He understands everything about us. He is our creator, but when a person receives Abba's salvation through the Lord Jesus, that is salvation. You will enjoy peace. Abba is the God of Peace. He alone can answer all your questions and make your dreams happen. Did you believe what she said about Nebo and Biliah?'

'Biliah's testimony really draws me close to the Prophet. He did not condemn her to death, even though she was caught in adultery. Instead, he saved her from death. And now, she has adopted a son and actively follows the Prophet.'

'Zara's testimony is even as amazing.'

'Now, I am curious!'

'Sure, but let us get something into our tummies first. I always have fresh bread because I work in Amos' Bakery. As soon as one is delivered from prostitution, you are free to engage in life outside prostitution. I told you that on one of my visits, didn't I?'

'Yes and your testimony.'

Chapter Twenty-Six

I have come to call the sinners to repentance
(Luke 5:32).

She watched Razi go about sorting out plates, the bread, soup, and tea for them both. She took the opportunity to think about some things she had heard. Razi, unlike Zara, was genuinely interested in receiving salvation and held nothing back by way of testimonies and her transparency. Zara, on the other hand, was interested in self-gain. She wanted to hold back her own testimony until she had heard hers. Even after telling Zara about the fire incident, she did not still share her testimony!! She thought sharing other people's own would eventually lure her into divulging her true life history, but not Razi. She realised she could trust Razi. *Life history? She didn't know. She might be an orphan, or maybe not.*

'Thank you, Razi,' she said, after her food was laid before her. It was then she felt her hunger—for food. *Talking about the Prophet or being around his followers keeps my sex urges at bay! Hmn.*

'Thanks to Abba. Enjoy,' Razi said, sitting opposite her.

As they ate, she studied Razi. This visit definitely drew them closer. She could confidently call Razi a friend, even though their lifestyles were the opposites. Razi was so beautiful within— personality-wise. No pretence or guile. She did not possess the serene attraction of Jewish women. Her nose and jaw were definitely Phoenician. Neither did she have those distinct feminine curves, but her inner beauty surpassed what she physically lacked as soon as she spoke. She suddenly wished she had that kind of inner beauty that spoke of wisdom and a benign personality.

'So,' Razi broke into her contemplations. 'Do you like the soup and tea?'

'It is great, Razi, thanks. I am curious about one thing, though.' Miriam asked

'Yes?'

'Did you have any hidden agenda when you followed Father Simeon out of that tavern, or was it all purely your desire to be saved from sin?'

'Miriam, I will tell you the truth. I discerned that Father Simeon was not fake. His testimonies of Jesus were compelling, stimulating, and pulled me away like a magnet. When I questioned my actions of following a stranger that night, I told myself I would stay with him if I were wrong but never go back to prostitution. And Miriam, I believe you have that gift from Abba. You can tell when people are sincere towards you or not.' Razi paused to drink some tea and saw her listener nod her head.

'That has really helped me in my business,' Miriam answered. 'I select who comes to my bed and who to manage my property.'

'When I was still a prostitute here on the outskirts of Jerusalem, about eight or nine years ago, I had this Egyptian client who began an interesting conversation with me. He said he had been to you, but you were too expensive for him. Then he said he had tried Zara a couple of times because she was a lot cheaper. He said her problem was that she always made him feel guilty, like he had been torturing her. So, on one of such occasions, guess what he did?' Razi asked.

'He told her how he felt and requested Zara to visit me. Yusuf, yes. I remember him,' Miriam replied.

'Exactly!' Razi exclaimed. 'Zara told me, and that was when I first heard about you. But as soon as I received this new life...'

'New life?' Miriam asked, puzzled. 'What is that?'

'New life? Oh, that is what the Lord Jesus calls people who repent, forsake their old nature or sinful life, and accept that he is the Way, the Truth, and the Life for everyone who wants deliverance, salvation, and talking to Abba. You get it?'

'Yes, I suppose so. Please go on. This is becoming very interesting.' They both laughed.

'So, when I received this new life,' Razi continued, 'I knew the truth about deliverance and salvation. I sought Zara out. She didn't know me then, of course. I told her how I had known about her through Yusuf, but I had showed her the best client, who would not have her body but deliver her from all her sins and give her a new life and peace. I told her some miracles I had witnessed and how I was saved, and Zara simply followed me to meet the Lord Jesus.'

'Ah, as soon as Zara received the new way of life, she told Jocheb and me, and that was how you met Jocheb, too,' Miriam said.

'I don't know him too well, though. I have heard a lot about him through Zara. I had met him only once when he was helping Zara move house. That was a while ago,' she sighed. 'Three years precisely.' Razi did not want to pursue the talk of Jocheb any further; she was very aware that Jocheb had feelings for Miriam. She changed the topic.

'So, did you find that amazing about how Zara found salvation?'

'Sort of. But not as dramatic as Biliah's.' She felt secretly amused that Razi had unwittingly revealed how she felt about Jocheb. So, *here was one more admirer. That makes us two...*

'Well. They have both been saved by the Prophet.'

'What makes you go out of your way to tell others about the Prophet?'

'Well, Miriam,' she sighed again and yawned. Unless you personally meet Jesus, you will not fully understand. All I can say is that I just felt my eyes were open to the truth, and I could see that my friends and people were suffering needlessly in ignorance. It is like showing someone the right direction to a place if they have missed the road.'

'Pointing them to the light away from darkness.'

'So to speak, yes!! I guess you too might be curious to meet the Prophet as well.'

'He is an extraordinary man, I admit. If I had heard all this about him 20 years ago, ten years ago, I would have gladly gone. But now, I have no parents, siblings, husband, or children. Just what I have worked very hard for. I am grateful for the new friends

I have like you. What more can the prophet give me or do for me? Truthfully, Razi, the sex keeps away my pain, losses, and the ugly side of my life. It has worked for me these past ten years.'

'It is your choice, Miriam. I mean, there is no harm in meeting Him. Forgive my manners. I should have asked you if you wanted more tea or bread,' she said, standing up from the dining table.

Standing up and helping with the packing up, she said, 'I am so full, thank you.'

Chapter Twenty-Seven

*Now faith is being sure of what we hope for and
certain of what we do not see (Hebrews 11:1).*

'Razi, I am glad that I chose to spend the New Year with you,' she said as soon as the washing up was over. They were seated in Razi's modest one-bedroom, which served as the dining and living room. *Not every prostitute was wealthy!*

'Abba must have planned it so. Usually, I would have been in Bethany, Capernaum with other new friends. Or with Zara herself. We occasionally rotate sleepovers.'

'Yes, I woke up with that need to visit both you and Zara. Do you think there is time to visit Zara?' she asked.

'Of course! Why not?' Razi replied cheerfully. She still could not believe that Miriam had purposely set the day aside to visit her.

'It was really my plan to see you both.'

'What stops you? We could both go together unless you want to discuss business matters with her. Then I can stay back.'

'Business?'

'Yes. I am aware that Jephthah, a former client of yours, helps run your estates and hers. Right?'

'Quite right.' *They are much closer than I thought.*

'If you need privacy, I will stay back.'

'No, Razi, please come. I did not set out today for business, and I definitely hate walking about alone.'

'I can understand the stares that will follow you. Your hair is so long, full, and thick. Miriam. You are so beautiful. Have you ever thought of having a family?'

'No.'

'Why not?' asked Razilla in great surprise. 'Your beauty would fetch you a prince or even a king.'

'Like it did for you and Zara.'

'My case is different, Miriam. I have told you my life story already. Besides, I do not have a great beauty like yours or the appealing one like Zara's. Master Jesus says that I am doing things that will enrich my life. You remember that I have told you before how I am a blessing to others through my charity actions?'

'Yes, I remember you did.' She noted Razi was quick to change conversations that veered towards her single status.

'That explains why I have not visited you for a while.'

'I understand. Don't worry. I owed you both visits, anyway. But yes, how is the charity work going for you?'

'Thanks, Miriam. Through the charity work I do, I experience peace and joy. Miriam, I believe I will have a family someday. I may not meet a prince or a king, but he will be someone who has the fear of God and lives the new life.'

'Good.'

'Even Zara lives a life to please Master Jesus. She really goes out of her way, sometimes. Watch out, Miriam. Special things will happen to us as we live our lives sowing good seeds.'

'I really hope so.'

'I don't want you to have all the money in the world and be miserable. I know how very intelligent you are, Miriam. Meet Master Jesus, and you will perform at your highest potential.'

'I already am, Razi.'

'I am not talking about your trade. I could take you to meet Master Jesus whenever you ask me to. I will be delighted to.'

'Fine. Let us go and see what Zara is up to.'

As they got up, straightened their clothing, and adorned their footwear, their conversation went on uninterrupted.

'Can't you guess what Zara is up to? It is easy to,' Razilla said with a smile.

'I know. Knitting and weaving.'

'Yes, but not mostly. She has joined our group of helpers. When the Master and his followers go about talking about Abba, healing people, casting out demons, and doing all manner of good works, we help minister to the Lord Jesus, his followers, and assist those he ministers to.'

'Really? How?'

'Since they go around the villages from town to town, they usually need their clothing washed, their stuff carried, their food cooked, and we help give immediate attention to those that have been healed from demons or other diseases.'

'You mean that Zara now enjoys doing this?'

'When we get there, ask her, and you will find out.

Chapter Twenty-Eight

For it is You, God, who works in me to will and to act according to Your good purpose (Philippians 2:13).

'Razi?'

'Hmm.'

'Has Zara really, really given up on her past life? Does her body not desire the former longings? How about the ghosts of her past she used to be so fearful of?' She bombarded her companion with questions that she knew would reveal the considerations of her mind.

'Miriam, you can trust me. She has really given up her prostitution life. She is completely free from the fears of her past and the devil's strongholds. Miriam, remember that anyone who meets the Lord Jesus can never be a victim of fear and their old sinful way of life. At least, that happened to me, and this is the testimony I hear from those who meet Him.' They continued their walk in silence, enjoying the evening setting and scenery of other people going about their business. A normal evening…

Their talks about Zara reminded Miriam of something Zara had mentioned, which she buried deeply away in her box of impossibilities but possible in her dreams in another world. The issue of love. She needed to review it further. This surprised her because usually, when love issues came her way, she didn't give it a chance. Somehow, she didn't throw what Zara had told her about love out of the window of oblivion. Now, she understood why Zara had once mentioned to her that the 'Lord Jesus offers the perfect love which casts out all fear'. *Was there anything like perfect love? Really?* She was intrigued.

'Razi, I don't think Zara believes in true love because of her past. What do you think?'

'I know little about her past love life, but I'm aware she used to sink into great depression whenever she thought of how the past led her to a hopeless life, although not a fault of hers.'

'I heard of her evil mother.'

'Exactly. Before she heard the sayings of the new way of life, Zara thought she could never find love and experience true peace of mind. All that has changed now. Moreover, Miriam, one should not dwell on the past. Let me tell you why you should never allow the past to weigh you down.'

More prophet talk! Miriam braced herself ready.

'...It might be a trick of the devil to drag one down to that pit of hopelessness and prevent one from having hope in the Lord Jesus and experience his true love. But do you know Zara's entire life story? You said you visited her a while ago.'

'Not from her own point of view, but I understand how very bitter she feels about her evil mother and why. She talked about the Lord Jesus too.'

'From whose point of view?'

'Jocheb's.'

'What did he say?'

'He told me it was Zara who recommended him to me.'

'Okay. What else?'

'He and Zara are siblings. Their mother betrayed and abandoned them.'

'Isn't that like everyone else's story? Okay, what story did you tell Zara and Jocheb about yourself?'

'The same as I told you, Razi!'

'I am an orphan. My family were all killed in a fire?' Razilla mimicked and sounded sarcastic.

Miriam did not confirm this. She had taken offence.

'I am sorry, Miriam. Please, do not be discouraged from coming out to visit. I promise to make more efforts to visit, no matter my busy schedule. I should never have stopped. That was wrong of me.'

When Miriam remained silent, she continued.

'Truthfully, Miriam, there is the occasional temptation to dwell on the past. It is a question of choice. Because of the Lord Jesus in our lives, our will is stronger. So, when temptation comes, we choose to fight it off and let our new life dominate us.'

Miriam's continued silence was becoming disconcerting.

'Thanks so much for coming out today and spending such a lovely time with me, Miriam. I really appreciate it. It is something I thought would never happen. I also believe your personal life story. Forgive my earlier jest. Please.'

My personal life story! You know nothing. Miriam was not fooled, but she nodded her head and maintained a secretive silence for a while as they continued walking the three miles to Zara's house. On the way, Miriam could not help but think further about the miracles that Razilla had told her long before their lunch about Prophet Jesus!! That was what had occupied their conversation all morning and afternoon and which had finally prompted Razilla to share her story! Prophet Jesus was making people have the ability to talk freely at will and eloquently with such conviction and without shame. She herself was not chatty at all like that. She knew she struggled to express herself where her emotions or life were concerned. Yet, here she was, having chatty conversations about him or with his followers: Jocheb, Jacob, Zara, and now Razilla. She noticed a great world of difference between how Razi and Zara had shared their life story from the way Jocheb had shared his. Razi had confidence and pride because she had met the Lord Jesus, and her pain, insecurities, and addiction to sex were all in the past. All her pain, loss, and betrayal were replaced with hope, fulfilment, and inner peace. Jocheb's story had one thing missing—he had not met the Lord Jesus physically! She had not seen him for two years, and the New Year would start the third year!! She would be 29!!! How time flew indeed! Would he avoid her this year as well?

This Prophet Jesus seemed to get very interesting to meet by the day. She was getting eager and curious, thinking she would not be afraid to step out of her comfort and the familiar world. But, eventually, she would have to go with Zara or Razilla and take a peep, just as Zacchaeus had done. That had been amusing, and she had laughed! It was good to laugh again. *Really good.* When did she laugh last? Years and years ago? When she was Dinah and knew the difference between love and lust! As Miriam, she did not cry nor laugh, but Prophet Jesus was making her laugh!!

During a very brief spell in their walk, she laughed out.

'What amuses you, Miriam?' Razilla asked, admiring this beautiful woman who looked pleasantly different when laughing.

'Short Zacchaeus climbing a tree to see Prophet Jesus!'

This time, they both laughed; the ice had been cracked, at least. Miriam felt Razi's relief.

Chapter Twenty-Nine

ABBA

The Lord God is a sun and shield (Psalm 84:11a).

Abba communicated several thoughts to His angels in their zillions. He continued to do this every second of every day to bless people and minister to their needs in their soul, body, and mind. He saw His angels all rejoicing in great joy for the salvation and deliverance of His loved ones on earth. This happened all the time when people repented sincerely of their wrongdoings or turned away from choosing wrong choices. His Son, Jesus, was doing an excellent job. Hearts turned towards Him in the right direction: many longed to know Abba to understand and devote their desires to live a new life to please Him.

Abba continued to commune with Jesus and transmit different thoughts to His angels—His beloved ministering spirits, and they offered their worship, praise, adulation, and service from the thoughts they received. The names He called them resonated with His divine qualities as He spoke His thoughts to them. Simultaneously, His thoughts came into Words and accomplished His purpose in the lives of over a zillion beings on earth. Many, like Miriam and Jocheb, who were not yet delivered from the ghosts of their past, were fortified in their souls to receive the spirits of forgiveness, deliverance, strength, hope, faith, trust, joy, love, salvation, peace, wisdom, and encouragement in readiness for when they met the Lord Jesus. Miriam's spirit was very needy. Abba despatched many angels bearing the various spirits to meet her at the point of her needs in response to prayer requests offered on her behalf.

Love: For Abba so loves you that He sent His only Son, Jesus, into the world!

Encouragement: Abba will calm all your fears with His love!

Salvation: Jesus has the authority and power to reverse evil.

Love: Even if your father and mother forsake you, Abba will not!

Hope: Abba has made everything beautiful in His time.

Strength: Abba will renew your strength and help you.

Salvation: What was meant for your harm will work to your advantage. Abba's Words are life to you. He is ready to save you.

Faith: Abba will not forsake those who are faithful.

Trust: Those who trust in Abba will lack no good thing.

Deliverance: Abba sent His Word and delivered you from your destructions.

Salvation: Work out your salvation in fear and trembling.

Wisdom: Iron sharpens iron, so one person sharpens another.

Faith: Abba is the Lord that heals you. Abba will take all sicknesses away from you.

Peace: Abba will bless you with peace.

Salvation: For sin shall no longer be your master.

Forgiveness: Do not repay evil with evil!

Chapter Thirty

Carry each other's burdens and in this way you will
fulfil the law of Christ (Galatians 6:2).

Zara was running late in her preparation for the Sabbath meal. All over Judea province, every Jew made the necessary preparations to celebrate Rosh Hashanah—the New Year. Many homes were at different stages of preparation. Zara knew she wanted an elaborate meal to celebrate her reunion with her mother and not just the need for a New Year's special meal. Now, she had to prepare not just for herself and Jocheb, but also for a starving woman. She prepared in excess. The culture emphasized preparing for extra guests. She prepared for seven people. It was a gut feeling that she was responding to. It never ceased to amaze her that at the beginning of every New Year, her thoughts would centre on the significance of the Passover celebrated in the month of Nisan [April]. Now, she consciously thought about the relevance of the Passover: It was a meal that symbolised the lamb sacrificed the night their forefathers were delivered from 400 years of slavery over a thousand years ago! In their present time, it was celebrating a journey from slavery to freedom, a celebration of new life and the ceremonial cleansing from being a slave to sin. Funny that she linked the importance of the Passover to the coming of the New Year. She asked herself the question—*is it because each New Year represents that I pass over from the old year to a new one? It has got to be since I am always consciously reminded that I have crossed over from death to life.* She decided there and then that she would find out what Jocheb's thoughts were on the importance of the beginning of each New Year in his life.

As she continued to warm up foods and prepare sauces, she thought of her mother then and how it was extraordinary that Mama had come about this time. The Rosh Hashanah celebration lasted two days, and her mother had appeared on the first day, which was also a Sabbath day—Saturday. She was delighted to have obeyed her gut feeling and prepared more than enough two days before. Maybe Jocheb might turn up starving too. He sometimes did. He had been the only family she had. Now, her mother had come. It was a celebration of a new life for herself, Jocheb, and now her mother!! Joy flooded her soul. The New Year had begun well. It had started with forgiveness. She felt strength, love, encouragement, and myriad blessings suffuse her soul as she became very hopeful of accomplishing her dreams in this new year. Pondering on her mother's coming into her life as a repentant and new personality created excitement and eagerness, so she was going to hear her mother's story!! *The unknown.* That would definitely get her to understand more of herself regarding her past. As she laid the table and brought the prepared food to the table, she began to croon the words from one of King David's psalms—Tehillim:

For this God is our God

Forever and ever

He will be our God

From now on even unto the end

Chapter Thirty-One

He makes the storm calm so that the waves are still
(Psalm 107:29).

After completely laying the table with special cutlery and crockery, she heats water in a big basin. She helped her mother wash from her hair down to her feet. Every part of the body was scrubbed thoroughly, and all the wounds on her back and feet received balms and ointments that gave her mother an instant soothing from pain. Her rags were fed to the fire, and she was adorned in clean, fresh garments with a new shawl for her head. The shawl was one of the handwoven ones she had made. What a world of difference with how Mama looked now! She thought to herself. Now that she was bathed clean with her hair and body massaged with oil, balms and ointments, she did not look aged, tired, worn out or saddled with grief. Zara decked her mother with jewellery and perfumed her generously. Then they sat a while, catching up on their neighbours and people they both knew in Nazareth—those who had passed on, married, or moved away—before proceeding to the Sabbath table. Mama had promised that she would tell of the miracle of how she had been able to locate her in Jerusalem after their meal. Zara could feel her eagerness, like a child that waits to unwrap a new gift.

'God has really blessed you, my daughter. I feel so much peace knowing that all the evil I did toward you did not harm you. Your blessings are God's mercy over me and proof that He is indeed a God of love. You said Josef is coming?'

'Yes, he always does.'

'I am scared, Johana. What if he makes a scene and doesn't want to forgive me? I cannot go through a second time what happened between us when you sent me out. Please, let me hide away in one of the rooms till you have prepared his heart to receive me back.'

'No, Mama. Abba has it all planned. If Abba made it possible for me to forgive you, He will do the same for Jocheb. Relax!' she said cheerfully as she picked up the match to light the candles.

'In the next few days, Mama, you will meet my friends. They will be excited to see you because they all believe I could never forgive you! It was Razi who introduced me to the Lord Jesus. It is Mother Mary, who is the mother of the Lord Jesus. She adopted me when I told her I was like an orphan. I am the Lord Jesus's sister as well, Mama!'

'Have you met Him face to face then?' her mother asked with the excitement of a child. At that moment, Zara halted her intention of lighting the candles and looked at her mother. Once the candles were lit, there could be no further conversation until the meal was over. She realized then that all the ugliness, dirt, and evil she saw in her mother hours ago were just what her mind wanted her to conceive. Now that she had forgiven her mother, she could see her in a different light. She was indeed still a beautiful woman, just ravaged by the effects of deprivation and poverty. All that had been hidden under her happiness and the rich clothes she now

119

wore. Who would ever have believed the picture she had seen when she first saw her mother three hours ago with what she saw now!!? The lighting of the candles could wait a little. She was quite hungry herself, but she decided to answer Mama this one question.

'It all began with Razi,' she replied before lighting the candles. Then, with a mischievous glint in her eye, she said, 'You will hear the full story after dinner, but she too was a...'

Both women exchanged looks at the sound of knocking. Zara saw fear in her mother's countenance. She was not surprised when she heard the knock on her door. She had just lit two Sabbath candles standing in urns of silver, each giving off a pleasant heady scent. Their family would be reunited that night. She thanked Abba in her heart that Jocheb, being a new convert in the new life, would understand the concept of forgiveness. *Would he?* She ignored the thoughts of doubt taking possession of her. He would. If she had forgiven Mama, despite everything, why would he not as well? She opened the door and was doubly surprised. After she had opened it, there at the door stood a beaming Razilla and a smiling Miriam!

'Shana Tovah!' they both wished Zara a New Year greeting at the same time.

'Shana Tovah Umetukah!!' *Not merely a happy new year but a sweet one as well!* Zara replied.

'I can see you were astonished to see us,' Razi added.

'More than surprised! I have to pinch myself that seeing you both is not a dream, especially seeing Miriam here as well?' She shook her head and rolled her eyes to show disbelief.

'I am more than so glad. Please, hurry over to get washed up. We were just about to begin the meal...'

'We?'

'Come on, run off girls. We are hungry!! You will find out after the meal!'

Miriam followed Razi excitedly as they both hurried to the kitchen to wash their faces, hands, feet and dust their clothing. She had noticed that Zara had been specially dressed! Moreover, what were those delightful and teasing smells that swam into her nose and teased her taste buds? She was sure that Razi too could smell the aroma of assorted dishes. *There was a feast. What would this New Year bring for her, too?*

Chapter Thirty-Two

*Set your minds on things above and not on earthly
things (Colossians 3:2).*

It was not quite sundown yet. Zara felt starving and knew her mother was too, but she waited for her friends, who were like family to her. As she made her way back to join her mother at the table, she controlled the intense sense of disappointment she felt at not seeing Jocheb deep down in her guts. Where was he, and why had he not turned up? He usually did, except the one time he had been too ill to come down until days later. Soon, she saw her friends join them at the table as each woman conveyed greetings with their palms clasped together and a bow of their heads to herself and her mother. She and her mother had responded likewise. She expected they knew that after their washing up to get clean for the meal, the rule of silence followed, and there was no further conversation. Therefore, they would not think it strange that she did not introduce her mother yet. She was relieved inwardly that they had both understood. *Razi must have educated Miriam!* Otherwise, how did Miriam, who probably grew up knowing none of the Jewish traditions, understand what to do? Her mother looked relieved that it had not been her Jocheb.

As soon as Razilla and Miriam sat at the table, Zara gesticulated to her mother, giving her the honour of saying the Sabbath prayer. She watched her mother, still in her mid-fifties, get up and begin the motions for the Sabbath ritual. That single act of giving the elderly woman the honour of the Sabbath prayer told Miriam that she was indeed the mother of Zara. Her quick, sensitive and intuitive mind confirmed all the similarities she noted between Zara and the woman. But she then realised that the facial features had an uncanny likeness to Jocheb. How strange! Yes, she remembered Jocheb said they were siblings. She watched surreptitiously as the woman waved her hands over the candles as if she was directing their light to her face.

Her intuitive mind picked up intimate details which only people gifted with the expert ability of discernment as she could do: the woman was frail, broken, undernourished, impoverished, had been afraid, crushed, embittered, and full of regrets of a past that was too shameful. Yet, she discerned that unmistakable ray of a budding hope, like a flicker of light shimmering and standing unquenched against the raging forces of self-condemnation. She was able to identify with her immediately in her spirit and soul. Next, she watched as the elderly woman proceeded to cover her eyes with her hands—Zara's hands! She uttered some prayerful blessings and was silent for a few seconds. The old tradition of silence when eating the meal was observed. It gave one time for reflection and was a sign of respect to the Almighty Provider for life and all that life entailed.

As this was her first time in this particular home, Miriam found herself admiring the tapestry which Zara had used as decoration over the walls. Whichever way she turned, a tapestry from India, Egypt, and Arabia greeted her eyes, and she realised that Zara too was very wealthy. Definitely, she and Zara had the same style and taste for acquiring the very best quality of whatever was purchased: the candle urn, the candle, the tablecloth and perfume all seemed way over the top. This was her style, and she slipped into an ease of comfort and felt relaxed. Zara and her mother were dressed like guests at a wedding. It was surreal. The dining table was spacious and could conveniently sit eight people at one sitting. The more Miriam noted things about Zara's abode, the further it suddenly struck her that this very style of decoration, quality of furniture, colour of the rugs, tapestry, curtains, type of crockery, and the interior décor and probably beddings, were identical to her own home. Then she remembered the chance meeting of Zara and herself about ten years ago. Was it less or more? She might have been turning twenty, and Zara, about five or six years older, basing her judgement of Zara's age on what she had learnt from Jocheb over two years ago. She couldn't accurately concentrate as her mind was eager to dig into that dark past...

Chapter Thirty-Three

Choose you this day whom you will serve
(Joshua 24:15).

Zara had come looking hopeful, eager, and wanting to please. There were quite a few occasions girls queued up to see her gain direct employment from her in one of her taverns. These girls did not want to go through the men managing her other taverns for reasons best known to them. Some came as clients who thought she was heterosexual. Zara had been on the queue to see her, not as a client, but as a 'friend', as she learnt within two minutes of their interaction. Zara had been very open and direct. Miriam learnt she had been referred to learn tricks from her to succeed in Capernaum by an Egyptian customer who had considered her 'insufficiently experienced'. Miriam had picked an instant likening to this woman who was older and had not looked down on her on discovering she was younger. Miriam's quick mind picked up her personality type: a novice in the trade. She did not delegate tasks to her mind, heart, and body and was unprofessional. She was too honest and not shrewd; neither did she know her worth. She lacked a magnetic pull, so customers came once and never returned…

'What is your name?'

'My real name is Johana, but my professional name is Zara.

'How old are you, Zara?'

'I am 24, but I tell clients I am 16.'

'Where are you based?'

'Capernaum.'

'Move to Jerusalem.'

'Do you enjoy sex?'

'Of course not! It was not the life I planned for myself.'

'I know, but now, do you enjoy your clients?'

'No!! Some of them are old, dirty, rough, and spiteful. Even some of the rich ones are not gentle but –

'I know, but why can't you enjoy sex?'

'I just told you why??'

'I know, but have YOU decided whether what you do is a career you want to enjoy or a job to cater for your needs?'

Zara had given her a blank stare, with silence as an answer.

'Which is it for you?'

'I don't know.'

'What tools do you have for your business?'

Zara had shrugged and said nothing.

'Zara, for me, this is a career that I enjoy and my job because of what I gain from it. You MUST enjoy sex to survive in this business...'

She had advised her to realise that she was priceless. It was she only who could offer her clients what they could not easily acquire, attain, or achieve without her help. Her abode and the price rates were magnets. These communicated her priceless quality. At an exorbitant price, no riff-raff would come near her bed. That done, she should keep her heart and emotions to herself while her body did the work...

They had not become intimate friends, and neither were they rivals. Nevertheless, each never forgot the other...

As a way to compensate for the advice she had been given, she had sent Miriam a very wealthy client—Jocheb. She was beginning to realise that Jocheb might have served both as a spy and a client. The more she thought about it, the more she realised it was a very strong possibility. So, she asked Zara again about Jocheb. Following the new life, as she did, she would be open with her about her true relationship with Jocheb.

Miriam wondered to herself if she should go home immediately after the meal. She knew that Razilla and Zara were very close, especially as they were following the new way of life. Razilla would most probably stay overnight. She had done so a couple of times, just as Zara too had stayed overnight at Razilla's house, as she had learnt during their conversation during the day. She suddenly felt self-conscious. Here were fellow 'colleagues' who were reformed. They were no longer sinners like her. They had accepted the Lord Jesus as their Master and were living the new life. This new life. It was a life without ghosts of their past, guilty conscience, regrets, self-condemnation, or inferiority complex. They were no longer slaves to their bodies and insatiable sex urges! This perplexed her. She would give the matter further thought when she returned home.

For now, she was curious about the elderly guest. More so, as this guest was always throwing looks her way, probably assuming that she was being observed. She felt a kindred spirit with this elderly woman and wanted to know why she and Zara were dressed so gorgeously, as if in celebration of something. This was not just New Year's dressing. She could hardly wait for the meal to be over for Zara to introduce the woman and find out what Jocheb was up to these days. She realised she had not seen him for three years!

A soft knock on the door startled them all, as it was most unusual for guests to arrive halfway during a Rosh Hashanah meal…

Chapter Thirty-Four

Teach me your ways O Lord; lead me to a straight path (Psalm 86:11).

Jocheb profoundly missed sharing the New Year meal with his sister and spending the first day of a new year in her company. As it was the first day of the new year, he thought about her. Having returned from the cities of Tyre, Sidon, and then to Joppa, where he had gone for business, he felt exhausted. Rather than go to his home, he stayed in a popular tavern. At least, he was sure of food. Travelling later that night to his home was a bit too risky health-wise, he thought. He reckoned that by the time he bathed, ate, and rested, it would be getting dark. There was no need to tempt the fates. Even if he hired a horse, he would be attracting unnecessary attraction to himself. He would stay the night at his usual inn and see her the following day. That was more reasonable. Besides, he had ferried timber logs from the port at Syria to Tyre. He felt too tired. He was sure that he would arrive after the Sabbath meal if he set off straight away. The 25 minutes' distance would take him an hour, as he was fatigued. For a second time, his thoughts of hiring a horse crossed his mind again, especially as he had not seen her for a whole year. And Miriam? Three years!! Had she changed from her sinful life? He knew there was a fierce battle between the pros and the cons in his mind. *Hiring a horse at this time would cause an unnecessary stir. Tomorrow would do.* He reckoned that common sense had taken sides with the pros.

It had been quite a long while since he was in Jerusalem. He remembered he had popped in briefly twelve months after learning about Zara's betrayal. He had not wanted to go then, but he was curious to find out if Zara had taken Miriam to see the Prophet. He had been thoroughly disappointed then that she had not kept to her promise to take Miriam, and so she remained a sinner! He ached to meet the Prophet. He missed hearing stories from Zara and wanted to share the stories of the Prophet he had heard in Tyre, Samaria, and the Mediterranean area while on business. News of the Prophet had spread all over the entire region of Judea! Zara had wanted him to meet a woman that had adopted her as a daughter, and this new mother had asked of him! He desired to meet her. It felt good to have a mother in his life. Zara had mentioned that the woman had advised that she and he were to forgive *every* member of their family who had hurt them. This was the way of the new life. He craved to see Zara, their new mother, but most of all, he longed for Miriam.

Jocheb thought of Miriam. Was she still a sinner? If he went there the following day, what would he find? Would she have changed? Zara and Razilla had changed. He had. Many people he knew had. He remembered the conversations he had overheard at the eating house in Tyre. It was stories about the Prophet. A professional, Matheus, was recounting how some of her clients who had ailments in different parts of their body had stopped coming for body treatment. Everywhere he went, people were talking about the wonderful deeds of the Prophet. Nebo himself had become a follower and had a new name. He tried to remember it but could not. All these things gave him food for thought. Should he change his name too or go back to his old name—Josef? He decided to go back to his old name. There was no need to hide from his past anymore. It was the new name—Jocheb—that he needed to drop off instantly. He got bored with staying indoors in his room and went to the bar, where there were still some customers.

As soon as he settled down, a pretty lady of the red trade came to offer her company. He reckoned she was not much older than 16. Obviously, she was not a Jew by the way she wore her sash.

'Hello, handsome,' the woman piped out from heavily coated red lips. She stood beside his table, obviously waiting for the green light.

'Hello, beautiful. What is your name?'

'Adah. I am willing to delight you, sir,' she answered coyly, still standing.

'What is your real name?'

'I just told you. Adah.'

'Well, Adah, my real name is Josef. I am a Jew. When I lived a life of sin as a prostitute, I told people that my name was Jocheb. Then I heard of Prophet Jesus, saw, and even heard him! My life has been easier—no more demons, guilt, lies, pretence, condemnation, and shame. This is what I benefitted from accepting the Lord Jesus as my Lord and living the new life as taught by him. I want this for you too, if you can believe me.'

'I believe you, Josef. There was news of the Prophet raising people from the dead! Also, a friend's brother who I know was dumb from birth now talks!'

'Oh yes. Prophet Jesus answers people who call for his help. Sometimes too, in some evenings, when he is not teaching people the new way of life, he heals all the sick brought to him out of compassion. He also casts out demons from all who are demon-possessed and performs miracles on those who are crippled, blind, deaf and leprous.'

'I heard,' Adah replied lamely.

She realised Josef was no customer for the night, but she saw through his transparency that he cared and reached out to help her. It was uncommon to hear a man admit that he was once a prostitute. She decided to sit down beside him rather than reach out to a willing customer. She knew that he knew she was a Samaritan, yet he spoke to her!!

'Why have you not gone to see this Prophet or listen to him?'

He was amazed to see the subtle transformation that the question ignited in her. Her sudden interest, the desire to learn about the Prophet and the raw pain that was naked in her eyes was immediately transparent. He knew then that she would have willingly followed him to find the Prophet if it were afternoon. She was beautiful, and it touched him that some circumstance akin to his might have pushed her into this lifestyle. Deep in his unconscious mind, he wondered what made it so difficult and impossible for Miriam. She had shown interest, but no willingness to stop sinning. She was surrounded by people living the new way of life, yet she stuck to her old ways. Here was this young girl, who this very evening hung on to his words as a lifeline. Maybe Miriam was tied up to her wealth. *Wanting to gather more and more and more...* Adah brought him back to awareness.

'...so, as you can see, I work all night and have to rest all day. When can I ever get the chance to go?'

There was hope, very faint. She hung on this hope that some solution could be reached.

'Do you really want to meet the Prophet and live a new way of life?'

She nodded.

'You mean you are ready this instant to enjoy the freedom, peace, love, and deliverance the Lord Jesus offers through believing that He can set you free and you can begin to live the new way of life?'

'Yes, Josef, I really want to, but I don't know how.'

'I am happy to take you to my sister's house. She, too, was in this trade since she was 12. For about 20 years, she had no hope until she met the Prophet. Now she is free. What is your real name?'

Adah hesitated. Was this a kind of scam? Was she being hypnotised? The voices in her head began to warn her and ring loud and clear warning bells. Yet, something else told her to trust this stranger. He was no kidnapper or slave hunter. He was like a big brother who wanted to help her. So, she decided to reach out. He was a link to Prophet Jesus.

'Amina.'

'Meaning "faithful" in Hebrew. Follow me now to my sister's house. She will take you to meet the Prophet. She knows where the Prophet's mother lives. Amina, your life will not be the same. I will go with you and my sister to visit Mother Mary and other followers of Prophet Jesus.'

'Josef, why are you helping me?'

'That is the way of the new life that Prophet Jesus teaches. We are all one big family of Abba. I see you as my younger sister. No matter where we come from or who we are, we are all to show love to each other by caring, helping, supporting, and guiding. This is the way to show that we are followers of Prophet Jesus.'

'Are you married and have a family?'

'No.'

'No?' she asked, as if not believing.

'That is the truth. A month ago, I was 29. I really want to settle down and have my own family. I am ready.'

'Are you betrothed then?'

'Not yet, but soon. I am hopeful.'

'But Josef, is there hope for people like us who have been in the trade of pleasures?'

'Yes. God will provide.'

'Is there already a lady for you?'

'Yes. You know Amina, if I start that story now, we will not get to my sister's house in a good time. We can continue our discussions on the way. It should take us about 30 minutes if we keep a fast pace. I returned from Tyre this evening from a business trip as tired as ever, but now, I have been imbued with renewed energy from on high.'

'Please, give me a few minutes to pack a few clothes and close up my business.'

'That is all right by me, but please, be time conscious as it is already dark. I do not want to suggest tomorrow as you might change your mind.'

Chapter Thirty-Five

Jesus answered them, 'Have faith in God'
(Mark 11:22).

Josef watched Amina walk away and wondered what he was doing. He was taking responsibility for a complete stranger who was a lady of red. What would his sister say? He had not seen her in a year, except once after he had that terrible experience with Miriam. He had gone to Zara for comfort. *Zara?* Why was she still holding on to her old name of sin? He decided he would no longer refer to her as Zara. At that moment, Amina returned. She was no longer a lady of red. Her dressing was decent, and her face had no make-up. She looked even younger and more beautiful, but there was a hardness to her features and shrewdness to her eyes, which were the unmistakable stamps of her trade. He carried her bag as they set off.

'Are you not taking a bag of clothing for changing,' Amina asked, surprised. 'Surely, you are not returning here this night!'

'I have some change of clothing at my sister's house. I also have my home not too far from hers.'

'What is her name? I can tell you are fond of her.'

'Johana. She is my big sister and my only sibling.'

'Married, of course.'

'No, not yet, but she is hopeful.'

'And the lady you intend to marry, who is she?'

'Miriam.'

'The only Miriam I know is a very wealthy harlot and very beautiful, too. Her reputation supersedes her. Do you know the meaning of Miriam?'

'No. I have never given it a thought. But I know that our ancestor, Moses, had a sister who bore that name and was a prophetess. Why?'

'Miriam means "Rebellion," or "Sea of sorrow."'

'How do you know?'

'No one in Samaria would bear that name owing to the interpretation. Does your own Miriam know about your past as a prostitute?'

'Yes, I told her.'

'And?'

'Amina, you are so curious! We need to walk faster than we are doing. Remind me to answer your question when we have settled down by tomorrow.'

'Okay, I will. I am eager. I too wish for a family of my own one day, if Abba will forgive me.'

'My sister said she learnt from the followers of the Prophet that it is important to resist temptation. Because when you change your life and stop sinning, temptation will always come. Prophet Jesus says Abba loves us and wants the best for us. So, you must believe what the Prophet tells you. Then, you will be able to enjoy a new life with a spirit of discipline to resist the temptation to sin.'

'Is that what you did at the bar? Resisting me?'

'Yes. I faced temptation. I have had to deal with temptations. I struggle with it when deciding not to become enslaved anymore to my past. I have decided never to give in to sin, and Abba has given me the strength to resist temptations. I always introduce the topic of Prophet Jesus when temptation comes.'

'Josef, why do you call God Abba?'

'Oh, God is Abba. I feel closer to Him like a father and son relationship. Calling Him Abba makes me feel He is nearer, personally closer, and I can relate with him better. That is how my sister and all the people we know call God. Abba. Easy. You too try it.'

'Josef, what is your own story? I am really curious about you. How I just saw a stranger, took his words completely, followed him just like that really makes me wonder.' She kept her gaze steady on him. It was not late to back off.

'Don't be afraid, Amina. No harm will come upon you; I was raised by evil parents. They betrayed my sister and me and led us to perverts for their own pleasure and profit. We knew no other life outside sin, especially as we were outcasts because of our mother. She was a fallen woman; she has never looked for us. Johana met Prophet Jesus and told me about him. That he was sent from God to set the captives free. She encouraged me to follow, and so I did. Now I am free. But the new way of life demands that we forgive our parents. That is very hard for Johana and me. Our parents are sometimes dead to us. Johana said Mother Mary was praying for our parents to change their ways and for us to be able to forgive them. I won't even bother. Abba has given us a new mother.'

He gave a deep sigh but was surprised that he felt no pain talking about his past. He did not feel the way he had felt when he had disclosed all this to Miriam. What really happened back then? It occurred to him he was no longer ashamed and scared to face Miriam again. He had kept away from Jerusalem because he did not want to face people who knew his past, including Johana, his sister. She had betrayed him. He had not forgiven her. Finally, he realised he had to face her, and he was glad that Amina would be a kind of camouflage. 'Now, you know my story. Please, don't be worried about following a complete stranger.'

'No Josef, I am not afraid. You are my brother now. I am glad to have a family. You said you will introduce me to your sister and Mother Mary. You have given me a family and a reason to live because I will have a family that accepts me for who I am.'

'You must be willing to be open, recognise your weaknesses or the areas you are tempted in so that the Prophet will help you. What is your own story?'

'My ancestors were slaves. When I was fourteen, I was separated from my family and sold to another man who used my body for his profits. One client pitied me and helped me escape from Egypt. After six months, I returned to Egypt in disguise as an old woman to visit my parents and found they had been so heartbroken. My father had died, and my mother followed on shortly. I came back to Jerusalem to seek a job, but no one would hire me. I found this bar. The manager gave me a room as long as I paid my rent, attended to customers, and agreed to delight him as often as he wanted. He was surprised to learn that I was following you, and he reminded me that some evil men disguised as friends and then did evil and horrible things to women like me who followed them home. I ignored his warning, paid him what I owed in rent, and followed you. That is my story.'

'Amina, the new way of life is in your path from now on. I will be your big brother and support you as best as I can if you can choose an honest trade.'

'I am ready for this new life. I am willing to forgive even Amon for what he did to my family and me...'

Amina realised they had stopped in front of a door. She still felt emotionally exhausted and choked from going down the memory lane of her past.

'You, knock on the door.'

She obeyed by giving a timid knock...

Chapter Thirty-Six

Anyone in Christ is a new creation
(2 Corinthians 5:17).

The Angels discerned the Spirit of the Lord hovering over the entire earth, bringing order where there was chaos and void in people's lives whose souls reached out to Him. He sent the Angels of faith, unity, victory, light, salvation, provision, mercy, and praise to communicate His thoughts to specific people that needed Abba's intervention.

Faith: Abba's faithfulness is all the evidence you need.

Healer: Sickness and disease are conquered in His presence.

Unity: Unity is restored in His presence.

Victory: In His presence, every battle is won; every division is conquered.

Light: Light always overcomes darkness.

Salvation: Believe on the Lord Jesus, and you shall be saved.

Provision: Abba meets our needs.

Mercy: Turn to me and have mercy on me.

Praise: Praise the Lord; the name of Abba is exalted.

Chapter Thirty-Seven

Jesus is the author and finisher of my faith
(Hebrews 12:2).

'It is our Jocheb!' shouted an excited Zara to her listeners at the dining area as she opened the door, 'and he has brought a friend!! Please, come in and join us at the table. There is enough of Halo Bread and Cholent Stew for everyone and more.'

'Good evening, Johana,' Josef greeted a bit on the cool side. 'This is Amina, our little sister. She wants to meet Prophet Jesus and his followers and start this New Year with the new way of life. She had turned her back to sin and followed me here when she learnt that we are all followers of Prophet Jesus and his new way of life.'

Zara hugged Amina in a welcome embrace as Josef dropped Amina's bag in the small room that would lead to the main house.

'You are welcome home, Jocheb and Amina! First of all, Jocheb, there are people already at the table. I must tell you something before you come into the dining room. Amina, please go through that door and make yourself comfortable at the table,' she spoke eagerly to an overwhelmed Amina.

'No, Johana. Give her time to freshen up a bit, and then you can introduce her. Meanwhile, I will freshen up a bit too and wait here for you.'

She nodded to all he had said with a smile, wondering at the name he had addressed her before she spoke. 'Please wait, Jocheb. Amina, I will introduce you, but you must come back here to the portico after you have freshened up. Again, you are very welcome. Give me a few seconds to talk to my brother, and I will show you where to wash up.'

Amina nodded, keeping a smile on her face while Josef wore a puzzled look, but said nothing. His sister had more to say.

'Jocheb, before I go off with Amina, I need to get this out of my chest.' She paused and had the look of one battling some issues in her mind. Kneeling down, she spoke, 'Please, forgive me for what I told Miriam. Please, I am truly sorry. Don't keep away from me this coming year!'

He smiled and nodded his head, pulled her up to her feet and stooped as he hugged his sister.

Chapter Thirty-Eight

Blessed are the merciful for they shall obtain mercy
(Matthew 5:7).

The arrival of Amina changed the dynamics of the atmosphere as far as Miriam was concerned. All protocol of the Sabbath silence was broken, and everyone wanted to know who was who. The elderly woman behaved strangely, and she was not restrained. She got up, looking scared, and sat down again. She had stopped eating, and this day was getting more exciting by the hour.

'My dear family,' began Zara, looking excited as she returned from the portico, 'please meet Amina, a new member of the family and great news, JOCHEB IS HERE! Jocheb will say more about Amina when he has freshened up.'

Amina waved at everyone in greeting and followed Zara out silently through the direction of the portico.

'I was expecting Josef. Who is Jocheb?' the elderly lady asked.

'Brother of Zara,' Miriam answered kindly.

'Who is Zara?' she asked, looking a bit confused when she realised that the younger ladies were looking at her with amused expressions.

'Mother, what name do you know our hostess?' Razi asked.

'Johana.'

'Johana is also Zara!'

Razilla beamed, and both she and Miriam turned their heads in time to see Zara beckon to the elderly lady to come with her. The lady got up slowly from the table, walked even more slowly towards the portico where her daughter stood, and finally disappeared with Zara. Amina returned to the table, looking fresh and a bit more subdued. Miriam knew Amina was a bit uneasy. However, that was not her concern. Instead, she was itching to ask a question before the elderly lady was beckoned away to confirm her suspicion.

'Razi, do you know the elderly lady?'

Amina answered, 'She is their mother.'

'Mother? Whose mother?' Miriam and Razilla exchanged looks as they realised they had asked the same question simultaneously.

'Johana and Josef.'

As Miriam was absorbing this shock of the unveiled truth, Razilla asked: 'Are you their sister too?'

'No, but Josef and Johana have just adopted me as their sister. Johana is trying to convince Josef to stay the night and not rush off. He insists he will go back this night to his own home, and Mother Abi is so upset about this. She, too, has happily agreed that I could be her daughter too! I am so overwhelmed. I am sorry if I sound pushy and forward, but I cannot believe all that is happening to me. I began this day as a lady of red with no family, no friends, and no prospects for the New Year. But now, I have a family. I will start a new life, meet Prophet Jesus and ha...' She had become emotional.

Miriam was touched to see this young girl weep out her heart and not finish her words. She reasoned within herself that if Josef was going out of the house, she would stay here, but if Jocheb changed his mind, she would go back to her own house. She did not want to examine her heart closely as to why she was making these decisions, or why she was relieved to hear that Amina was just like a sister to Josef or why she also felt overwhelmed and emotional by all that was happening around her. She unconsciously watched Razi make small talk with Amina. Probably trying to persuade her to eat and not get carried away by her sudden fortune! At that moment, Zara, Jocheb, and the elderly lady reappeared. Their eyes were red. Razilla, on impulse, got up and went to embrace all three in turns and finally gave the elderly lady another long hug. She had followed Razi's cue. Jocheb had embraced her tightly before he had released her. The hugs brought fresh tears from everyone. She felt very emotional and was sure her eyes were brimming with tears. She knew she was remembering her own life and wishing she could experience the joy of a family reunion. *Abba, this is what I want too. Reunite me with my husband and children, since You are the God of miracles. I don't know how you have managed to unite this very evil woman to the children she abandoned and harmed grievously!!! This is an astonishing miracle!*

'We have an announcement to make,' Zara said, suddenly getting everyone's rapt attention when she could seize a moment. She suddenly felt like a big sister in the family, sharing duties

147

amongst younger family members. The room became still with an air of expectancy.

'With me here today is my mother—Mother Abigail, Josef my younger brother, and Amina our little sister. I wish to be called Johana, and Jocheb wishes to henceforth be called Josef.' Razi clapped, and soon Amina joined in. Zara had more to say.

'As you may have all noticed, my mother and I are wearing very special clothes. This is because today marks a new chapter in our lives and relationship as mother and daughter. Mama has found salvation with Jesus. She has repented of the past, and Josef and I have forgiven her.

'Abba, be praised,' Mother Abigail said, cleaning her eyes again with a bright pink cloth she was given for that purpose.

'After breakfast tomorrow, we will all sit together here and share testimonies. Mama wants to share how God led her to me. She is keeping that back for all of us to hear. The day after tomorrow, we will visit Mother Mary and the friends of Prophet Jesus, where we have been invited for a New Year's party. For tonight and tomorrow, everyone is my guest. Amina, I know you will be happy to help Razilla with the table and dishes after our meal.

'Of course,' Razi said, looking towards Amina, who smiled sweetly as she nodded her head.

'Thank you, Miriam. I know you would be glad to do the rooms upstairs with me. Yes?'

'Why not? My pleasure.'

'Thank you, Josef. I know you are eager to keep Mama's company and hear her testimony.' Josef merely raised his eyebrows at that.

How clever Zara is, Miriam thought to herself! She decided to go a step further, 'Johana, just tell me what you want done in each room, and I will do it alone. I am sure you too would want to hear your mother's story.'

'Thanks, Miriam. I have it all sorted out, but Mama will live permanently with me, so I can always hear her story over and over again, but Jocheb, oops, I mean Josef will be leaving after the visit to Mother Mary. Thank you all the same for your good intention. Let's go upstairs once we have finished eating and said the Sabbath Blessings.'

Chapter Thirty-Nine

Now therefore I pray You, if I have found favour in
Your sight, let me know Your ways that I may now You
(Exodus 33:13).

Miriam tried her best not to dwell mentally on the picture of the twenty-five-year-old girl who had come to get tips from her on how to be an expert lady of the red. Luckily, her mind was instantly pulled along from such thoughts as she was drawn to admire the rich tapestry on the stairs landing and thick quality carpets on the stairs and walls. They were just like hers, but in different colours. She wondered again and remembered. Jocheb, at the beginning, had admired her interior decoration and had asked her for the decorator that helped her. He had also asked her about the whereabouts of her purchases while praising her for her good tastes. Would Zara own up if she were asked about all this? Zara saved her the trouble.

'Miriam, I want to apologise for not being open to you about my brother, Josef. As you must have realised, he was not just a client to you initially. Now, of course, you know he is a true friend of yours.'

'So, he was your spy at the beginning?'

'Sort of,' she replied, giving a short laugh as she opened a window and went over to a cupboard to bring out beddings. 'Do you remember when I came for advice from you?

'Yes.'

'You advised me to *up* my tastes and my value. I wasn't trying to rival you. Just wanted to up my game then. I am sorry…'

'There is really nothing to apologise for. It was all part of your business strategy. I would have done the same. I do not take any offence at all.' This was greeted with a firm hug from Zara.

Miriam wondered about Mother Abigail as they spread the beddings, wore on the pillowcases, puffed up the pillows, and ensured a lavender candle was glowing. Miriam noticed they repeated the same pattern for each of the four bedrooms. At the fourth bedroom, she asked, 'So, have you thought about the sleeping arrangement?'

'Yes. You and I will take my room. Razilla and Amina will take one. Josef will take one, and Mama will take the one next to my room.'

'Johana, I am so happy for you. You look different. I see you are contented and filled with true happiness.'

'Yes, but my true happiness will be complete with holding my own child, having many children, and a good man who fears the Lord to love me. Miriam, I have something in that regard to share with you. But firstly, what are your own dreams? You still have not told me your real name. Is it so hard for you, then?'

'Yes, because I have had four different lives.'

'Still, you began with your first original name. What was it?'

'Eliana.'

'Lovely name! Let me call you that. I want you to know that we love you as a sister and care for you. The Prophet said that our kindness and love should be seen by others in everything we do, like shining lights. I am glad we are all going to sit together as a family and hear Mama's testimonies. She hasn't told me all of it. She wanted Josef to be around as well. For a start, will you be glad for us all to call you Eliana?'

'No Johana, please don't call me that name. I will give myself a completely new name. I am thinking about it. People don't change overnight. I am glad to start the New Year with God's people in your house tomorrow. I appreciate all your efforts to help me. I don't know why I feel afraid and still think I am the one who will not be lucky like you lot.'

'Miriam, please tell me your full story this night; please. God brings people across our paths to shine His light so we can see the right way to go.'

'Why not?' But tell me, how did your mother find you in Jerusalem when she last saw you in Capernaum several years ago and knew you by Johana?'

'Ahhhh, that was the first question Josef asked her after their reconciliation! She will tell us all that later and even about my father. After your story this night, I want to tell you what really made Josef and I forgive our mother. Truly, Miriam, our steps are ordered by the Lord! Let us go downstairs and see what everyone else is up to.'

Even from upstairs, all the way to the living room, they heard voices and realised that everyone else had seated themselves and were listening to either Razilla or Mother Abigail tell her listeners some miracles of Prophet Jesus. They joined the listeners, and Miriam realised that Mother Abigail was responding to a question.

'...Prophet Jesus had answered that question when his friends had asked him about Celidonius, who was blind from birth. He had said it was for God's glory and not because Celedonius was being punished due to his sin or the sins of his parents.'

'This is becoming more confusing! So, do some of us suffer afflictions for God's glory?' Miriam was glad when Amina asked a question that reflected her thoughts aptly.

'Mother Abigail, let me understand you. Will it be for God's glory if a child is orphaned and abused in many ways in this life?'

'Think about it this way, Amina,' Razi offered, 'it is because of Jesus we are all here today. We have become a family, and God takes glory for that. Never for evil. Whatever the devil did to each of us here, we did not die. God reverses the evil to benefit us in the end. Lord Jesus said he is the way to Abba, and he has come to call sinners like us to repent so that we will not die in our sins. What is this sin—not believing that the Lord Jesus came from Abba to set the captives free. Abba will take the glory for our freedom.'

'I remember Razi that you said you heard the Lord Jesus say that salvation had come to Zacchaeus when he gave out the money he had stolen from the poor. Remember?'

'Yes! And to Mother Ahuva, the Samaritan lady he met at the well. He said salvation is from the Jews. This is good news for the captive. She was set free that day when she believed he was the Chosen One.'

'I understand now. So, whatever afflictions we are bound to by the devil, it is through believing in the Lord Jesus that will get us saved by Abba's mercy. Salvation,' Amina affirmed.

'That is my understanding, too. He is the captive's rescuer from all sins,' Mother Abigail answered back.

'Well, it is late now,' Johana cut in. 'Tomorrow is the day we all get to listen to Mama's testimony. She says it is very special and wants every one of us to be blessed when we hear it. That was what you said, Mama, right?' Johana added, waiting for her mother's confirmation.

'That is correct, my daughter.'

Miriam could feel Josef's eyes trying to magnet hers to his. She heard his sister ask him to lead the night prayers.

'Dear God of Abraham, Isaac, and Jacob and all of us here, thank you for this Sabbath. Thank you for our meal. Thank you for this new year you have brought us into as a family. Make it special for us. Set us all free from whatever may be holding us back so that we can each wear the crown of freedom. Thank you for every one of us here again. Thank you for Prophet Jesus and how he is helping people everywhere. Bless our sleep this night; bless tomorrow for every one of us here. Accept this prayer in the name of our Lord Jesus, amen.

'AMEN,' everyone chorused.

Something new and revealing was etched in Miriam's mind that night from all that was shared. *It was a sin not to believe that Abba sent Jesus. It was a sin not to listen to Him!* What gladdened her soul, especially was when Razi said, *'It is because of the Lord Jesus we are all here today. We are a family because of Jesus.'* Abba had just given her a family! How else was this new year going to be special? One thing she knew as she stood up to get ready for bed—she was eager for tomorrow to hear the special testimony. How would it bless her...?

Chapter Forty

We conquer the enemy by the word of our testimony;
God's message is near you; on your lips and in your
heart (Revelation 12:11).

'My son, what a wonderful prayer! How did you get to know how to pray like that or even know the Lord Jesus?'

Everyone's ears in the room pricked up as they all stared at Josef. Gone was the mood for bedtime. Miriam realised she was not the only one who could not wait for tomorrow.

'Mama, God is in control even if things in our lives are out of control. I saw wonderful miracles starting from our Johana. I saw her change from being a lady of red to being a follower of the Lord Jesus. Mama, how did *you* hear about Prophet Jesus?'

He had asked everyone's question. Was Johana going to ask them all to wait for tomorrow?

Miriam noticed everyone shifted their attention to Mother Abigail. It seemed that for all of them present, it was this moment of revelation they had been looking forward to. Her mind was keen as she listened with rapt attention. *This was that very evil woman.* She discerned that Mother Abigail appeared to have received new strength and firmer will to relive her life the way she would have wished for thirty or even forty years back. Miriam longed for a mother. She felt Mother Abigail's eyes on her. As if calling back her wandering thoughts...

'...I became destitute for ten years: I had a genital disease that slowly killed me. I spent all I had, sold all my possessions, but that did not cure me. All my lovers had abandoned and rejected me. They thought that I was being punished for my sinful life. I thought so too...'

Miriam saw she had paused, but no one said anything, and Mother Abigail continued,

'I took to the streets as a beggar for eight years. Then I could no longer bear life in abject poverty. Gathering all my savings from begging, I set off. I started looking for you and your sister and found out you both had left Capernaum. No one could help me with any information. As I went through the town on foot, I saw a great crowd gathered at the door of someone's house. Something important was definitely happening because some members of the Scribes, Pharisees, and all manner of people were gathered at this house. I asked what was happening, and someone said, "Rabbi Jesus is teaching." I didn't really know who he was, but I joined the crowd. It was a good place to beg.'

Another pause, 'There, a miracle happened!'

She paused to recollect her thoughts. Miriam saw that Josef was impatient.

'A miracle, Mama?'

'Yes. I saw that lots of people had come from neighbouring towns. I even recognised some beggars from Nazareth and Bethany who told me that the Rabbi was a miracle worker. Soon, I understood why they had called him a miracle worker. I saw the unbelievable. I recognised Jonah, a paralytic who used to beg for money in Nazareth. He was being carried up to the roof. I saw helpers get several ladders, and his family lifted him to the rooftop. They were so bold! We all taught them crazy. As if that was not enough, they started removing the roof tiles as quickly as possible, but no one stopped them.

My depression left me at once as curiosity and wonder took over. While my eyes were glued to the roof in amazement, I thought about my own disease and began to have hope. I began to cry like some others, too. We were so touched to see Jonah hunched up in a basket held with strong ropes disappear down the hole in the roof!

It was as if time stood still. No one came out to examine the roof's damage or seize the men who were so tenacious as to damage it. Then we outside heard the prophet shout, *"My son, your sins are forgiven. Now you can get up, pick up your bed, and go home. You are thoroughly healed!"* Soon, everyone made a path for Jonah all the way from right inside the house to where I was outside, amidst deafening cheers of praises to God. Some beggars and wretched people like me all tried to rush in. Some of us managed to squeeze in. We begged him to have mercy on us too: to heal, save, and forgive us.

I wept and begged for forgiveness, healing, and his mercy. I shouted, "I WILL SIN NO MORE, I PROMISE." There were so many of us, and we all wanted to be near him, but we were being pushed away by his helpers. It was chaotic.

I couldn't get any closer. A miracle had happened to me there and then after I had shouted. At that same moment, a lot of miracles happened to all those who had cried out for his mercy. Well, I was healed spiritually and physically. Ruth from Nazareth said she could hear the Rabbi's voice! We became friends. She had been deaf!'

'You heard him say, *"Your sins are forgiven"* to Jonah, a paralytic?' Mother Abigail nodded. Her eyes were misty.

'And you also received your healing as soon as you claimed you would sin no more?' Josef asked.

'Yes.'

Miriam was confused. She had heard from Razilla earlier that it was not the sins of Celidonius or his parents that caused his blindness. She realised that Mother Abigail continued speaking after a drink of water offered to her by her daughter.

'After his preaching, he came out, and I followed on, waiting for an opportunity to thank him. That opportunity came much later—two men, one woman, and me who had patiently waited, went to meet the Rabbi. We thanked him for what Abba had done for us. He spoke to us all at the same time and said we should sin no more, and we would regain all that we had lost. Then I heard someone ask one of his disciples, Jude, if one's sins could cause sickness!'

'Mama, how was the question answered?' Johana asked.

'Jude said he heard learnt that sin could come in various ways, such as a person being a slave of the things they do, doing evil things or adopting a wrong attitude in life which is against Abba's will.'

159

Amina became inquisitive and lost more of her shyness, 'Mother, why did the Master refer to Jonah's sin?'

Mother Abigail answered after a sigh, 'I am not sure, but once I know my sins are forgiven, I am confident that God will meet whatever needs I have. That is my understanding of what some people said when they went to be baptised by Prophet John the Baptist. That was what enabled me to shout for forgiveness and healing. Now that Prophet Jesus has healed and forgiven me my sins, I have stopped feeling guilty or condemning myself for my past life of sin. I used to feel that Abba saw me as an outcast because of my lifestyle and how I treated my children. But all that is over. I have been set free. Abba has put a crown on my head. I fully belong to Him now.'

'We are all happy for you, mother,' Josef said softly.

'But my dear son, the miracle is that the Lord Jesus has the power on earth to heal and forgive sins!! He said so the day he healed Jonah. I heard people arguing amongst themselves about how a mere human like the Prophet could claim such power and authority to forgive sins like God!! I don't care about such arguments. I just thank God for that day I met him. Now, I am a totally a new person and born again!'

As Mother Abigail smiled, they clapped and praised Abba for her life, and she said, 'This is not the special miracle I meant to share. What I will share tomorrow will blow your mind. Abba is a God of miracles!'

Josef was witnessing a miracle; he could not believe his ears. His mother was discerning and repentant, even preaching and testifying. She had seen the light, put an end to the negative cycle in her life, and created a new standard for herself in her faith. She had experienced healing and restoration by taking that one step to follow the life the Lord Jesus had given her. She believed in him. *My soul blesses God.* He was far from sleepy, and so was his sister!

'So Mama, apart from not going back to your old life, what else has changed in your life? I know you promised Abba you would sin no longer.' Miriam discerned that Johana did not want to let go of this magical night. She looked around them all; no one wanted to. She was glad, so she sat tight and listened on…

'Well, from that day onwards, I continued to follow him and his helpers for about a year. I learnt to identify what my sin was, and I stopped avoiding the laws of God. I started to pray and fellowship with God's people. Finally, I began to believe the Prophet's words, and that he was the Chosen One. I had been like Adam, who hid from God's presence because he had disobeyed Abba's command. I had also been living in self-pity: being an orphan sold into slavery and later led to prostitution. All that was no excuse or a reason to live an evil life, but it was clear that I had failed to do what was good. I had the wrong attitude as a mother and as a daughter of Abraham. Of course, I knew God condemns sins such as stealing, fornication, and other vices. But I asked myself this one crucial question: *how will I stand before God if my own heart is condemning me for not keeping His commandments?*

The answer was to change my wrong attitudes and be guilt-free. You know he is from our village; I used to look down on him. Many people did too. He didn't do miracles in our village because of people like me. Well, I know better now, and so after my healing, I continued to follow him and his followers in Galilee and Capernaum. As I listened to his words, my thinking and attitude towards life changed. I have a new identity and personality. I understand what love is. I have eaten the blessed bread he shared miraculously in Capernaum. I spoke to him once, and I asked how I could be saved? I was told to receive the good news. My son, do you know the *good news*?'

Josef's action softened Miriam's heart. She remembered her motherly love when she was Dinah. Josef embraced his mother and while hugging her, she replied quietly: 'What God wants you to do is to believe in the one he sent.'

'Mama, were you really in that crowd of the bread sharing?'

He broke their embrace and saw that she was crying. So emotional did she feel that she could not trust herself to speak then, so she nodded.

At this point, as if to some secret agreement between them all, Miriam found herself getting up with the rest of the family after the goodnight blessings. Privacy was given to mother and son to bond as the rest were shown their allotted bedrooms upstairs. *How blessed to have a mother…family…*

Chapter Forty-One

Be still and know that I am God (Psalm 46:10).

'Mama, I was there at the sharing of bread in Galilee!! To think my mother was there and I never knew!! Mama, I too was healed of a disease,' he said quietly to his mother, who was staring at him in surprise. 'Yes, I was healed from male prostitution and a life of fornication for 15 years, Mama!! As soon as I left you as a nine-year-old, I lived with our Johana. When she gave her body to men, I gave mine to perverts when I turned 12. When I became fourteen, a client rented me a room where I lived for another two years. At 16, I left Johana in Capernaum and came to Jerusalem with the help of some of my clients. I soon became wealthy, but I was so miserable, unhappy and often suffered from serious depression. I could not get out of my lifestyle, didn't seem to know how to, and longed to be normal and have my own family. I ate the bread of Prophet Jesus, and I have never gone back to that debased life. I am now engaged in timber transport. It amazes me how I never thought I could be involved in another way of life other than the one I saw around me. I never thought it possible that the son of a leper and a fallen woman could be accepted into society till I ate that bread and fish. Mama, stop crying!!!'

'I am so happy, so thankful to God. He has done so much. Now, I see that you have also brought home your future wife. Am I right?'

'No, Mama. She is your new daughter now, remember? I see her as my little sister. The woman I love is *Miriam,*' he suddenly whispered, 'but she is afraid of her past to accept my love.'

'I can discern Miriam is a lady of red. Am I right?'

'Yes, but she is beginning to change. How did you know?'

'It takes one to know another, that's all. I believe she will change when she meets the Lord Jesus this week. No one who meets the Lord remains the same. I now know that. Then, she will have a change of heart towards you.'

'I believe so, too. Razi and Johana told me she was beginning to open up. She hardly ever visits, and she has begun to do so, neither has she refused the idea of visiting the Prophet.'

'You know, Josef; she reminds me so much of a lady I sat next to in Galilee! I have forgotten her name now. She was with another younger lady and two young boys from Nazareth. Do you know anything about her family and where she comes from? She kind of looks foreign. Is she a Jew?'

'Of course, she is Jewish, Mama. Don't let the hair deceive you. She is an orphan, Mama. All her family died a long time ago in a fire. She doesn't talk much about her life. I know nothing else about her.'

'How many Jewish females have you met with such hair, and why do you want her to be your wife? Her beauty and prowess in pleasuring?'

'Mama, you are full of questions. One at a time!! Yes, I want her because of her beauty and pleasuring as you say. I know not many Jewish ladies with such hair beauty, but she is Jewish. I really want her as my wife. Do you want to know why? Well, because I know we would always understand each other, considering where we are both coming from in our past sins.'

'Speak to the Lord Jesus about this, maybe after the first weeks in the New Year, Josef. No mother is happy for a son to marry a lady of red, even if she were the most beautiful woman on earth!'

'No mother would want her daughter to marry an ex-male prostitute even if he were the most charming and as tall as Saul. I wouldn't bother the Prophet with such personal stuff, and by the way, why do you call the Prophet Jesus, Lord?'

'Changing the topic, are you?' she sighed. 'About the Prophet? Everyone does. What kind of man is able to heal all who are broken-hearted? Makes the lame to walk? Sets people free from blindness and deafness? Makes the mute speak? Frees people from being slaves to sex addiction and all manner of diseases, including leprosy? Frees the demon-possessed or feed thousands of people with only a few loaves of bread and fish twice? And the greatest? He raises the dead to life!! Elijah, the greatest of our prophets, did not do some of these things, Josef. I witnessed a man called Lazarus raised to life! I was there; everyone praised God for sending Himself in the flesh. Jesus is *My LORD*, Josef.'

'And *My Lord* too, Mama!'

Abigail knew the night was far spent. She did not want this dream to end, and she held on to her son and wouldn't let go of him. She had never felt motherly. Motherhood was sweet. How had she avoided it?

'So Josef, why are you confident that only Miriam and not some other woman would understand your past?'

She saw her answer come quickly as Josef himself stood up, giving a full stretch of his tall, handsome body. What a very handsome man. What lovely grandchildren she would have, but she was disappointed at his answer.

'Mama, my past is buried and to be forgotten. Never to be mentioned in my new life. I have no plans to tell anyone else. Goodnight, Mama,' he said with affection reflecting in his eyes as he embraced her and felt her gripping embrace. He listened as she spoke in their reunion embrace.

'Good night, my beloved son. Thank you so much for forgiving me for all the evil I caused you and your sister in the past. I love you so much. Whoever you bring as your wife will be a daughter to me. I will love her equally, too—even Miriam. I still have so much more to share with you both together about those years I was in the wilderness. I have come a long, long way.' As he broke off from their hug, he wondered how she had managed what she had just said with a clear voice, considering the number of tears he saw in her eyes!!

Chapter Forty-Two

Angels are singing: You are worthy O Lord
(Revelations 4:11).

Abba's angels were excited and eager to carry out their messages, which they considered very important to those that would receive them into their souls. Like cotton kites, they floated invisibly in their zillions. They understood that communicating Abba's thoughts would eventually be discerned by those who were earmarked. It was their appointed time, and they shared in the joy of the blessed recipients.

Life: *Life is in His name.*

Faith: *According to your faith, it will be done to you.*

Wisdom: *If you obey and serve Abba, you will spend your days in pleasure and prosperity.*

Deliverance: *Forget the former things. Do not dwell on the past.*

Salvation: *Unbelief is sin. Do not consent to sin.*

Strength: *Abba has armed you with strength for every battle.*

Salvation: *If anyone comes after Abba, he must deny himself, take up his cross, and follow Abba.*

Hope: If we ask anything according to Abba's will, He hears us.

Knowledge: Abba is the stem; you are the branches.

Deliverance: Abba, You are my God. Earnestly I seek You.

Wisdom: Cast all your anxiety on Abba because He cares for you.

Chapter Forty-Three

*Your heart and mind must be made completely new
and you must put on the new self which is created in
God's likeness (Ephesians 4:23).*

Amina was reminiscing the entire evening. She had felt immediately disappointed when she saw she had been paired up with Razilla for the night. She had instantly recognised Miriam. Her business was so famous that her 'name and fame' had preceded her. Either she didn't know it, or she acted like she didn't know it. Amina had continued to study her surreptitiously throughout the evening. Her facial expressions were completely blank and gave nothing away. She knew that if she had such great, uncommon but natural beauty, she would have been proud and self-conscious. She would have made a lot of money and gone off to settle in a palace, have her own man, maidservants, children, and live a life of luxury. She would feast and look opulent and wear only the best apparel. Wealthy people should always wear their best.

She had studied her heroine. She had been aspiring to be like her, even dreamt of a chance meeting. Miriam's clothing was the only thing that gave off her wealthy status. It sparkled high quality, and she wore gold ornaments on her wrists and neck. *It had to be gold! She was so wealthy, right?* She suddenly felt a desire and longing for such fineries. What other kind of job could she take on? Taking a new life would make her even poorer. What was she going to do now? Work as a house servant? Work in the fields? And where would she live? It would be an answered prayer to marry a rich man. Josef was obviously smitten by Miriam, she realised. Who would not? The other women were all beautiful in their own rights, but only enhancement would make them as stunning as Miriam. Without the makeup, their beauty was not extra striking.

Amina tried to catch Miriam's eyes. Miriam did not pretend to be unaware of people staring at her or stealing glances. She would return the stare with those lover's eyes!! One could drown in them; they were not common eyes. They were laced with such thick long lashes. How did she achieve such a waistline? She had the best and perfect curves she had ever seen in a female. Yet, she carried herself innocently, unaware of her assets. Amina looked at Josef and realised she was not the only one vying for a return gaze. She was watching Josef, trying unsuccessfully to communicate something between him and Miriam. Miriam kept a client smile on her face while Josef was actually wooing her openly with a very warm smile and eyes that were pleading. She glanced away, wondering. How could a man living the new life of the Lord still be attracted to a prostitute? Was it her beauty making Josef ignore her sin? Why was she here? Was she also leaving her sinful life like herself?

'Have some more wine, Amina,' Razilla had whispered into her ears during the evening dinner. 'The wine will help you feel at ease, like everyone else. You are far away. Where are your thoughts?' She knew Razilla had seen her new protégé blush.

Amina did not answer immediately. For two seconds, she regretted she had been caught red-handed staring at Josef. It might have sent the wrong message to Razilla, who was probably trying to get her to back off the wrong tree! She had felt so mortified.

'Truthfully, Razi, I was thinking about where the future would lead me.'

'We will discuss that when we get together. Let that not worry you for now. Enjoy the wine and the fellowship.'

'True.'

The dining table was solid oak, Amina realised. Their host was evidently wealthy as well. Was she as rich as Miriam? How had they become friends? Would she ever get this rich? She shifted her gaze momentarily to Johana, who was in the middle of telling a tale to a listening group that had included her!! How had she strayed from listening to the story? She reconnected again, but it was the very end, and she heard the last bit.

Johana: 'So, eating without washing your hands doesn't make you as a person unclean!'

Josef: When I was in Tyre, the Lord himself was there. I heard about this lady from Canaan who had clung to his feet, begging the Master to heal her daughter from a demon. You know the daughter was not there, but because she had *believed* the Lord's words could heal, the daughter was cured and rid of the demon! The lady was a gentile, but the Lord did not move away from her.

Mother Abigail: What of Lydia, who suffered for 12 years with a blood issue? She was unclean according to the laws of Moses for women who are in their monthly time. So she touched Jesus' clothes, believing in a miracle for her healing. And guess what? She got instantly healed. The Lord did not become unclean…'

Chapter Forty-Four

*He hath chosen us in Him before the foundation of the
world that we should that we should be holy and
without blame before Him in love (Ephesians 1:4).*

These different conversations after their dining were twirling around Amina's thoughts. She, like everyone else after Josef's prayers, listened to Mother Abigail's life story before and after she met the Lord. Afterwards, they climbed up the heavily carpeted stairs, and each went into their allotted room with their secret thoughts like hers. She and Razi had cleared the table and done the dishes. As she reflected on Razilla, it seemed she was the kind of woman who got on with chores and did not talk much. Maybe she did not want any distraction, which might get some of the expensive crockery ruined. Or had she been engrossed in her own secret thoughts too? She had dominated their conversation, which had centred on the various ways she prepared the Sabbath meal compared to some other people she knew. Was she trying to get her relaxed or something?

At last, she was not surprised when Razi had asked for her life story!! That was quite bold and presumptuous of Razi! She noted Razi had listened in spellbound silence and sometimes even opened her mouth to let out a gasping sound. *Razi must be so soft-hearted...*

When Razi began narrating her own story, Amina realised why Razi had been so affected. She had stopped drying the dishes and turned to gaze star-eyed! How uncanny that they both had the same fate!! Razi was a gentile like herself! She had been an only child who lost her parents for the same reasons she had lost hers — slavery! Razi had started her road to whoredom in the same bar that Josef had found her!! Three years ago, a man named Simeon had come to call her out of that life, saying, 'The Master wants to change your life forever.' That was how she turned her back to being a lady of red three years earlier. At the end of Razi's story, they had hugged each other and wept. Amina knew she had found a friend and a senior sister. She felt more confident and developed an immediate attraction and bond with Razilla. When they got to their room, it had already been prepared! Then she remembered that Johana and Miriam had been assigned the duty of making the rooms.

Chapter Forty-Five

The Lord will guide you continually and satisfy your
soul in drought (Isaiah 58:11).

Miriam had begun her reflection even before she got to their assigned room. She talked to God: *Abba, I can see You have been busy changing everyone's lives. I can't change my own life or the circumstances that have made me become Miriam. Can You change me and my circumstances too? Please create a new me; then I can become joyful and appreciative of these new friends You have given me. Thank you, but I want to be transformed too. If You could transform Mother Abigail's heart, then You can transform my mind and heart. Please, Abba. Don't leave me out again. I am going to trust You. I will give You the gift of my Nerd for all that You have done for my friends, especially Mother Abigail!! It is my most precious perfume. Everyone is taking, receiving and gaining from You. What do they give you in return for their gratitude other than just a mere 'Thank You! I wonder, Abba…*

It had occurred to her that her mind was not preoccupied with the splendour of Johana's wealth, as she knew some others might have done. There were many battles in her mind. She fought each one at a time and at the opportune time. The one currently facing her was the question of divulging her past completely to Zara, who now called herself Johana. True, she had mentioned that she had four lives, but she had not given the details of each life. Who knows, Zara might want her to change her name. Zara had insisted she started from her original name, Eliana. *Did she want to?* It was *Miriam who* had brought her wealth, fame, individuality and had sheltered and protected her from her past. What was all this sentimentality? Did she really want to be drawn to it? She jerked when she realised Zara had broken into her eerie.

'Here we are, Eliana!! Hope you are not having second thoughts about tomorrow?'

'No Zara, I...'

'Johana! Eliana, please remember,' she sounded irritated and had spoken in formal Hebrew reserved for mere acquaintances, 'That name is dead to me now.'

'I understand, Johana. I am hoping you too will respect my preference where names are concerned,' she replied quietly as she watched Zara close the bedroom door.

She saw Zara did not say anything, even though they were now alone in the bedroom. She instantly noticed the big difference between Zara's bedroom and hers. It was not designed to tease or give pleasure. Instead, it seemed a plain room decorated with a sense of good taste. Instinctively, she pictured her thick, deep wine curtains, custom-made with splashes of nudity at different stages of undress. Her bed was much higher, with a raised arch framing the headrest and sides. It held jars of soothing balms, scented oils, hair jellies, cleansing cloths, tantalizing perfumes, and other lubricating gels. Her friend broke into her eerie again.

'I hope you agree with the white curtain blinds, curtains, and the pink and white striped beddings?'

Did she honestly think that white represented purity! 'Johana, those are not my thoughts.' She looked at her friend directly with a gaze that explained her thoughts, and she was successful.

'Miriam, please listen to me first.' Then after a pause, she spoke her heart out to this beauty in a very soft voice intended to aim at her stony, cold, and doubt-filling heart. She had deliberately reverted to the usual Hebrew tongue used for family and very close friends.

'Our faith grows by facing our problems. Take small steps of faith and watch the Lord meet all your needs. I understand you do not wish to unburden and share your past with me. Fine. Give all that to the Lord whenever you meet him. All I will ask you now is—do you know the meaning of *Miriam?*'

'Some customers or two might have mentioned it at some point in time, Johana. And I thank you for accepting to respect my wishes this night.'

She saw her friend nodded, and this greatly relieved her. Too much had been taken in this one day, and she was not even given a chance to ponder and meditate. Jacob was patient and knew how to give her time without creating tension. He had never pressured her to say her past to him, even though she had sensed that was what he wanted to know. He had said so much about himself and did not make her feel guilty for withholding information about herself. Yet, Johana, Josef, and Razi could not handle her silence on her past. Were they themselves not leaving a trade that had ingrained so much patience, like farmers who waited for their crops and seasons to give a bumper harvest? She brought back to mind how she had waited patiently for many of her clients to reach their climax. There was no rush. It was a pity that there could be no further conversations between them this night. She had wanted to be told more about Mother Abigail, Josef, Amina, and other things relating to the Prophet.

She had not been surprised to feel the invisible barrier, so impenetrable, which Johana had built between them. Johana had asked her the meaning of 'Miriam', but she had not given her the meaning. It had been a friend's way to offer a final truce, and she had declined it as it seemed. Each had gone through the motions of bathing and dressing for bed. She had been handed a brand-new nightgown with a false air of gaiety. As she got into bed, it occurred to her she would never in her lifetime, in her own home, have worn such a gown that was not sexy in colour and style! She found herself smiling inwardly. This new life!! However, not wanting to seem so impossible, she had adorned herself in the white gown. There is always a first time for every experience in life, she told herself. She wondered if Johana was waiting for her to succumb to guilt and give her a tap and say, '*Okay, Johana. I am sorry about all this. I don't know the meaning of Miriam. Do you? I chose it because it was the name of Moses' sister. What else would you like me to share about my past? Please, sit up and let us talk a little.* She soon heard the way Johana breathed. She had slept off!

Chapter Forty-Six

Your Word is a lamp unto my feet and a light unto my path (Psalm 119:105).

Abba sent out His angels as usual, who communicated His thoughts for the benefit of many on earth, like Miriam. It would be a lifeline...

Wisdom: Commit everything you do to the Lord; trust Him, and He will help you.

Instruction: *Remember the Sabbath day and keep it holy.*

Beauty: *Abba has made everything beautiful in His time.*

Salvation: Rejoice in the day of your salvation.

Deliverance: Arise from the depression in which the circumstances have kept you.

Peace: Let us make every effort to enter the rest of Abba.

Hope: *There is hope for a tree cut down.*

Justice: *Abba is just and will settle the cases of His people.*

Faith: *Be fully persuaded that Abba is able to do what He has promised.*

Knowledge: *Abba founded the world and all that is in it.*

For by Abba, all things were created: things in heaven and on earth, visible and invisible, whether thrones or powers or rulers or authorities; all things were created by Him and for Him.

Chapter Forty-Seven

Pour out your heart like water in prayer to the Lord
(Lamentations 2:19).

For a while, Miriam engrossed herself by listening to Johana's breathing, the silence, the darkness, and taking in the newness of her present surrounding. She was conscious of the New Year. It was pregnant. Her soul was immersed in the swirls of all the testimonies she had heard this day, from the moment she stepped into Razi's house to the end of the evening in Johana's house. Something was cooking up for her. *Miriam* was pregnant, and she wondered what this personality would birth out for her. Just as she was waiting for sleep, her body, mind, and heart attacked her. Her body wanted sex. This was not unusual. When this happened, the body was fed with sordid imaginations of her best two clients: Kazim or Jocheb, and sometimes 'Elizabeth's husband.' It was her way of masturbation. This time around, however, her mind won over her body and asked her the meaning of her name. Her thoughts shifted. *My name? What is important about that? I have borne it for seven years with no mishap...*

Eliana – which is my childhood name, had brought me no luck, she thought. *Did I kill my own mother at childbirth? No one told me the truth of how I became an orphan or my true origin, and so I had to make up the story of the fire incident destroying my family...*

She summoned up her memory to when she grew up in a 'Charity home' for orphans and seemingly abandoned children in the city of Ramah. She had stayed there long enough to know that some of the children were sold to childless couples or hired as servants, and the worst—sent to the prostitution industry. She shook her head with tears brimming in her eyes. Many things happened to the children who were 'orphans': those who were deemed stubborn, lazy, or not good-looking were sent away, but then she did not know where. If the child was a particularly good-looking female or male, it was groomed for the pleasure industry. Such children were taught to dance, sing, read, and serve visitors that visited the centre. Now, looking at it from a different perspective, she understood the picture better. The value of such children with their extra talents would fetch a handsome price. She remembered the little boy called N. Everyone called him N, and he had called her E as everyone else did. N was brought there as a baby, too, so they had bonded over the years until she was taken away. She still felt the grief just thinking about N...

He was the only 'family' she ever had, and she remembers him being sorrowful at their separation. Then she saw babies and older children come into The Charity Home and fade into the unknown.

She asked herself the question she often did: Am I beautiful? Why do I feel worthless, unloved, miserable, and filthy?

Then her mind flashed back to a memory of how the personality of Eliana's life really began: She had been sexually groomed right from a tender age, and she was sold to a particular client, and that was when she knew both her name and age. As soon as that client saw her, he had hurled insults at Jibril. *'What do you think I am? A pervert? Why?!! She's just a filthy, ugly five-year-old without teeth and all hair!!!'* She heard her trader say, *'Be patient, Kabul! If you are not happy, return Eliana, and I promise to refund you.'*

It was the first time she was referred to as Eliana. It was when she was a bit older she realised E stood for Eliana. She wondered what N stood for. Nathaniel? Nathan? She pictured herself at that tender age, like an obedient puppy, doing all that she had been asked to do—Kabul turned out to be a pervert. He was a glass merchant in Sidon, but he opened up his own pleasure tavern where he took her. Then he asked her to choose a new name for herself. She remembered considering carefully about that before she had renamed herself Reubena. She still recalled why she had chosen that name. Another little seven-year-old girl had been called Reubena, and she had witnessed her being adopted by loving parents. Kabul had told her then that her life would be the best thing that ever happened to her. She would become rich, and she could use the money to find her birth parents or go off and start her own business in the best part of the world! Poor Reubena. She was so young and worked very hard and as faithfully as she could. She was put to work instantly, making money for Kabul. She served and amused other clients, singing, strip dancing, massaging till she was ten. Her body had developed fast, and by eleven, she was initiated into the real world of prostitution. That same year she was eleven, her life changed again when she met a client called Al Basrah.

Chapter Forty-Eight

Do not sorrow, for the joy of the Lord is your strength
(Nehemiah 8:10).

Miriam reminisced about how Al Basrah had been tender and showing care and concern, even teaching her how to read. He had promised her freedom. He was working on it; he had said. At the right time, he would let her know. He had kept on at this till she did not believe him any longer. Still, she liked him. He had shown he cared in various ways for her feelings…

'Reubena, I am very pleased with your reading progress!'

'I knew a little from Ramah before I came here.'

'You are quick at learning. You should not stay here forever. I will help you out Reubena, and you too can start your business.'

'That is what you always say, Al,' she replied, tugging at his sidelocks.

'You know I mean it, my beautiful.' He squeezed her delicate-looking hands lightly before planting a kiss on them. 'I know you will make lots of fortune, Reubena. You have a rare exotic beauty, and you are extremely caring to clients. Get them to give you generous tips.'

'Most do without my asking, but I don't bother. Kabul takes it from me. He always does. I give him all my tips so that he can trust me.'

'Kabul is not being fair!' Al Basrah said angrily, 'I will talk to him, or he will lose his best clienteles. This is what you will do meanwhile. Tell your clients to drop their tips for you with me. I am saving some for you as well. Don't worry, my pet. I will take you to Sidon, and we could do business together. Maybe even get married...'

Then six months later, after Al Basrah had lain with her, he told her to follow him to Samaria. On their arrival at Samaria, after they had something to eat and drink, Al Basrah told her how he had drugged Kabul with his guards and looted all his money. He had promised to give her some. He actually fulfilled his promise by giving her some money, but she eventually realised that he had resold her to Gwabar, the inn manager of where they had eaten. After that, she never saw or heard of Al Basrah. It was her first taste of betrayal and treachery. It was bitter than gall. How she had been able to move on to what she had become still baffled her till now.

In Samaria, she changed her name. It meant a new start and the dawn of a new personality. Reubena had been kind, honest, and caring, yet she was dealt with treacherously. Reubena's sterling qualities were signs of weakness, which did not go well with business. She had to learn that business lesson the hard and brutal way. She promptly lost faith in friendship and love, not trusting anyone ever. She had developed feelings for Al Basrah. If she ever got rich, she had told herself then that she would return to Sidon and have her revenge. Thinking about it now, how she went back to Sidon, hoping to find Basrah, she had hoped to find him and really discover what had happened. She still could not bring herself to believe that a man who had been so caring and tender would go that far as betraying her. It was too bitter a pill to swallow. Could she ever be able to trust any man?

Her mind naturally moved on to contemplate on Safirah, her next persona, who was on the verge of her twelfth year. Over the next three years of her life there, she had eventually become demonic and bestial. She vented her hatred, bitterness, and anger on everyone, whether they sought her for pleasure or just her mere acquaintanceship. She did not care if a client killed her, or her trader beat her up. She would fight till she died. Yet, there were clients with masochistic tendencies who thrived tremendously on the pleasures of a sadist. By thirteen, she had realized her power, strength, resilience, and realised she could hold even Gwabar, her trader and manager, to ransom. He gave her almost a third of the profits she made each night. At least, she was grateful to Al Basrah for ensuring that the deal was in place before she worked for Gwabar. Gwabar tried to outsmart her once when he reduced her earnings, even though he came to her for free. On that occasion, when he had come to her for his pleasure, she unleashed the beast in her with all her fury and hatred. Gwabar had received the beating of his life and had nearly died. She had punched him a hard blow on his naked manhood, the one spot she had realised that men were delicately vulnerable. She threatened to leave if he did not deal half the profits she made from clients henceforth and pay for his own pleasure.

Abba must have watched her back! Gwabar did not punish her or get her attacked or sacked. She was the star of his business.

Safirah had eventually become wealthy and reckoned with, but she was also emotionally wrecked. She wanted a real home, a husband, and children. It was an impossible dream, but she clung to the hope that she could live such a life in dreams. She could at least try it and chase her dream. Surely, there is a man out there looking for a wife. If that man did not know her past and what she really was, then it could happen. Having this hope and feeding it daily gave her the determination, boldness, and faith to accomplish her dreams. One morning, she left Gwabar's lodge house with just her purse hidden under her sarong and said she was taking fresh air and exercise. She paid for an escort to travel with her to Sidon.

At Sidon, a fourteen-year-old Dinah, later to be known as Miriam, was hired as a house servant because she accepted a low rate from Sosthenes and his wife, Keturah. She would never forget them as she mentally drew up their pictures before the visual screen of her mind. They were her role model. She got her first taste of real family life, something she had never seen, experienced or imagined. Her longing to become a wife and mother became very strong. She maintained a reputation of being humble, hardworking, patient, obedient and a faithful ideal house servant. As soon as sexual urges attacked her, she would drown herself in hard work in and around the house. Never did she ever once heed the suggestion of her mind to seduce Sosthenes, her master, when the wife was away. She found nothing too demeaning. She was resourceful, and the family prospered more with her service in the home. She had been so devoted to their own six children as if they were hers. Her dream came true a year later when a cousin of Keturah came to ask Sosthenes if she could become his wife! She became Lucas' wife for two years.

She reviewed how she had felt all those years ago. Her dream had come true!! Lucas was not a rich man, but he was a good man.

A family man and a righteous Jew. He wore the prayer shawl and the inner garment to remind him of his devotion to God. Lucas gave his heart to her, and she perceived she still had a heart to give in return. She did her best as a wife, and Lucas began to prosper, as she was so resourceful. A week into their marriage, she willingly gave him a bag of some of her past earnings. The only secrets she had totally kept back from him were her different names as a prostitute when she was Eliana, Reubena, and Safirah.

Also, the remaining money she kept in her body sarong. It was her security. Up till now, she could still recollect clearly and would never forget the look of surprise and adoration Lucas had given her when she handed him the money. He had not questioned her background or the money. He was content to believe that she was an orphan. With her help, he had invested the money into a profitable boat-building business. He treasured her so much. There was so much trust, faith, and love invested in her that she thought God had finally remembered her. She was able to develop trust and love in God and Lucas. Before then, she had never thought of God. But as Dinah, she had felt His nearness. She was no longer an outcast. She had been on the outside from when she had her earliest memories. Now, she had her own home. She had been accepted. She knew love. The best thing that happened the same month she became Lucas' wife was when she realised she was with child. She told him. *'My lord, I am with child...'*

Chapter Forty-Nine

My heart and flesh cry out for the living God
(Psalm 84:2).

At this point in her thoughts, Miriam felt as if some dry sand had been thrown into her eyes, and she felt her throat constrict. It was painful to have these thoughts, and as she shed silent tears, the storm within her was building up and getting ready to burst her dam. Where was God when this beautiful life came to a sudden crash? She remembered her little son. Where was he? Was he still alive? Was he a slave? Who had taken him? Was he living a life of abuse like the little boys with her in the Charity Home? The likes of N. There had been another child before she finally left Sidon at eighteen, conceived without Lucas' awareness. Leah was being fostered in safe hands. Even if her foster parents moved away to an unknown address to adopt Leah, she knew she was safe and would grow up in a home where she would receive love. But her son? She suddenly felt the heaviness of a dark shadow fall on her. She became so restless, tensed, and sorrowful and sobbed silently at first but gave in to deep, racking, loud wails. She saw she had woken Johana, who reached out to her. She willingly yielded, and Johana had embraced her in a motherly fashion, just as she used to do with those clients who needed comfort; the way she had embraced Keturah's children and had soothed their son, Levi. Lucas had named him Levi. She had called him Adam. To her, he was a new creation, born out of pure love without corruption.

She couldn't stop weeping and could not be comforted. God had thrown her back outside where she belonged, and Lucas had taken Levi. She was not shocked that her weeping in the early hours of dawn had stirred the entire household. The house was astir, but she did not care as she continued to cogitate about how Dinah's life had been abruptly turned over. She kept her eyes closed as they felt full of the dust of her past life. She wailed like she would die, and she did not know how long or what the different people were saying to her, all at the same time as they came into the room to offer her comfort.

'Miriam, what is it?'

'Did you and Johana quarrel?'

'Please, let me help you.'

'Let us take her to Jesus–'

'What shall we do?'

'Are you in pain?'

'Is it a bad dream?'

'Miriam, Miriam, it is me.'

'Abba help!'

'Miriam, we love you–'

'We are here for you—'

'Miriam–'

'Johana, what did you do to her?'

The weight of her bitterness and sorrow drowned all the balm they offered. Someone or everyone had tried to drag her out of bed, but she had forcefully resisted. It was not how much she had invested in her two-year marriage and all that she had gained that was most painful. It was her love for Lucas: he was her god, her love, and life. She could not erase the brokenness and look of betrayal on his face as she turned her back to leave him. It was so painful. She had not cried then, but the tears for the past were now released in torrents until the dust was out of her eyes, and they no longer hurt. Despite her pain and groaning in sorrow, her mind was still conscious that the house had become quiet, but she did not want to open her eyes. She felt Johana shift from holding on to her while she felt someone else take over from Johana. She dreamt of her son...

A young sixteen-year-old woman was nurturing her son at the breast—a good, healthy son she fondly called Adam. She wondered how any person would maltreat, abandon, or do evil to such as these. She caressed his plump left foot and fondly planted a kiss on his head. As the child nuzzled, she stroked his soft head. He was so much his father in every way. What had he taken from her? Nothing really, she thought, except just one thing—the birthmark. Like hers, it was on the lowest area of his back and centrally lodged at the junction of his bottom cheeks. It always made her wonder if one of her parents might have had the same birthmark! At this stage, she knew she was half-awake and consciously established that she had inherited hers from her own mother.

When she was consciously awake, she kept her eyes shut. Mother Abigail was administering a facial massage with calming balms. It was gentle and soothing. She did not have the grit of sand feeling in her eyes anymore. Her throat had lost that heavy lump of pain, and she felt no constriction. Her heart felt lighter, and the sleep may have done her some good. In no time, she stretched herself...

Chapter Fifty

Remember me oh Lord. Visit me with your salvation
(Psalm 106:4).

'Good morning, my daughter,' Mother Abigail greeted as she stopped the massaging, seeing that Miriam was fully awake.

'Good morning, Mother', she returned the greeting as she sat up. She felt refreshed, hearing the Hebrew language accent used by Mother Abigail. It also felt good to call someone 'mother'.

'The family has gone about their individual businesses, meetings, and chores. I hear there is an evening fellowship somewhere else. Razi will know. Don't worry. I will go with you to that one, should you want to go.'

She felt herself panic. Not at the thought of having missed listening to the special testimony with others, but knowing that this meeting she was to make with the Lord was inevitable. There was no escape. It meant she would become transparent and metamorphose like everyone else around her. Her name, livelihood, language, and lifestyle would all change. She panicked because Dinah's dream had ended after all the hope she had for a good life and a clean break from her past. It had not worked out for her. She had not become like a normal woman. She felt her bile releasing the pain slowly again into her system. She was lucky that Mother Abigail was sensitive and distracted her train of thoughts.

'There is a feast in two evening's time. Even if you will not attend any fellowship, you can come to the feast. Our Lord will be there. Johana said she would send the message to Mother Mary to tell the Lord to expect you. Don't think of returning home without meeting him.'

'Feast? Mother, what is there for me to rejoice about when I don't know where my son is? I once had a family and lived in bliss for two years. On my son's second birthday, a client from Samaria, who had known me as Safirah the harlot, arrived. I was exposed and stripped of all that I had. I was disgraced, and my Levi was taken away that very evening. It was a miracle that I was not stoned to death. My husband there and then claimed that he was not the father of our child. I had conceived our son that same month I came into his house. I had not cried then because I felt I deserved my punishment for being an evil woman. If I were not evil, all that had befallen me would not have happened...'

Abigail was the perfect listening ear. She remained still as her daughter's protégé poured out her entire life history from her life as Eliana through all her other personas to her life as Miriam. She unconsciously kept on a blank face. She felt triumphant that Miriam had been able to unburden herself, which she had been unable to do. When she realised Miriam was silent, she paused for some seconds and held both her hands in hers.

Then she spoke to God inwardly, begging Him to help Miriam as He had helped her. She asked God to give her the right words to draw Miriam closer to salvation and not put her off. Miriam was strangely calm. She hoped Miriam's mind had not retreated to that faraway place beyond feelings and emotions, but was present and listening.

'Miriam. See what happened to me!' Miriam found herself listening in awe as Abigail poured out her own life story.

'Now, you know my entire life story: waywardness, lust, greed, selfishness, wickedness, and evil. Yet, the Lord restored my health, sanity, and children to me in the end. It will be the same for you. Please, trust the Lord; you are not evil. You were a loving and wonderful mother—a much better mother than I was. You were a perfect wife introduced to a sinful life right from infancy. I deliberately walked into a sinful life because I was too lazy. I just wanted pleasure and wealth without having to labour. I did not have to follow in such footsteps. If I had not destroyed Johana's dreams, she would have walked away from the life she had known from me. Did she tell you she is engaged?'

It was remarkable that Miriam could keep her emotions under such firm control. She had shown no surprise at the news!

'No. I did not give her the chance. She wanted to hear my life story first, and I wasn't ready. So, she slept off.' She saw Abigail smile and then shake her head.

'Johana forgave me despite the great evil I did to her and her brother! She obeyed the Lord's command to forgive me. It was tough, but she did it. Well,' she sighed softly, 'her engagement is another testimony. I will let her tell you herself; I will be so happy and blessed to become your mother, too. I see that you and Josef have plans. Don't be scared to show your love. You deserve to be happy in that way again.'

Miriam remained quiet and passive.

195

'When you meet the Lord, whatever he tells you to do, just do it. He might tell you to forgive Lucas.' Then she stopped. *Was she talking too much and probably scaring Miriam? Why did she just say what she had said?*

'Don't mind me. We do not want you remembering the past and feeling anguished again. Let us talk about this party.' Miriam nodded her head.

'Can you guess where the feast is taking place?' Then she replied without waiting for Miriam to try a guess.

'At Simeon the Pharisee's house!' she spoke out with disdain, and she was not surprised to hear her listener gasp. Abigail continued to pour out her heart to Miriam. She was so drawn to her she could not explain why. She went as far as revealing things she could not mention to her own children. She was ready to adopt this woman as her daughter. Was that not the way Johana was blessed with Mother Mary in her absence? The Lord was in the habit of matching 'fathers' to 'sons', 'mothers' to 'daughters', and vice versa. Johana had said that some weeks ago, the Lord had given Nebo a 'father' and a 'mother'! Then, like lightning, a brainwave flashed in her memory, and she realised why she had been staring at Miriam during the Saturday Shabbat. *Hold on,* she thought! The morning was far spent, and neither had bathed and eaten. She played the mother.

'Come on, Miriam, go and wash while I see what Johana has in the house for us all. It is almost noon, and they will soon be back...'

'Mother, please, you go and eat something. I don't feel hungry. I will have some fruits when I am done. I will wait for dinner. I will go to the washroom now.'

Chapter Fifty-One

But now lord, what do I look for? My hope is in You!
(Psalm 39:7).

In the washroom, she reflected upon all that she had heard. *Why not give it a try? I will take small steps of faith as someone once advised me and cling to hope.* She called to mind how devoted Lucas was to God. He talked about everything to God. It was through him she learnt about the Shema, a Jewish prayer in the Torah that affirms that there is only one God who demands the love of every Jew with every aspect of their being—heart, soul, and mind. Lucas was a devout Jew, and he prayed the Shema three times daily without fail. She spoke to God now:

'Abba, I know You are here and listening because You are omnipresent. I know some facts about You from Lucas when I was Dinah and went to the synagogue with him. Like David said, there is no way we can hide from You: whether we go into the heavens, the seabeds or the darkness, You will be there. I know You are the potter, and we are the clay. It is my turn, God. Do for me what you have done for Abigail, Johana, Razi, Amina, Nebo, and many others. It is **my** turn. Turn to me and have mercy on me, please. Teach me Your ways too. I desire Your miracle too. Whatever You want me to do, tell me. Please, help me find Levi. Let Lucas forgive me. I did not come to his house with evil intentions. And God, I am no longer angry with Kabul, Al Basrah, Gwabar, Lucas, and whoever took me away from my own family. Please God, also remember dear Jacob and N.

When she came out of the washroom, she heard the voices of Johana and Josef below talking to their mother. She resisted the temptation to eavesdrop and went into the room to oil her body, hair, and dress up. Johana had come upstairs to meet her in the room. She seemed so full of joy. She remembered what Abigail had told her about Johana. *She must really be in love.*

'You look refreshed, Eliana. I mean Miriam. Do you...'

'Call me Eliana. It is okay, now. I have had a long chat with Mother Abigail.'

'Oh, Eliana!! I am so happy for you. Give me a hug.' She did, and she saw tears in Johana's eyes. 'That is a better name. Mother Mary Magdalene said Miriam means sea *of bitterness or sorrow,* but Eliana means *my God has answered me.* I had recently inquired when I asked about my own names, too.

'What do Zara and Johana mean?'

'Zara means something about the morning. Not so sure now, but Johana means *God is gracious.* I was going to ask you if you felt much better.'

'Yes, much better. Thanks. I also think the meaning of Johana is certainly much better than Zara,' she told Johana while completing the last stages of dressing up. She did not want to ask her about Josef's name. She was not ready for love. She had a sudden strong determination to find her son first. Maybe Josef, with so much burning love for her, could be instrumental in going back to look for Levi, who would be a ten-year-old boy now! So, she deliberately changed the topic on names.

'Johana, tell me. How have you been able to forgive your mother for the past? You also never mentioned to me that you had met with the Lord personally.'

'I didn't?!!' She was certain that she mentioned it and it had fallen on deaf ears. Her friend had not listened.

'No!'

'I did mention to you how I had met the Lord Jesus's mother, his brothers, and the disciples. How did I skip the most important thing? Razi must have told you, though.'

'Yes. About how she led you to believe in the Prophet.'

'Concerning my forgiving Mama, the Lord helped me, Eliana. It is called God's grace. As soon as he laid his hands on me and blessed me, I knew I was healed instantly. I wept out my heart in gratitude. I will never forget that day in all my life. He gave me new eyes and a heart to see and feel things differently. Before you and Razi came yesterday evening, Mama and I had talked a great deal. I realised Mama, too, had been crippled with very low self-esteem, addiction, and bad role models all her life. The Lord has enabled me to have compassion, which helped me to forgive her. I know it is the prayers of Mother Mary and her group of brethren which they prayed to God that helped prepare my heart.'

'Have you prayed for me, too?'

'Yes, all of us have been praying for you. You know I have from the moment I first received my salvation and started talking to you about Prophet Jesus almost three years ago. I remember those who matter to me, and I keep begging God to let His light come into their lives.'

Eliana confirmed this, but she said nothing. Instead, she hugged her friend and whispered *thank you* very softly. They went downstairs together. She was told that Razi had already taken Amina to see her house but that they would return for them all to meet at Simeon's house in two evenings' time. Miriam knew she needed a change of clothing and refused Johana's offer of fresh clothing. She kept her eyes stayed on Johana's.

'I need to change my clothes,' she told her new family, still maintaining eye contact with Johana. 'I promise to be back here to join you all. I do not want to miss the special testimony. Thank you, Johana, for the offer, but I will be more comfortable in my own clothes, please.'

'That is fine, Miriam,' Josef put in. 'I will come with you.' He started in her direction while his sister watched on a bit anxiously. The devil was so subtle and would do anything to fight for her soul.

'No, you don't have to, Josef,' she called back forcefully, with a smile as he neared her. 'Thank you very much. I really want to meet the Lord. I will come back.' As she stepped out the door, she saw Mother Abigail follow her. She was stunned, but she could not turn her away.

'We shall both be back by tomorrow. I will share my testimony then, and after that, we can all travel together,' Abigail told her children, who looked amazed. Their mother had been given renewed strength from above and the zeal of a caring mother over an adopted daughter!

Chapter Fifty-Two

Joy comes in the morning (Psalm 30:5b).

'My daughter, please walk more slowly. You remember how many miles I had walked in Capernaum all last week?'

'Mother, why have you come with me? Don't you trust me after all I have heard from you this morning and everyone last evening?'

'Just the chance to see where you live, my daughter.'

She decided not to reply. The walk would do her good. On the other hand, taking a horse would attract her to those roguish Romans who used any opportunity to claim the property of rich Jews.

'It is just to pick a few garments, isn't it?'

'Yes, mother. Thank you. You didn't need to put yourself into all this trouble.'

'If you had let Josef come, I wouldn't have needed to follow you.'

'True.'

'Are you going to tell Josef all that you told me this morning?'

'No.'

Abigail then caught on that Eliana did not like conversations as they walked, but she couldn't help herself. So, a little while later, she said,

'My daughter, I thought for a few seconds that I knew you when you first came into the house yesterday.'

'Hmn?'

'Yes. You reminded me of a lady who sat next to me at Galilee, where the Lord fed us with bread and fish.'

'Really?'

'She was about my age and had two children with her. One of the boys was so tall for his age. I remember gasping to learn that he was just nine at the time. He made me think of my Josef.'

'Interesting.'

'God was talking to me, and I did not know it. My Josef was in that crowd!'

'Hmn.'

'Can you believe the Lord got the meal he shared out miraculously from one of the boys? Few loaves of bread. I think five. And two small fish. Timothy gave it all up to the helpers of our Lord! I can never forget his name. I had thought the Lord was hungry and needed to eat. You know, for energy to do amazing miracles. Guess what happened, Eliana?'

'I heard the story from Johana, Josef, and Razi. He prayed to God, and that meal kept multiplying!!'

'There were twelve baskets full of extras!!'

'If you and Josef had not witnessed it, it would have been hard to believe. I can't wait to meet him. Mother look! We have arrived. Come now.'

Presently, Abigail saw they had come to a very large dwelling. She welcomed the news of their arrival with so much gladness. She saw the house was a bit secluded and detached from other houses in the area. It was a building originally designed to be an inn but converted to private property. She had considered Johana, her daughter, very rich, but now she realised that Miriam was extremely wealthier by far in her estimation. She had pipe water and massive rooms, one of which was richly furnished to fit a queen. Could it be her wealth holding her back from the new life, she wondered?

Miriam showed her where to wash up while she also went to another part of the house to get refreshed.

Afterwards, she listened to more miracles of the Lord Jesus and what he had said about himself.

'Miriam, the Lord Jesus said he is the Way, the Truth, and Life to get to God.' She kept these words in her heart.

Chapter Fifty-Three

Come to me, all you who are weary and burdened and
I will give you rest (Matthew 11:28).

It was not just Abigail and Amina who noticed the sparkle in Josef's eyes. They both assumed they understood the sparkle. Amina's thoughts were: *At last, his dreams are coming true. Miriam will become a believer in the Lord Jesus, and she can then become his wife...*

Mother Abigail was also thinking: I should be the proudest mother on earth. Miriam will soon be my daughter through Josef. They are such a beautiful couple! I will be a grandmother soon. See how God is increasing me. Johana is betrothed to Jephthah, an inn owner!

Two days later, as the entire group started their four-day journey to Capernaum by walking through shortcuts during the day and resting in inns along their route, Miriam noticed everyone looked hopeful. It seemed they were all happy for her sake and Amina's. They were going to be introduced to the Lord. They had gathered from Biliah that the Lord would be at Simeon's party. It was wonderful that Abigail knew the house, as this would save time asking and looking for directions as soon as they got off the boat.

Miriam could not understand that Prophet Jesus mingled with everyone, even tax collectors, she had learnt, like Matthew! A traitor. A thief. Not that she was any better reputation-wise, but at least, she did not betray her own people. Surely, she brought help and pleasure to people who needed such favours, but Matthew brought no favours to anyone. Who knew who would be at Simeon's party? She was going there only because that was the only way to meet Prophet Jesus.

Moreover, she had learnt in conversations with her new friends that Matthew had been reformed! The Lord would give her that wonder look, and the miracle would be achieved, and she would be transformed too forever!! Just like that and for free!! She tried not to doubt the possibility. Her mind kept telling her that what had happened to Dinah would happen all over again. She knew she was curious. Also, her inner fears and doubts were all enshrouded in hope.

Hope never harmed anyone. She encouraged herself that at least she had gained more friends and family, and there was a chance of getting Josef to help her find her son. *Why did she have this hope that she would be reformed and healed? She reasoned that she had friends and family now who would pray for her as soon as they knew her quest. Why had she not tried to find him all these ten years? The fear of being stoned to death. The fear of the past haunting her. Self-condemnation. Failure and facing rejection from those she had truly loved. She had turned her back on that episode of her life. Dinah no longer existed. Her past pain was rearing its head as Dinah was beginning to seep into the surface of her calm. She decided to engage with the others in their conversation...*

Amina asked: 'Does this mean that we outcasts or sinners should not expect to deserve normal people in relationships?'

'No. Don't use my case as an example. I know Jephthah was once a client of mine occasionally, but he is a devoted Jew and respects my new faith. I told Mother Mary about it, and she approved of our relationship,' Johana confirmed.

Miriam wasn't so sure about Johana's views, but felt Amina was just being realistic. Would Lucas have married Dinah if he had known she was a harlot? At that moment, her eyes met with Mother Abigail, and she smiled back.

She heard Mother Abigail say: 'People will see things from God's view if they have been healed emotionally. That is my experience and understanding. If I were still a young woman and had met the Lord Jesus, I would not turn away a leper or a tax collector as friends because I will see them as the Lord Jesus does.'

Josef remembered his mother's views concerning him getting married to a prostitute, but said nothing.

'You are right, mother!' Razi sounded very impressed. 'Is that not why we are going to Simeon's party to celebrate and rejoice with those entering the new life? Look at Matthew, the tax collector, for example. I hear he was at work in his tax collecting office with others like him. The Lord called him to change his life with two words—"FOLLOW ME," and he did. If our Lord Jesus considers him worthy, then we, too, are worthy. When our Lord saves us, we are saved. We are all walking away from darkness into light. Our past is gone and wiped clean; Amina, don't ever see yourself with your old eyes. We are not outcasts. We are the beloved of God.'

Josef added, 'Razi, I think what Amina is suggesting really is this: If she comes upon a perfect person, should she let that person know about her past? Did I get you right, Amina?'

'Yes, Josef.'

'Well, for me,' Josef continued, 'I would not mind at all for someone with a past like mine. That person and I would both understand each other very well.'

'You would know for sure that person truly loves you despite your past,' Johana added.

'All I know,' Mother Abigail added, 'is that we should all be delighted to be alive in the time of the Lord Jesus. Some of us are what we are because of life's afflictions and the great injustice and tragic circumstances that happened to us right from birth. But we are privileged that we are alive to the One who will give us rest from all our sufferings which our ancestors did not have. Let us thank Abba for what we are all about to receive from the Lord Jesus this new year.

When no one had anything more to say, Razilla gave her opinion:

'Our Lord Jesus tells us not to be like the Pharisees, who think they are perfect people. No one is perfect. Our Lord always emphasizes this. We are free, released from darkness. Instead of shame, we now have joy, healing, and freedom. Let us not look back. Miriam, you are so quiet. What do you think?'

Josef kept his gaze steady on Razilla as she spoke. She radiated an inner beauty, and watching her keenly, he realised she was quite pretty and actually the first amongst them to be a follower of the Lord. He saw her in a different light, and he wondered why he had never asked his sister about her own story. How old was she? He realised he had not accepted her dignity. He assessed her attributes as a woman and realised that though she was not as alluring as his sister or youthful as Amina or beautiful like Eliana; she had a transparent personality that was quite appealing. He promised himself to find out more about her from his sister, or he could ask her directly and see if indeed she was proud to flash out the sordid details of her past. He suddenly took his mind off her and paid keen attention to Eliana's response.

'People shy away from the facts of their dark pasts. Only God can make other people accept them with love.' She remembered Lucas.

'True, Miriam. I mean Eliana,' she corrected herself hastily, 'the important thing is to trust God. Anything is possible to those who trust God. Look at Mother Mary, for example. She was a virgin when she was betrothed to her husband, Joseph. Yet, God told her she would have a baby without knowing a man. That was how our Lord Jesus was born. His father, Joseph, did not reject Mary and her child. God has our lives all planned for His glory. The invisible God becomes visible in our Lord Jesus.'

Chapter Fifty-Four

I will declare that Your love stands firm forever
(Psalm 89:2a)

That first night at the inn, Josef remembered Razi's words and became intrigued. *Who was this lady? What did her name mean? Did she have a family? How had she become lost?* He realised his heart was fond of her. His spirit affirmed this, but his flesh stuck stubbornly to wanting Miriam. She was the only woman he had been able to have proper sexual relations aside from his sexual version to men. He knew he was no longer attracted to men sexually, but he still found out that he could not think of women in a sexual way. It meant to him that Miriam was his only hope.

As they all sat on the lodge's balcony enjoying the evening air and scenery of the Judean hills and valleys, rested, washed up and their bellies full, Amina asked a question that made everyone so delighted.

'Mama, can you tell us all that special testimony you wanted to tell us all?' Everyone clapped and hoorayed.

'Yes, Mama! Tell us now. I had not forgotten; I just didn't want to be pushy,' Johana chimed.

'Me too. Didn't want to rush you,' Josef piped in.

'Of course, I had not forgotten as well, especially as Mother Abigail said it would bless us. I have been waiting,' Razi said.

'I am still waiting,' Miriam finally jumped on board, smiling as she kept her gaze on Mother Abigail.

'I did not forget,' Mother Abigail began. 'I was waiting to be asked. I didn't want to stuff you all up about just me.'

'Don't say that, Mama!' Johana chided lovingly. 'You don't know how much you have been blessing us with your testimonies.'

'Josef asked me a question, the first time he saw me last week on New Year's Day. He asked, "How did you find Johana's home here in Jerusalem?" It is everyone's question as well. I told him and his sister that it is a miracle I would like to share not only with them but with the company of their friends as well. I will tell you.

As you know, after being healed in Capernaum where I had gone to look for my children, I stayed with the Lord Jesus and his followers. I, at least, always got something to eat. There were some wealthy women and even men who ensured feeding for the Master, his disciples, and helpers. I made myself useful in helping with fetching water, cooking, going on errands, helping to carry stuff, and just helping with anything anyone needed doing. However, sometimes, the Lord would stay in the homes of one of his disciples. I usually got invited to stay a day or two with very kind women like Dorcas and Phoebe. Phoebe was not married, but when I stayed with Dorcas, I served her and her family. Whenever I stayed with Dorcas and her family, I would become so sorrowful because her family reminded me of what I had thrown away. Last week, I was in Dorcas' house when she mentioned that the Lord was going to Jerusalem. I got the hint. I left her house and followed the Lord and his troupe.

When we got to Jerusalem, he spoke to specific people, and I was one of them. He said to me, 'Abigail, remain in Jerusalem. Your new home and family are here. Thank you for all your help.'

'Where, Lord?' I had asked eagerly.

And he said, 'Just ask for directions towards the East Gate. You will find a helper there.'

'I thanked him. I remember thinking to myself then that I would no longer be hanging about in people's homes for charity. And no more travelling around the villages and towns. It was time to rest. The Lord must have known that I clung to this hope that he would restore my children to me. That day, I was hopeful and glad that he gave me another chance at family life. I went in the direction he pointed out, hoping to find a family that would take me in for good. You see, the Lord was always restoring people to their families, uniting people together, and placing people in new families. I never stopped thinking of my children, and deep inside me, because it was the Lord Jesus, I believed I would find my heart's desires—my children.

At the East gate, I was hoping to see either of you. I didn't. I spoke to the first person I saw. A man with his two sons leading their sheep herd. I asked, 'Please, are you the helper the Lord Jesus said would help me?'

'Yes, follow me,' he said. Then he asked his sons to continue without him. We said nothing more to one another until we got to the front of a big white house. He pointed at it and said, 'That is your Johana's house!'

'I looked towards the house with my heart beating so fast, and my mouth had suddenly become dry. I was too shocked beyond words that he knew my daughter's name. I turned to my companion to ask him how he knew it was Johana's house and thank him. He was gone. Just like that! He had disappeared. We had not spoken because my thoughts concentrated on what life held next for me. I was ill, tired, dirty, and unkempt.' She stopped talking when she realised her audience was looking at her in utter wonder. It dawned on her listeners that Abba had sent an angel to help Mother Abigail find her daughter's house.

Miriam was so overcome that she began to cry. She wasn't the only one, but that was not her concern. Her crown was in sight! She was going to meet this same man. Lord Jesus!! *Abba was a loving God. He had sent the Lord Jesus to set her free. If He could set Mother Abigail free, then He could set her free and restore her to Lucas and Levi!!* Mother Abigail took her indoors, and that in itself seemed to be a sign that it was time for them to all turn in, get rested, and refreshed for their journey the following day.

By the next day, Amina was glad they had arrived in Capernaum, and she could tell by looking at everyone else's face that they were all glad. Miriam's face had remained unfathomable. The others? Expectant. The conversation centred on what they expected to see at the party. Not on the miracle they had heard about the angel the previous evening.

'Simeon is rich. Sure, there is going to be lots of food.'

'Josef, don't get your hopes too high,' his sister warned with a laugh.

'Why not!? Rich people like to show off.'

After about ten minutes, Mother Abigail said, 'I can lead us all to his house. These sycamore trees always remain a landmark in my memory of Simeon's house.'

'How do you know his house?' Josef asked in surprise.

'My son, the house of a rich man, whoever he is, is like a magnet to beggars. Yes, I have been here. I was able to pay for my upkeep from here to Nazareth and from here to Jerusalem. He might have been a tax collector before, but now that the Lord set him free, he is kind to beggars. Follow me...'

'See! We are near Simeon's house! We have to clean ourselves at his well situated at the back of the house!' exclaimed Mother Abigail excitedly.

'Mother, I know Mother Mary's home. Let us go there instead and refresh ourselves there. Her home is a second home to me, and I promised that I would bring you lots to meet her and her group.'

'Johana is right. She will be delighted to see us,' Razilla added.

'I thought the party was for noontime?' Amina asked.

'No, evening time. Remember Amina, the lady I spoke to when we were on our way to my house? She is Biliah. She brings foodstuff and other wares from Capernaum twice a week to sell in Jerusalem. She, too, lives the new life now. She has a handsome son named Justine.'

'Feeling over-eager then, Amina?' Josef teased.

'Yes, but also, I keep having doubts that my miracle will never come.' She felt comforted, as they all encouraged her at the same time.

Josef said, 'Wait and see,' and turning towards Miriam, he asked, 'and you Miriam? Are you excited?'

Before she could reply him, Johana said, 'By the way, everyone, Miriam does not mind if we call her Eliana, as that is her real name.'

'That is good to know! So, Eliana, are you excited?'

Eliana heaved a huge sigh and replied, 'Yes. For many reasons.' Everyone turned to look in her direction, but no one asked her reasons. She saw that they all followed Johana's leading to the home of her adopted mother—Mother Mary.

Abba dispatched two angels with His thoughts for those children of His going to meet up with His Son, Jesus. It was urgent that His angels were on guard to ensure their safety and success.

Praise: I will praise Abba's name in song and glorify Him with thanksgiving.

Deliverance: The sacrifices of Abba are a broken spirit, a broken and contrite heart.

Chapter Fifty-Five

Examine me and test me, Lord; judge my desires and thoughts (Psalm 26:2).

It occurred to Josef that Simeon's party began before the roosters and fowls of the air went to roost. By then, most fishermen, mongers of different trades, and artisans were done for the day. But to his utmost surprise and that of his troupe from Jerusalem, he was visibly shocked to see tax collectors from the various Galilean and even Judean provinces, prostitutes, and people who looked mentally ill or had the palsy. He looked sharply towards their Capernaum hosts: Mother Mary, her senior sister Mary the Elder, Aunt Adah, Aunt Rachel, Uncle Jonathan, a few younger men he couldn't remember their names and James, the Lord's brother. They did not look nonplussed. Together, they had all come to this party. He was sure that he and the rest from Jerusalem had very high expectations and must have been so disappointed and shocked at the calibre of people they saw.

'Take your seats,' Mother Mary said sweetly. They all trooped to some vacant seats in the large airy room, adjoined to the main house. It was obviously built for occasions like this. He was sure weddings and other important events took place here. *Where was the Lord?* He looked towards the high table where some distinguished guests who were well dressed sat. His eyes scanned another group, and they were mostly people he would normally look down upon because of how they were dressed. They were very poor. Surely, it seemed wherever there was a gathering expecting the prophet, all manner of people, including sinners, were there. The Lord had not arrived but then looking around, he witnessed something interesting and was momentarily distracted.

Eliana had reverted to her Miriam persona. She had taken off her veil and flung it carelessly on her shoulder. Her bosom cleavage was showing; her curves were obvious, and she let all the wealth of her hair flow like a cascade of lace veils over her lower back and down to her ankles. Having left her overnight bag in Mother Mary's house, she brought with her a smaller bag she had hidden under her sarong. This time, she held it in her hands. Jocheb noticed the persona switch. The meekness in her seemed to have evaporated from her into thin air. He swallowed twice before speaking to her. Didn't she know everyone would obviously know that she was a sinner? She was dressed richly as usual and had a bag with what he thought was her toiletry purse. He walked towards her and drew her back outside with everyone's eyes watching.

'Eliana, please put on your veil. You do not want to give our Lord and people here a wrong impression.'

'Let him see me for what I am!'

'Why!!? You are not that anymore. You don't want people thinking you have come to seduce a holy man!'

'Don't trouble yourself on my account, Josef. The Lord will discern my heart.'

'I know that, but what of others?' Josef asked.

'Which others? Can't you see that most of the women are sinners like me? Why should I pretend?'

Feeling exasperated, he replied firmly: 'All right, you are not going in like that. You will take my advice now. I will not see you disrespect our family. Woman, have some pride, please.'

Miriam looked at him and then made to go inside, and he held her arm and pulled her back.

'Josef, you do not want to know Safirah. Please, let go of my hand.' Her tone was hard, and her eyes had become dangerous.

This was a side of her that was completely unknown to him. *So be it*, he thought.

'*You* don't really know Jocheb,' he said in a flint tone as he gripped her arm even more firmly. 'I am telling you, it won't do for you to hang out your soiled undergarments for the whole world. HAVE SOME PRIDE, WOMAN!!'

She acquiesced for the moment. She would need his help to find her Adam. She put on back her veil, and they both went in just as Mother Abigail had come out to see what they both were about. She looked at them both and smiled. Before they sat, Mother Mary beckoned to them and Amina to follow her to the Master. A long queue had already started.

Chapter Fifty-Six

Live in love, as Christ loved and gave Himself up for us,
a fragrant offering and sacrifice to God
(Ephesians 5:2).

The Lord gave each one his attention. There were many people lined up in a queue to see him. Amina saw a holy man with a kind heart, who laid his hand on her head and said a word of prayer as she knelt before him: 'Go in peace, your sins are forgiven.' She found herself inhaling the peace as it spread all over her. It pervaded her entire being, and she knew she had been spiritually healed. It was a miraculous experience. This great prophet. This miracle worker. The Lord who had done all those wonderful things she had heard had actually laid his hands on her head. He did not condemn her, and she felt his love for her infuse her body the way the sun's rays permeated her being on a sunny day. She was so overcome with emotion that she began to sob profusely. She felt Razilla's embrace and another helper of the Lord. The Lord called out a young man to attend to Amina. Razilla recognised him to be Nebo.

As he came out, the Lord said, 'Nebo, love and cherish Amina. She completes you.' Some people gasped as they had understood what the Lord had done. Nebo had been given a wife! Amina, completely oblivious to the miracle that had just happened to her, was taken aside to be ministered to.

Josef was next. He was amazed that the Lord was like any other man, dressed casually and sat amongst the 'sinners' and those who were poor. He remembered he had scanned the group earlier but never imagined that the Lord looked like any other in appearance. He was dressed neatly in a simple outfit. Then, as he was about to kneel, he heard him ask, 'Josef, son of Kazi, what shall I do for you?' Josef realised he was momentarily speechless. *What did he want? What should he say?* He was no longer a sinner. Ah yes, he knew now what to say, 'I want a family. Please, Lord, bless me with the bone of my bone and the flesh of my flesh.' *Surely, the Lord knew he meant Eliana!*

'Your desires have already been granted.' Gratitude and healing flooded his heart, and he suddenly felt overwhelmed and embraced the Lord, sobbing.

'Abba, Lord. Please, I want to be one of your disciples if you think I am worthy.'

'You are already a disciple! Go in peace. Your sins have been totally blotted. You have what you have believed for—a wife and a family.' That was what pleased Josef the most as he was led away by his helpers.

'Rabbi, the party is starting now! You cannot see the rest now. You can continue as soon as You have had a meal and rested.'

Miriam could not believe her ears. Her own miracle was about to be denied her as his disciples began to shoo them away like unruly kids. She tore off from one of the helpers, and to the utter dismay of everyone in the room, she threw open her veil and ran to the Lord Jesus, throwing herself at his feet and weeping her heart out. She clung to his feet and refused to listen to the disciples bullying her. The Lord did not rebuke her, and she became bold.

'Leave me alone!' she said gruffly to a disciple who forcefully tried to pull her up. Then she heard his voice…

'Philip, let her be. For such like her, I have come.'

'Mother Mary, my mother, says you are Eliana. As your name is, so shall it be for you.'

'Yes, Lord,' she sobbed. Words failed her. There were over a multitude of words from over the years. She sobbed on his feet and continually used her hair to clean the tears off his feet. She heard the Lord speak to the celebrant. She did not hear what he said, as she dwelt on the words he spoke when they tried to drag her away. Her soul connected to the Lord:

You said You are here for me, Lord? Please, save me from myself. I want to sin no more. I want to belong to you. I want to be free. I don't want to be crushed by the weight of my sin, loss, and pain. Deliver me from sex. Deliver me from pride. Deliver me from fear. Show me who I am. Make me whole; help me to love again. Give me a new heart. Give me a new reason to live. Bless me like you have blessed my friends with a crown of victory on their heads. Make me yours too. I want to be a mother again. I want to feel worthy and have my family back. Give me this miracle. Help me trust You with all my heart and keep my hope alive.

They said you came to set the captives free. Free me from all that has held me captive: free me from loneliness; free me from my sins. I don't want to die in them. Free me from all the curses the devil has put on me. Save me. I want the captive's crown. I believe You are Abba!

Eliana wept and wept as her soul spoke of her needs to the Lord. She was oblivious to her surroundings and the people in the room. She wept on his foot as she clasped his legs and rubbed her face on the tunic covering his legs. Her tears fell fast on his feet, and she used her hair, again and again, to wipe his feet as she kissed them. She wept for Lucas. She wept for Levi, her Adam. She wept for Dinah, Safirah, Reubena, Miriam, and Eliana. She felt the Lord stroking her hair, and eventually, he lifted her face towards his, and she looked into his eyes. She heard his soul speak to hers:

My daughter, I will be your God; my kindness shall not depart from you. Be transformed by the renewing of your mind. I have given you the authority to trample on snakes and scorpions and overcome all the power of the enemy. I will pay you back double for all the unfair things that have happened to you. You shall love the Lord God with all your heart, soul, and strength. I have set you free. You wear the captive's crown. You are free!

She experienced boldness, calm, assurance, love, and a feeling of peace beyond her human understanding. She knew then that she had received healing in her mind, soul, and body. She opened her bag confidently and brought out the most expensive of all her perfumes from Arabia. She had planned for this moment. She had her prize ready for when the Master saved her. She uncorked its lid, and its titillating scent engulfed the entire atmosphere as flames of a hungry fire. She poured it out on his feet carefully and lovingly began to massage both feet up to his knees and kissed his feet repeatedly. The party began, but she was no longer hungry for food.

She heard her actions being criticised openly by his helpers and other people around, but she went on doing what she was doing. She heard the Master defend her actions. Finally, she heard him speak again to her in a voice loud for all to hear.

"Your sins are forgiven. Your faith has saved you. Go in peace. What you have done for me today will always be remembered of you wherever this gospel is preached."

Instantly, possessed by the Holy Spirit, her soul began to praise the Lord, and it was so much it bubbled out, and she found herself amid that entire congregation, not feeling any shame, begin to praise the Master in worship:

Intoxicating love, flowing from your heart to mine up to the brim. Your love, oh Lord, makes me bolder than he who has drunk earthly wine. But this is love from heaven that overflows the cup of my heart and the vessel of my soul. And all this is for me. Oh my Lord, truly, your love is more than anything one can describe on earth. You have forgiven me, and I feel good, oh Lord! You abound in love, overflowing to all who call to You. I give You my heart, soul, and body. Everything. *You are the reason for my ecstasy, boundless joy, deliverance, and salvation. Thank you so much, my Lord.*

On and on she went as she gathered the empty jar, and as she was wrapping her veil over her head, she heard the Master call a woman.

'Rachel!' the Lord called. Thomas, a disciple, quickly went and fetched her from amongst the guests. When she was near where Eliana and the Master were, he said, 'Rachel, here is your own daughter, Eliana.'

'Thank you, my Lord,' she replied, beaming happily.

He smiled. Then to Eliana, he said, 'You have your own mother now. Stay with her and remain at peace.'

She nodded her head. She kept her eyes on the Master, and he gave her an assuring smile that spoke of peace, rest, and love. Eliana understood so many things at once in her mind concerning her future that she could not grasp. She knew at that moment all would be well with her life. As she walked away feeling heady, dazed, and with mixed emotions, she was vaguely aware that she had been asked to follow a strange woman. She was not aware of disapproving stares.

'Let us sit here,' her new mother said to her, 'I am Rachel. I heard your name is Miriam, but you now want to be called Eliana.'

'Eliana was speechless and remained silent as she kept her gaze on the Master.'

'I can understand how you must be feeling. That is how we all feel when we have a personal encounter with the Lord.'

Chapter Fifty-Seven

A blessing if you obey the commands of the Lord your
God that I am giving you today (Deuteronomy 11:27).

Still, Eliana could not keep her eyes from being fixed on him. He was now attending to another person, who was also being very emotional. She felt her new mother dragging her gently to where there was a group of people welcoming her to the family. She was not yet settled in her mind to listen properly to the introductions as her mother introduced her to some guests she said were family to her. She felt a lot of people's eyes on her, considering what she had just done to the Master. She did not feel abashed or self-conscious as she perceived the perfume scent which was all over the entire hall. Instead, she watched the Master intently. *What an opportunity to meet with the Lord.*

When would be the next opportunity? Her new mother let her be, and she was very grateful. Eliana realised she was not interested in looking out for the rest of the Jerusalem family. She was just so content keeping her gaze on the Lord Jesus. He was an elixir to her soul and a balm to her heart. Gazing at him brought utter solace to her whole being. She felt as if she was soaked in the presence of some overwhelming state of everlasting euphoria. Her whole being felt refreshed and revived. The weariness she felt from the burden of her lost family drained out of her as she fed her eyes on the Lord Jesus. She knew her soul was worshipping the Lord in the beauty of his holiness. After this experience, her lips would always overflow with his praise and testimony of what she had experienced this evening. God's love had been poured out to her physically, and she would remain overwhelmed and drunk from it for a very long while.

Eliana did not know for how long she was transfixed by the Lord's presence. She was not interested in eating, but she knew some mothers had gathered their toddlers and babies. They wanted their children to be blessed by the Lord. Of course, who wouldn't? She heard her new mother prompting two youngsters to join the waiting crowd of children and their mothers.

Again, she saw some of the Lord's disciples come out to send away the children and the mothers who were waiting to be beckoned. His disciples argued that the Master had no moment to himself to rest or even eat. Then Eliana heard his voice again:

'Oh please, do not send the children away. I want to bless them too. Anyone who does not receive the kingdom of Abba God like a child will not enter it.'

She pondered the meaning of that statement as she saw the Lord laying his hands on each child and their mothers while blessing them. When the Lord had given everyone attention, he sat still and calm, with his eyes closed. His hands were clasped. He appeared as if he were reabsorbing and recharging his spiritual energy from above. She continued to watch him. His facial features exuded serenity and wisdom. Other than this, he was just as plain as everyone else in his dressing and outward appearance. She still could not believe that she had encountered such an extraordinary and phenomenal moment with him. She desired to ask him directly many of the unanswered questions she harboured deep in the safety of her heart.

Many guests came to congratulate Rachel, her new mother and herself, including her Jerusalem family, as soon as they all stepped outside Simeon's portico. She was hugged by both Johana and Razi. They had tears in their eyes, and she noticed Mother Abigail embracing Amina. Indeed, many guests were greeting each other with hugs, and a lot of congratulatory wishes filled the atmosphere. Eliana turned her eyes, searching for the Lord. She could not see him. It had to be now; she reasoned. She broke away from those who were greeting and spoke to Rachel.

'Mother, I won't be long. I have just one question to ask the Lord Jesus.'

Rachel was doubtful. His disciples were so protective of the Lord and might have taken him to an inner room to eat or rest. Or they might have taken another exit out of the building to their home. Still, she did not attempt to dissuade her. It was the way of the new believer. She had once been like that not too long ago.

'Why is she going back?' young Ariel broke into her thoughts as he followed his mother.

'You heard her.'

'Yes. She wants to ask the Master more questions. Mama, when are you going to ask him for a gift of a father for me?'

'You already have one, my dear son. Let us wait here for your sister.'

'You always say I have a father, and you would tell me the full story one day! When Mama?'

'Maybe this night so that your new sister can get to know you as well.'

'Are you disappointed, Mama? You don't seem cheerful,' Ariel observed. His mother did not answer him. He got the message and kept his peace.

Eliana meandered her way with some struggle back into Simeon's portico. It was an enormous and impressive structure with several exits. She kept her eyes intent on her purpose, thereby discouraging people who wanted a bit of her attention. She discerned the Jerusalem group wondering why she was returning into the portico, but they let her be. After all, the Lord had seen it fit to place her in another family. She was in good hands.

Soon, Eliana was inside the portico, and her eyes opened wide with surprise. There he was, but where were his family and helpers!!? Seeing him quite alone was more of a mystery to her than a miracle. Today was the luckiest day in her life, she thought as she ran to the Master before any of his helpers suddenly appeared to prevent her.

'My Lord, My Lord!!'

'Eliana. I was waiting for you. I have sent my disciples to see that everyone is out safely and to attend to people who might need help or just have questions. I knew you would return.'

'Did someone tell you to expect me back, my Lord?'

'No, Eliana. I know you have pondered in your heart the concept of people receiving the Kingdom of God like a child if they wanted to enter it.'

'My Lord, I am a truly blessed woman this day!!! You are my Lord, and I believe You are sent from God. I have heard all the miraculous things you have done which no human being can do except by God's authority. I want to receive the Kingdom of God like a child. I also have other questions.'

'Ask, and you will receive.'

'My Lord, why did I face an evil life right from childhood? Will I be judged for this at the end of my life?'

She looked down. She could not bear to hear anything unpleasant.

The Lord lifted her chin and said, 'Eliana, look at me. I shall tell you the truth, and the truth shall make you free. Whatever evil was meant for your harm, it will turn round for your own good. Abba has removed your sins as far as the East is to the West. You will not be judged as you think. You are saved because you believe in Me. You have made Me your Lord, and you have confessed your sins. If you pray for anything and have faith, you will receive it. That is how to enter the Kingdom of God. Do you understand that children innocently believe what they are told, which makes their faith strong?'

She nodded…

Chapter Fifty-Eight

For all the promises of God in Him are yes and in Him
Amen (2 Corinthians 1:20).

Even in Heaven, there was excitement. The angels of Abba could not wait for events to unfold. In moments like this, they wished they could see the end from the beginning. They were affected by the great love that Abba had for mankind through His promises, which they chanted in unison and awe. They knew that their words from Abba would minister to several people on earth:

Promise: Abba said, be still and know that I am God.

Abba's promises to you are yes and amen.

Abba said you would lend and not borrow.

Abba said He would restore to you what the enemy has stolen.

Abba said He would prosper you even in a desert.

Abba said whatever you touch will prosper.

Abba said your cup would run over.

Abba said you and your house would serve the Lord.

Abba said the seed of the righteous is blessed.

Abba said your children would be mighty in the land.

Abba said your end would be better than your beginning.

Abba said all things work for your good.

Abba said He would go before you and make the crooked paths straight.

Abba said He would give you beauty for ashes.

Abba said He would pay you back double for the unfair things that have happened.

Abba said He would give you the desires of your heart.

Love: As Abba has loved Jesus, so He has loved you.

Salvation: If you confess your sins, Abba is faithful and righteous to forgive your sins and cleanse you of all unrighteousness.

Knowledge: Abba looks down from Heaven on the sons of men to see if there are any who understand, any who seek Him.

Knowledge: Nothing in all creation is hidden from Abba's sight.

Knowledge: Abba is not slow in keeping His promises.

Promise: Abba will cleanse you from all impurities and your idols.

Love: Love your enemies, bless those who curse you, do good to those who hate you and pray for those who persecute you that you may be sons of Abba in Heaven.

Knowledge: Abba did not call us to be impure but to live a holy life.

Love: Love one another as Abba has loved you.

Love: What is man that You Abba are mindful of him?

Chapter Fifty-Nine

It is Abba who gives you the true bread of Heaven
(John 6:32).

It was the following morning, and all the invited guests were returning to their respective homes with the gist of Miriam's behaviour on their tongues. The Jerusalem family, as well, were returning to their homes, and they chatted in a high beat tone with their feelings of astonishment and joy. They spoke of the marvels they witnessed at Simeon's. However, Josef returned to the home of their host after escorting the family to the harbour. He had a burning desire to talk with Eliana. He remembered how he had wished her a happy new year before they had set off from Jerusalem.

'Happy New Year, my beautiful beloved. May this new year celebrate us together in our new lives together.'

He had embraced her. He did not want her to break off his embrace until she had replied positively to his greeting or confirmed it with an Amen, but she did no such thing. He remembered the advice of both his sister and mother: *Wait until she has met the Lord Jesus, the Master.* Well, now she had. The eyes of her heart were surely opened. He wanted her love and intimacy almost to desperation. They should get married so that it would not be a sin for him to be with her. He could still hear her melodious voice. She had sung after being blessed by the Lord. What a magnificent voice! He felt hopeful as he knocked on the door of Mother Mary's abode.

'Josef! You returned? Did you forget something?' She momentarily glanced around the small room where her guests from Jerusalem had spent the night. Then she made way for him to enter the house. He sat down when she had taken a seat.

'No, Mother Mary. I just want to greet Eliana and her new family before leaving for Jerusalem. But I do not know Mother Rachel's house.'

'Oh, they live not too far from here.' She paused a while, as if to dig out a mental route. 'Get to the town square and ask for her house from Amos, the milkman. He sits beside two big brown female cows. He sells milk. You can't miss him.' She perceived Josef had other issues on his mind: 'Is there anything else I can help you with, Josef?'

He rubbed his two hands together and replied after some seconds of silence. 'Yes, mother'.

'How?'

'I want to ask Eliana to be my wife. I want to ask permission first from Aunty Rachel, her new mother. I need to get this sorted before I travel off for my business. The Lord clearly told me that my wishes to have a wife and family had been granted. It has always been my wish to wed Eliana.'

'Listen to me, my son. Your mother confided in me concerning Eliana because I had to speak to the Master about her. Mother

Abigail also mentioned the possibility that you would want to wed her.'

She gave a soft sigh. Her pretty face was calm, and she spoke unhurriedly, 'This is my suggestion. Eliana and Rachel will be here tomorrow, as they informed me before leaving. I do not know their further plans, but you can wait here till then and talk to Eliana first. She needs time to be mentored in the new way of life and find her own family.'

'Family?'

'Yes. Did you not know that she was married and has a ten-year-old son?'

'No, this is a surprise! I can't believe it!!'

'You see! Get to know each other better first.'

Chapter Sixty

Be anxious for nothing (Philippians 4:6).

Josef was restless all day and evening. At night, it was no better. He could not blame anyone for not telling him anything. They had all gone about their different businesses, leaving his mother and Eliana behind the following day, which is Sunday. Soon, after everyone was gathered back to the house, his mother and Eliana took off. He was sure that no one else knew Eliana's true story. Before he came into bed, he had tried getting further information about Eliana from Mother Mary, but she had advised it was better for Eliana to tell him herself. Why had she never told him this information? What had made her open up to his mother? Did she hope for his mother to tell him?

And that very disgraceful behaviour of hers at the party!! Unbelievable!! The camera in his eyes opened up the specific episode captioned 'DISGRACEFUL' at Simeon's party, and he felt so ashamed for Eliana. Like at a demented lady with her head uncovered and all that mass of untamed hair, she threw herself on the Lord's feet! As if that were not enough, she began to cry like someone responding to the lashes of an invisible whip and sometimes, as it sounded to him, a woman undergoing some orgy of the flesh. He had looked around and seen the horror expressed in people's faces. He heard their unspoken comments: 'slut' and 'how shameless!' He heard the whispered questions—'Can't someone take her out? Is that not Miriam the harlot from Jerusalem? What does she think she is doing? Does she not know the Master is a holy man?'

He looked at the Lord's helpers. They, too, were looking in shock. One of them had tried to drag her away, but the Lord had stopped him! He didn't want to hurt her feelings. He felt so angry. Hadn't he warned her? The women in the hall were so horrified at what they witnessed! They covered their children's eyes when they saw Eliana kissing the Lord's feet. Did she think she was in her pleasure house? She had made it clear to everyone that she was indeed a sinful woman. As he pondered the effect of her behaviour on the party crowd, it suddenly dawned on him the depth of Eliana's sorrow. She had lost her parents, been abused as a child, and like his sister, led into prostitution. She had also lost her marriage! He realised he would not judge her anymore. He was aware of the compassion he felt towards her and his desire to make everything all right. She was the only woman with whom he could make a family. She must be the woman Abba wanted him to take as a wife.

After a while, sleep mercifully took him over. When next he woke up, it was the noise of people going to fetch water or getting ready for their business in the early dawn that caught his ears. There was also the sound of cock crows and someone knocking...

Mother Rachel had been taken unawares by being entrusted with a daughter! It was not what she had hoped and prayed for, but she was surprised that the Lord considered her worthy to have another addition to her family. There were other women like Felicia or Ahuva, or yes, even Atarah! Why her? She was neither an active worker nor one of those that followed the Lord and his disciples on their evangelical tours, as some of these women were. All the same, she was glad for the honour, even though she had hoped for a father for her Ariel. Eliana was extremely beautiful and would be helpful with housework. What was her story? She was clearly a lady of the red in her past life and rich. She would take her to visit Mother Mary and the other women who would tell her the wise sayings of the Prophet now and again. Or they could attend the New Believers' gatherings.

They both had been extremely exhausted emotionally from the previous evening: Eliana, with a new life and family while she had a new daughter. A big responsibility!! Where was she to start from? She had been a virtuous, humble bride to Asher, her husband till her derangement. She heard that the perfume Eliana had splashed so liberally over the Master had cost a fortune! Eliana was rich, but she was very poor. How would such a wealthy woman cope in the one-room she shared with her son, property, and domestic animals? What was the Master up to? He must have been so tired. This was surely a mistake! After the party, they had bid her family a good night and came home, and it was straight to bed!

Having lost her three children thirty-three years ago and finally, the love and protection of her husband, she had lost faith in God. People had treated her as one with a deranged mind owing to the loss of her family. Then two years ago, she had followed her neighbours, Adah and her son, Timothy, to a big gathering of people wanting to hear the Master. She did not care to go, but her son, Ariel, had wept his eyes out. He was Timothy's best friend, and they were about the same age, so she had to consent to her son's wishes if she did not want a headache following. She had eaten the bread shared by the Master. She had been enthralled by the miracle she had witnessed. Timothy's meal had been multiplied miraculously to feed all that crowd of people!! Her faith in God returned.

Her life changed gradually as she occasionally followed Adah and Timothy to hear the Prophet, and she began to attend the Believers' fellowship regularly. Soon, she became a part of a big loving and caring family. She had spoken to one of the disciples to give her audience with the Master. He had blessed her with His peace, and she remained hopeful. Ariel needed a father. Through Adah, she had heard her neighbour how the Master gave people the family members they needed. She was just 42 then. Surely, the Lord should give her a husband for the sake of her son, Ariel. Eliana was too old for Ariel to play with. She could still have children because she still flowed. Could she still be hopeful when she had been entrusted with a much younger beautiful woman who needed a husband?

She turned from her back position on the mat where she lay with her new daughter to face the other direction towards the window. It couldn't be past the second watch of the night. There were no cock crows yet. She tried to sleep. She comforted herself with the fact that in the morning, after some breakfast, she and her new daughter would go back to Mother Mary's house. If there were no mistakes, she would get advice on mentoring the mature woman in her care.

Eliana lay awake. She knew precisely when her new mother fell asleep. She sensed that, like her, Rachel could not sleep off as soon as they came to bed. She discerned her new mother's worries accurately: her new daughter was too rich to fit in their home; her son needed a father or a brother and not a sister too old for him. What would each offer the other, seeing they were completely two different people? Her little brother had followed Timothy's family. She was sleeping on Timothy's bed. When Timothy returned, what would be the sleeping arrangement in this tiny room already stuffed with all they possessed on earth! Ariel looked malnourished and small for his age compared to his friend, Timothy. What was her story? It was obvious. She was a poor widow working odd jobs for those who were rich enough to pay her well. This was what she used to fend for herself and her son, but this was not often. She also occasionally depended on the charity of the Master and his disciples. She supplemented her rent through other menial jobs such as water and animal feed fetching, childminding, baking, and anything else people needed her to do for a pittance for her labour.

She had a plan. It had to be the plan of the Prophet to bless this family through her. First, she would ask her new mother and Ariel to move in with her to Jerusalem. Surely, it was also the Prophet's plan to give her a sibling who would be like a son in place of the one she had lost. Next, she would confide to Mother Rachel her plans for the family. Also, she wanted to see Mother Mary tomorrow and ask her something that lay uppermost in her mind. Soon, she found herself listening to the soft snores of her new mother and revisiting the incidents of the evening.

About Amina – *Was she being given to Nebo as a daughter, sister or wife?* Most likely a wife. How lucky can one get in the space of less than seven days!!

About Mother Abigail – *She confirmed that Mother Rachel was the lady she had sat with at that miracle of feeding thousands of people with Timothy's meal!! Both ladies had embraced each other.* What a coincidence!! *Another sister believer. The family is expanding!*

About Josef – *Had been granted the desires of his heart for a wife and family by the Master!!! But he was not attached to any other woman!!? What had he been told? He did not go back to Jerusalem with the rest of the family! He said he wanted to share with her what the Lord Jesus had told him.*

About Johana – *Was she being briefed on all that had transpired in her absence between her mother and me when the family were all away at their various businesses? Most likely. Or they might have been talking about wedding plans between Johana and the innkeeper. What was his name????*

About Razi – *Sat with Josef. Did they both share their stories with each other? Was Razi hiding her feelings for a man in love with someone else? She seemed to keep Amina away from Josef. The path is clear now...*

The Master. Prophet. Lord. Rabbi Jesus. God. *What had he said to her?* She slept off while gathering her thoughts. She would wake up, knowing that she had dreamt of the Lord and what he had told her.

Chapter Sixty-One

Do not cling to events of the past or dwell on what happened long ago (Isaiah 43:18).

Josef jumped up instantly from his mat as soon as he heard the knock, feeling surprised he had been able to sleep so well and peacefully on a mat! What a contrast to his plush bedroom and bed. He had no time to freshen himself before facing Mother Rachel, and her 'new daughter', he assumed was at the door. He felt tickled, remembering his mother was hoping for 'something' from the Master when he had blessed her with longevity. He had seen the look of disappointment after he had blessed her. Did she forget he had restored her health and her two children to her? Where did he find the strength to bless everyone as he did last night?

As he opened the door, he was so surprised, and at the same time, disappointed. At the door stood Nebo, Amina, and four other people he did not know. After exchanging warm greetings between them all, Mother Mary herself came in from the adjoining multipurpose room. She had obviously freshened up, and after greeting her early morning guests, she led them to her living room. Josef excused himself and went out to the communal well in front of the courtyard. On his way, a smart maiden offered him her pitcher of water. He took it gratefully and refilled the empty one in his room. He was reluctant to ask for her name as he thanked her, as this might begin a road he was not prepared to walk on. He gave out money, and his peace of mind returned. Then, carrying the water pitcher, he took himself to a low-roofed chamber to bathe and visited the latrine for his other needs.

Chapter Sixty-Two

*He is good to everyone and has compassion on all He
made (Psalm 145:9).*

It did not take Eliana long to realise that there was no privacy in a room like Mother Rachel's. As soon as it was the third cock row, a cock crowed in the room! Soon, everyone's cocks began to crow, and Mother Rachel's neighbours spilt out of their little one or two-room dwellings. The lamps lit from many homes suddenly illuminated the neighbourhood. Young Ariel was back. He had been told that his new sister and mother needed to talk, so he agreed to sleep in Timothy's house.

'Good morning, Mama,' Eliana greeted.

'Good morning, Mama and good morning, big sister,' Ariel greeted as he rushed into the room.

'Good morning, my children. My daughter, this is when we get up to fetch water for people who will pay me in one way or the other. Then we will either use what we receive towards breakfast or just wait for the midday meal. You can use Ariel's pitcher.'

'That's fine, Mama. Good morning, Ariel. Did you sleep well?'

'Yes. I know you and Mama did not talk. Mama, please, I want to sleep here tonight. Also, Timothy will get more denarii than me if we don't go now. We have a competition, so please, Mama, let me go with my big sister too.'

'Then look for a spare pail from someone, and you can show your sister where we supply water.'

'Okay, Mama. Am I sleeping here tonight?'

'Your sister is waiting. Hurry before we lose our customers!'

'Mama, you rest a bit more. Ariel and I will be very fine. When I return, I will help you with whatever else is needed to be done.'

Eliana was impressed with Ariel. He was very intelligent. He had figured out that giving up his bed had been in vain. She decided to engage him in conversation to keep off their neighbour's gaze at her and debar the opportunity of opening up conversations with her. The news of her behaviour at Simeon's party had spread around the village, as well as her reputation in her past life. Before she spoke, Ariel opened up their chatting.

'Big sis, I am going to take you somewhere special.'

'Somewhere special,' she laughed softly. 'Why is it special?'

'It is a rich man's house. He has plenty of animals and needs help with plenty of water.'

'Do you go there with your mother?'

'Never! Mama said the rich man is evil.' Then stopping to look at her, he said, 'I hope you will not be scared. Timothy earned lots of money when he went there without his parents. They eventually got to know and made him promise never to go there without them.'

This boy reminded her of someone, but her excellent mind seemed to fail her at this instance. 'No, I am not scared. We are children of God now, and no evil can harm us.'

'I know. Mama said still to be careful. She said this rich man sells people as slaves from here to other faraway cities.'

'So, where are you going to get a spare pitcher because I can carry two at a time?'

'The man has many. Look, we are reaching there now!'

'Don't worry, Ariel. We can tell him about Jesus.'

'But please, don't tell Mama.'

'Okay.'

Eliana saw that there were already a couple of hands there. It was quite a large ranch-like structure, and they helped fill up troughs of water for the animals. They could have worked the whole day, but their mother would have guessed where they went. During a moment of rest, she called Ariel, who was already involved in a ball game with some kids.

'Ariel! Come. I have remembered something important.' The boy stopped his game immediately and obediently came to her, wondering what was happening. 'You know I cannot tell lies and deceive Mama because of my new life. So, let us get paid and go.'

To her alarm, Ariel drew everyone's attention to them as he started crying. 'Mama made me promise never to come here!! Please don't say anything!' he shouted. 'She said this man steals children,' he wailed aloud. Everyone came closer, suddenly interested. Eliana was not impressed by his weakness. She was so disappointed because she had thought he was intelligent. He was a foolish boy, after all!

Eliana was confused. God was testing her. Should she deceive Ariel or stick with what she had said? She decided to stick with what she had said and hushed the crying child, but he would not till she promised she would not tell. Some people had tried to comfort him as well. When the rich man came out, Eliana came face to face with Kabul, the man who had bought her from Jibril and with whom she had renamed herself Reubena to work as a harlot in Sidon 16 years ago. Time stood still. To her own surprise, she experienced no hatred or wrath and greeted him coolly.

'My brother and I want to go now. We have been here since 7 am, and it is noon now.' She watched him nod his head with no display of emotion or sign that he knew her so well. Even his eyes did not betray anything.

'That is fine. I will get your pay, but why is that youngster crying?'

'Don't worry yourself on his account. I will take care of him.' He nodded his head and went off to get their pay. When he returned, he held a plastic pouch and switched from the Hebrew language to the Phoenician language; one he knew only her could understand. Some people were amazed, and others became suspicious.

'Please, forgive me, Reubena. Since I met the Lord Jesus, I have been a changed man. I do honest work with my hands and try to help the poor as best as possible. I am very sorry for the past. Here are the wages I owe, had you not left of your own volition.' He handed her a bag, which she received. Speaking back in Hebrew, he said, 'Peace and God bless you.'

With no show of emotion, she took it from him and thanked him. Then he withdrew inside.

'Ariel, you see. This man used to be a bad man, but now, he knows Jesus, and he has turned over a new leaf. He has returned to me what he stole from me many years ago!! Don't be afraid. I will explain everything to Mama. God wanted us to come here and be blessed.'

'You don't understand. Mama will not listen to you or even take that payment.' She saw that he really looked sad and worried.

'Then I will get Mother Mary to talk to her! By the way, Ariel, what was all that shouting in public for?'

'Well, that is the only way I sometimes get Mama to let me have my way.'

'That is wrong.'

'No, it is not.'

'Did you and Mama not eat out of Prophet Jesus's bread?'

'We did, and we are still very poor and sometimes cold and hungry.'

'Ariel, now we are a family. We are rich because I will use all my savings for our good.'

'What savings?'

'You know I used to be bad. Evil and a sinner like that rich man, Kabul, but I have been eating God's bread in a different way.'

'What way?'

'Well, listening to all the good things the Lord Jesus does and trying to live a life that will make Abba God happy. Then, when we go to Jerusalem, you will understand better.'

'Jerusalem? Mama will go nowhere! She wants to live near Mother Mary and the Prophet. She is waiting for a miracle.'

'What miracle? Because I am that miracle.'

He laughed. Then, becoming serious, he said, 'She wants me to have a father. So, big sis, you tell me how the Prophet can give me a father if we follow you to Jerusalem? You have been sorted. You now have what you wanted.'

'How do you know what I want? You could be wrong!'

'You wanted a mother and a brother, and you got it all. So, I am going to wait for mine.'

As they got into the house, a surprise awaited Ariel and his new sister. There was Mother Mary in the company of a very tall, handsome man. *This must be my new father*! Ariel thought excitedly...

Chapter Sixty-Three

I have hid Your word in my heart that I might not sin against you (Psalm 119:11).

Josef felt his heart swell for this beautiful woman who had immediately acclimatised to her new life and family. He had been regaled by her seemingly homely virtues from Mother Rachel, who had told him how she did not feel anxious over Eliana's adjusting to her new life. Eliana had slept on the mat with no complaint, got on with house chores, and was bonding with her little brother. Watching her now, he could imagine what their family life would look like. Mother Mary was busy making a fuss over her and her little brother. Finally, Mother Rachel broke into his thoughts.

'Josef, please, tell Eliana and Ariel the good news you have brought.'

'I know the good news!' shouted an excited Ariel as everyone looked towards him. His mother scolded him instantly.

'Ariel, you don't butt into conversations. That is not right. Go over to Aunt Adah; next door right now with no protests!' He did, but looked at Josef with pleading eyes.

'What a great lad you have,' remarked Josef after Ariel left. He watched as Mother Mary, Mother Rachel, and Eliana made themselves comfortable as they sat on the mats. All eyes were now fixed on him as he spoke.

'Mother Mary and I bring the good news of Amina's engagement to Nebo!!' he began. 'They brought the good news this early morning.' Everyone began to remark how both Nebo and Amina had been extraordinarily blessed. Things had moved swiftly for each of them within a very short space of time. Then Mother Mary turned her attention to the new family.

'We thought you were both coming over to the house but realised you both would be busy getting to know each other first. So, we have come along to see how you are all doing. Well done, Eliana. Mother Rachel says you are doing so well. You already look like your new mother!' Eliana merely smiled.

'Thank you, Mother Mary. I have good news too. Today, I met Kabul, who repented and apologised for the evil he did to me 16 years ago in Sidon! That was when I worked for him as Reubena in his tavern. Today, he gave me back my wages.' She brought out the plastic pouch amidst everyone's cheers. 'He says he is now a believer. I discovered I was not angry, and neither felt hatred nor revenge. I praise God. Here, Mama.' Her new mother received the parcel with surprise in her eyes and mixed emotions of gratitude and wonder. Josef was touched.

Mother Mary embraced Eliana with tears in her eyes. 'Yes, we know Kabul. The Lord blessed him and told him to live honestly, and like Zacchaeus, pay back to all the people he had cheated. I am sure he had kept that money for you for a time like this. Mother Rachel, have you told Eliana your story?'

'We will bond this night. Ariel will have to sleep next door.' Her eyes, too, had the wet and shiny look.

'No, Mama. It is all right with me. Let him stay.'

'But the story I am going to share with you is too gruesome for such a young boy. What do you think, Mother Mary?'

'If Eliana doesn't mind, let him stay. He's got to know about his own true origin some time anyway and truly learn about your past. We underestimate children. He is not too young. It will benefit Eliana somehow, too, as you all will get closer.'

'Mother, I have even greater news!' Eliana remarked as she directed her attention to Rachel. 'Kabul is a key to my past! He should know where Jibril who sold me to him is and...'

'If I may come in here, Eliana,' Mother Mary cut in hastily, 'this is your family now. The Lord knows why he asked you to stay here. Be patient. Forget the searching of your past through Kabul. It is not the Lord's way. Stay with your new family.'

Josef saw that everyone agreed to Mother Mary's suggestion, and he felt sorry for Mother Rachel, who looked hurt. He could see that Eliana felt so disappointed. Only he knew that, even though she hid it well from others. At that very moment, Eliana knew she would still find time to catch up with Kabul. She was so close to getting a link to her past. He might know where Jibril was. Jibril might know how she came to be in the Charity home. Josef drew her out of her mind's maze.

'Eliana?'

'Oh, pardon me!!'

At that moment, Mother Mary stood up. 'Josef, I am going back to my house. Are you coming now or…?

'Erm, I think I will take the advice you gave me earlier on.'

Mother Mary had looked confused, and then she remembered she had told Josef about Eliana already being married and his getting to know her better. She smiled encouragingly to Josef as she made to leave.

'Eliana,' Josef called softly, 'please, let us escort Mother Mary…'

Chapter Sixty-Four

*'My thoughts' says the Lord, 'are not like yours, and
my ways are different from yours' (Isaiah 55:8).*

'Let us sit by this old unused well, Eliana. People can't see or hear us here.'

'Don't even worry about that, Josef. I am no longer fearful of my past. I am a new person. Are you still fearful about your old life?'

'Possibly.'

'I feel inner peace. Just let go.'

'Eliana?'

'Hmn.'

'When I asked us to escort Mother Mary, did anything come to your mind?'

'No.'

'Okay. I just wanted the opportunity to get you alone so that we can talk.'

'Okay. I was going to ask for your help on a very personal matter. Also, Josef, I am curious to know what the Lord Jesus told you. Is this what you want to talk about?' She saw him swing his head from side to side to signify that it was a possibility.

'Partly, but yesterday, Mother Mary advised I get to know you very well first. She assumed I had known you were married before with a kid! It kind of came up when I told her I was staying back to see how we both could become betrothed. Later last night, she shared some more details, but I would prefer you to tell me yourself. The Lord Jesus said I would have the desires of my heart where marriage is concerned. I want you to know that my feelings for you have not changed, and we could spend some time now knowing things about each other better.'

'That's okay, Josef. I told your mother everything about my past. You can always ask her.'

'How about you tell me yourself?' he asked softly, and he reached out to hold her left hand, but as always, she remained calm and did not resist. It would be foolish for him to make assumptions. He could not wait to find out how she felt about him. He unclasped her hand.

'My telling you my story will be a waste of time since you already know the details, Josef. I planned to ask Mother Mary's advice about going after the link to my childhood, but see how she handled Kabul's case. It doesn't make sense to me. So, I have decided to ask for your help instead.'

'I am willing. How may I help you?' he asked, noting that she had not expressed how she felt towards him or made any comment about what he had said about his intention for their betrothal.

'Josef, can you help me convince my new family to move with me to Jerusalem? Ariel told me it would be a difficult task convincing them to move.'

'Okay, but why not wait until you all have bonded? Test the grounds first and let me know by tomorrow. I am very certain that if she is offered a better living apartment, she will jump at it.'

'Thank you. Also, Josef, I want to travel to Sidon to look for my son. I plan to visit Sosthenes' family first. It was they who recommended me to Lucas, my husband. Please, will you come with me?'

'Why ask? I will come, but again, please tell your mother tonight.' Then, after a moment's silence, he decided to be bold.

'Eliana?'

'Yes, Josef.'

'If I confide in you on a very personal issue, will you give me your honest response?'

'Why not, Josef! We are family, and more importantly, believers and followers of the new life. Was that not the purpose of you telling me your real name and your past? Like Johana and Razilla, I do not want to be involved in any form of deceit or falsehood in my life.'

Josef rewarded her with an embrace and cleared his throat.

'Eliana, I am still very much in love with you. Do you feel the same way about me?' His heart began to beat fast. What would he hear?

She was quiet for a while. 'Josef, I am going to be very honest. You know my life has been very different from yours. I had had the privilege of experiencing true love when I was Dinah. It cannot be compared to what Miriam felt with her clients, which was all lust and pure business. I know we both became personally involved in mixing friendship and business. Still, you were a client paying for your pleasure. It was lust. I love you now, like a family member. Even now, I am training my emotions and senses to forget what was between Miriam and Jocheb. That was the past. You are my brother now.'

'I hear you, Eliana. What about Jephthah and Johana? Why is Johana not reasoning like you? He had been a client before, too. Or Biliah, whom I gather is getting married to her client too?'

'I don't know the details of their relationships with the men each is engaged to now. Josef, is this about you not being able to tell another woman about your past?'

'What do you think, Eliana? If your husband were to have you back today, would you be bold enough to tell him about your entire past?'

She bent her head and began to cry softly, but Josef made no move to lend a shoulder. He let her be.

'No, Josef. I would not want to wound his heart; I don't think I could. But that does not change how I feel towards you now. Josef, I know someone who is very much in love with you.' The crying had suddenly stopped.

'I don't want to know her. Go home and think of my love and how both of us will raise your son together and have more of our own.' He stood up.

She stood up, too. She sensed she had hurt his feelings. 'It is getting very hot, Josef. Let us go before Mother Rachel thinks I have run away.'

He ignored the joke, which was her way of lightening the mood between them.'

'Josef, has my response changed your desire to help me find my son?'

'Never!'

'Josef, Razilla cares a lot about you. She didn't tell me. I just know it. She once said that God does not use our pasts to determine our future when she was encouraging me. I use those same words too to encourage you now. Please, ask Mother Mary what she thinks about us and tell me her opinion. She approved of Johana and Jephthah. Whatever she says, I promise you, Josef, that I will abide by it.'

Before he replied, he thought about what Eliana had said concerning Razi. He knew Eliana was discerning. It was a gift she didn't seem to know that she possessed.

'Thank you, Eliana. You have finally given me hope and gladdened my heart. Let us meet here same time tomorrow afternoon. I will tell you what Mother Mary thinks about us for the future, and you will also give me feedback on your new family. Let me escort you to your home.'

Chapter Sixty-Five

Abba makes all things beautiful in their time
(Ecclesiastes 3:11).

Eliana was excited. It had been a day of accomplishments. She lay on her bed, pleasantly exhausted and going through many thoughts. Soon, her family in Capernaum would join her. She could not believe how two weeks had flown by so quickly.

Nevertheless, she was confident that her Jerusalem home would be suitable for her new family by the end of the week. Josef had been right. She recalled the extreme joy she had seen on her mother's face when she got back home that afternoon after Josef had left.

'Eliana! Eliana! Look what Kabul paid you. Your wages are worth four months' pay! I can change to a bigger room and start selling things like Biliah does. Abba!! See what You are doing for me. I praise You, God!!'

She remembered how her excitement had been so infectious that even Ariel started singing, and she embraced her mother and told her she had even a more exciting plan. Ariel could not wait.

'Mama, God has given us a big house in Jerusalem. You can use this money from Kabul to keep you and Ariel going while I go and get the house and shop ready for you.'

So, they had talked about her Jerusalem home: where it was in Jerusalem and what it looked like; what Mother Rachel would do in her new role as a shop owner; when and how they could all move in. They had further talked about how the Lord Jesus had blessed every one of them that evening at Simeon's. Also, Ariel too had talked about his witnessing the Lord Jesus multiplying Timothy's lunch to feed a huge crowd of people. Eliana told him she heard it was 5,000! That had led to a whole new discussion on the miracles they heard he had been performing in Judea. Finally, when everyone was tired and sleepy, she had asked Mother Rachel when it was best to go to Jerusalem. She had agreed for her to travel the very next day so that no time was wasted! She had smiled, remembering all this. Mother Rachel was keen to start a new life. Every plan to bond that night did not take place. She and Josef had gone to Jerusalem the following day.

Josef had mentioned to her that the evening he and she had talked, Mother Mary had asked for an update concerning his plans. So, he had told Mother Mary their plans to find Levi, her son in Sidon. Mother Mary had not reacted to that but had listened patiently. Even after she heard their intention to get married with her approval, she had said nothing. But the moment Josef had mentioned the plan to settle her new family in Jerusalem, Mother Mary had been more than elated.

Eliana marvelled at the way God was sorting out her life; just the way blocks were placed one on top of the other to build a magnificent and splendid house! Her thoughts reviewed her conversation with Josef.

'Eliana, Mother Mary was excited about your new family moving to Jerusalem! She gave God praise and was so happy that you were, at last, finding peace and happiness in your life. She said you should not rush any other plans yet, especially about our marriage, but pray to God. She promised me that she would tell the other believers to pray for you, Mother Rachel, and me...'

So, Mother Mary was not supporting her looking for her son or tying herself up with Josef? Josef could not discern this, but she knew. It was something she had discerned deep in her soul but had not acknowledged it. She wanted to find her son, and Josef was happy to help. And if Johana had been wedded to Jephthah, her former client, what was wrong with her getting wedded to Josef? She found her mind switching thoughts from herself and Josef.

Her mind went to the two weddings that jointly took place seven days ago. Johana and Jephthah. Amina and Nebo. She remembered what Razilla had said: *to the pure, all things were pure.* This was indeed true. Eliana was sure she saw the love and peace that radiated from the newlyweds' hearts reflect in their eyes. No one, unless told, would ever believe or imagine where those four newlyweds were coming from! Especially Nebo!! He testified how he had been an orphan growing up in a charity home for orphans and was called N by everyone with no family. But in one evening, the Lord Jesus gave him a family. Eliana's heart lurched. *N was both the Nebo she had heard about and the little boy who had grown up with her in their infanthood!!!* Somehow, she did not feel it was right to introduce herself yet. Instead, she thanked and praised God that N had been blessed with new parents and now a wife!! The weddings had been a huge success, and their Capernaum and Jerusalem acquaintances had all attended, including her new mother and Ariel.

Mother Rachel had wanted to see the house, but she had been able to put her curiosity off. *Not yet.* Instead, she had been consoled that she could stay the night with her friend, Mother Abigail. Both women had spent the entire night telling tales. Well, it was what Ariel had informed her, and she didn't doubt it. She thought about her new mother. They had not told each other their personal stories, but were learning about one another through other people in bits. She smiled to herself when she learnt that Mother Rachel, too, had gotten details of her past life from Mother Abigail and Mother Mary. Then she remembered, gasping in surprise at what Mother Abigail told her during an opportune moment at the weddings.

- Has Mother Rachel, your mother, forgiven Father Asher?

- Who is Father Asher!!?

- What! Do you not know who Father Asher is?

- No!! Please, tell me.

Oh, he is the husband who put her away when she became mentally ill!!

- Noo! She had gasped in shock. I thought she was a widow!

- No! God forbid! She had her own children: two boys and a girl.

- Really!! So Ariel and I have other siblings!! Where are they, Mother Abigail?

- The two boys were killed during the time the Lord Jesus was born. They lived in Ramah then.

- My God!! And the girl?

- Asher gave her away! We are not sure how! She was a baby. She was very ill and didn't look like she would survive. The story is that he gave her to a childless middle-aged couple, who eventually moved away from Ramah. Unfortunately, no one has been able to trace the couple or their daughter. Mother Rachel has not been able to forgive Father Asher for callously putting her away and giving up on their daughter, who was just four months old. We are all praying for her to forgive Father Asher, especially now that she is a follower of the Lord Jesus.

- Does Father Asher still live in Ramah?

- I don't know. I see you both have not told each other your stories.

- No, not yet. One distraction after the other keeps happening. Do you know her life story?

- It is just the bit of her life before she met the Lord Jesus and how he healed her. Don't worry; she will tell you all in good time.

Yes. Lord Jesus has given me parents! I will help Mother Rachel to forgive her husband.

That will be another miracle, Eliana. Let us join the dancing procession...

She knew now she had the task of ensuring that Mother Rachel forgave Father Asher in her heart. If she could forgive all the men who had hands in exploiting her as a child all her life through human trafficking and sexual abuse, then Mother Rachel should be persuaded to forgive Asher. After all, Mother Rachel had applauded her when she said she had no hatred for Kabul. She directed her thoughts towards considering what she had achieved for the day. She could feel the emotions of pleasure and satisfaction blending into one indistinguishable wrap around her state of mind.

Today, she had completed changing the wall tapestries, curtains, blinds, and beddings. She employed people of various skills and assigned them to the appropriate tasks to get the whole house changed. It had taken approximately seven days, but today, it was all finally completed, and she was delighted. The house did not look like a harlot's den any longer. She had taken down her office emblem: *Miriam's house of pleasures.* Tomorrow, she would set up the shop. Mama would sell off her perfumes, spices, jewellery, fabrics from India, beddings, and all the pottery she no longer needed, or which were in excess. She had thought about a line of business for herself. She could stock the shop while Mama sold the stuff or start a weaving loom business on a grand scale. Perhaps those wealthy aristocrats could hire her to teach their daughters about home running, business, and rearing children. She would personally teach Ariel, and what she could not, he could get through paying scholars to educate him. She could not wait for this life to start...

Chapter Sixty-Six

Turn to the Lord and pray to Him now that he is near
(Isaiah 55:6).

Finally, her thoughts returned to Josef, and she found bitter tears brimming in her eyes. Had she loved him all the while and did not know it? She realised she was beginning to welcome and dwell on the hope that they would wed, raise Levi if he were found and have their own children. And Leah? God would take care of that. Her mind was beginning to suck up entertaining daydreams of Josef and herself. She knew it was lust. The signs were there; it was a forbidden passion that seduced one. It was sweetness mixed with the unreal. It felt so good with tinges of guilt at its edges. She found her mind wanting to go down the dark lane of sexual fantasy with Josef. For the first few seconds, she wallowed in it and then, like sudden lightning, she remembered what the Lord had told her: *Love God with all your heart, soul, and strength…I will give you double for all the unfair things that have happened to you…*

She was eventually able to stop and blot out the erotic images from her mind of Josef with her.

Mother Mary had said she would pray and ask Abba. The verdict had come back against them; it seemed. It was devastating news. Why was it that fate would deny her when it was her turn to experience what was good in life? What had she done that differed from Amina or Johana? Why could she not enjoy that which she so much yearned? It would be difficult to accept this verdict—*Eliana already had a husband and should seek reconciliation.* What if Lucas had remarried? Then what next? The hope of reconciling with Lucas seemed as impossible as it had seemed for Johana reconciling with her mother or being free from her sinful life. So, who was going to be Josef's wife? Not her. Not Amina. Not Biliah. Not even Razilla. Razilla and Josef were not even close, and Josef could not bring himself to open up about his past to anyone. *Oh, Lord!! Would she be able to open up to her husband if she even saw him?*

Why had she never thought it wise to tell him? He loved her so much. She knew that if she had, he would have forgiven her. Deep down, she knew what really hurt was the way he had found out. Her mind went back to a conversation between them both one afternoon when their son was just a year old:

'I wish both our parents were alive to see this beautiful boy God has given us.'

'My lord, he is so perfect; that is why I call him my Adam.' He laughed abruptly, but it still had the desired impact on her senses.

'What about relations of your parents, Dinah? We must let them know all that is happening to us?'

'If I had relations, I would not have been abandoned in an orphanage, my lord.' He said nothing but waited for her to say more. When she didn't, he told her more about his own family and why he was far from his sister.

'My love, it is a pity that Rebecca lives here in Sidon, but we are strangers.'

'Where does she live, my lord?

'The last house on Ephraim's Street, but I forbid you to ever go there.'

'Of course, my lord. I will never disobey you.'

'I know it. Even if I hear the worst said about you, I will always trust you, my love.'

'Thank you, my lord. I love you so much.'

'More than your own life. I know that too.'

'You and Rebecca would have got on so well.'

'What did she do to you, my lord?'

'Nothing, my love. She disobeyed our father's choice with her marriage, and our father disowned her. He placed a curse on any sibling who sided up with her against him. He even said such a sibling was to drop the family name and forfeit their inheritance.'

'I understand. Poor Rebecca.'

'Come here, my beautiful Dinah. I want to take advantage to enjoy our love while the baby sleeps...'

Their coming together was natural and spontaneous, as their love juices lubricated every fibre in their body, leaving them pleasurably intoxicated. She had always felt deliriously passionate with her love for Lucas, and she discerned he felt the same with her by his response. Their souls were love mates for life. She had never felt the same way about any man. Marital love was from heaven:

pure and surreal. Lucas had been a husband and not a client. She still loved him! He was gone, and she now had to face reality and go for second best.

Just then, as if receiving a thought wave, she realised she could reason and see things better from Josef's point of view, as she spoke her thoughts out aloud: *we are already friends; we already know each other very well. Our pasts are not secrets, and there is no shame between us. Why have I not realised how I felt about Josef until I had asked him to ask Mother Mary? Am I going to remain single now?* She found herself crying as compared to the exhilarated feeling she had felt when she was coming to bed. Both Josef and she had truly never expected a negative verdict! She had not even bothered to ask how and when he had gotten the message.

Oh Lord, You better sort me out! I have forgiven Lucas. Do you want us to be reconciled? Let Lucas forgive me, too. Please, work on his heart the way You did for Mother Abigail and her children. Thank You...

Abba dispatched His angels at once who bore the names of the spirits for Hope, Faith, Deliverance, Counsel, Peace, Intervention, Wisdom and Comfort...which were to be bestowed on the designated people.

Oh Josef, I think I love you. I want you. I want to be with you so much. What shall we do? She remembered their last evening together: how he had looked at her with so much passion and longing, held her hands tenderly with deliberate warmth, and she was certain there was a lot of chemistry between them both that night. How had she been able to resist the urge then? Why now? *Why were the eyes of her heart always closed and particularly that night?*

As her mind searched for answers to all these questions, she drifted into a deep sleep.

Something woke her up. She realised it was the need to visit the toilet. Getting back to sleep was difficult. Soon, she caught the tails of her dream before fully waking up. She had dreamt of Lucas! She sometimes did, but she would quickly bury it as a forbidden subject because of the pain and depression it brought on her. But now, she realised she wanted to grab the ladder of her dream and climb right into it, and she didn't feel guilty or suffer any pain of bitter regret.

As she settled back into bed with her thoughts on Lucas, she was sure that her feelings for Lucas remained strong. It was she who had deceived him. She did not have those same strong feelings for Josef. Her feelings for Josef were admiration and lust. She cast her mind back to the first days of her becoming Lucas's wife. Then, it was simply a different life in a different world, with love on a different level. Could she ever love a man like that again? Could any man like Lucas have that smile that set her heart bomb ticking away to a near explosion? Even now, she felt shy remembering her first day in his home...the things he said...

'My beloved Dinah, I could not take my eyes off you throughout the wedding ceremony. The pleasure a husband feels when about to enjoy his consummation rights, no woman's mind can fathom! Come to me, my darling, and let my eyes start with the feast of loving...'

Chapter Sixty-Seven

This is the confidence we have in approaching God:
that if we ask anything according to His will, He hears
us (I John 5:14).

osef could not believe how time flew so fast—two weeks gone already! He went through some of the highlights as he lay on his bed in his Jerusalem mansion. Immediately the feasting and merriments of Johana and Amina's weddings were over, he realised everyone went home feeling great and praising God. He knew he, too, like everyone else, was happy for them, but at the same time, he was wondering how his wishes for such a glorious wedding could take place. The Lord had clearly said *his wishes had been granted. He wondered if it was his own wishful thinking he had listened to and not the voice of the Lord.*

He certainly noticed the effect of Mother Mary's counsel on Eliana's countenance when he told her. It was like seeing a mask physically unmasked from her face! It was such a great revelation to how she really felt about him. He knew this revelation fuelled his hope and desire for their lives together, even stronger than ever. *What was the way out?* Coming to think of it, Nebo, who had been a male prostitute like he was, had gotten married to Amina, a former harlot. How about his sister? She was a harlot married to

Jephthah, a former client. Why did Mother Mary and the other elders not frown at these relationships and frown at his? Then his brain threw up a solution, and he caught it deftly in his mind. *Biliah had been formally put away by Rabbi Dodo in their Synagogue!* That made her free to marry again. He became excited. Once Eliana's husband was contacted, he would surely put away the harlot that camouflaged as a virtuous lady and wormed her way into his life with the pregnancy of another man! He concluded that this was what Eliana's husband had thought. Otherwise, as his mother had emphasised, he would not have put away both mother and child.

He thought of Eliana and wondered what she would do then. Was she asleep or thinking of her new life, new family, her son, or him? His mother had told him something that made him realise Eliana had some strange traits to her personality. The fact that Eliana had just walked away from her husband and child without a single word of defence, protest, or explanation was mind-boggling. She had not wept or pleaded, but just walked away. Where did she go? Who did she go to meet to unburden her fears and sorrow? He would find out when they travelled together to look for her son. What was she doing right now? He found himself crashing into sexual longing and desire, and he welcomed it with some guilt. He conjured an erotic image of her mentally and soon was masturbating. As soon as he had a release and felt gratification, he felt the hands of sleep beckoning.

He could not submit to sleep without first considering his plans for the next day. He remembered that Mother Mary constantly lived with four other women in their mid or late forties as herself: Mother Ahuva, Mother Atarah, Mother Felicia, and her older sister, Mother Mary the Senior. They had kindly stayed elsewhere for the Jerusalem troupe to be well accommodated. When they followed the Prophet to Jerusalem, he learnt they stayed in the house of Mother Tamar, who was married to a scribe and teacher of the law. He knew no one else who could direct him to the home of the scribe other than Biliah and Razilla.

He realised that going to Biliah might make her feel awkward as well as himself, even though he knew she had found someone she was considering. Biliah used to have a deep crush on him that was not cold yet. It was better to go to Razilla. She was neutral and everyone's friend. He tried to remember the first time he had seen her apart, from their trip together to Capernaum. Ha! His brain was fighting to keep sleep at bay while trying to dig into the past. This time, the hands of sleep succeeded.

Chapter Sixty-Eight

Why are you cast down oh my soul? (Psalm 42:5).

The New Year was just two weeks old, yet Razilla was surprised at how time had flown. She was sure it was all the events from the previous month leading to the last two weeks—the weddings of some of her closest friends: Johana and Jephthah, Amina, and Nebo. Soon, she was sure that Biliah and Tobias would wed. They had secretly confided in her about their betrothal. She found herself falling into the mood of frequent reflections about her new life as a believer while denying herself a full night's sleep. It was not yet the fourth-night watch, from three to six am, when the roosters would herald the arrival of daylight. Soon, she would get up and prepare for the day.

Since joining the family of believers, her life has been full. Was it not just three years ago she gave up her life of prostitution? *My! That made her 24? Wait a minute, 27!!!* She instantly changed the direction of her thoughts because they made her soul downcast.

Young believers often came for advice and counselling. They mentioned that her counsel was wise. She gave them the words of the Lord, where she gained wisdom in those first two years. The Lord's words brought her listeners peace, love, unity, and hope.

She recalled what the Master had said when she was first introduced to him. *'As your name is, so shall you be'*. Mother Felicia said her name meant *WISDOM*. Was she wise? If the Lord said so, then *she was*.

She remembered the Lord's advice when she was being blessed at the night of Simeon's party:

Remain in Jerusalem, my daughter. Continue to live by faith and not by fear. Your day of visitation is near!

She had been so encouraged. How did the Lord discern she was fearful of growing older and yet no one had asked her hand in marriage? Or that she wondered why all her friends were receiving marriage blessings while it seemed to bypass her? What had he meant by *'Your day of visitation is near'*? Who was going to visit her? Since the beginning of the year, she became more expectant and hopeful of all who came for advice. They could be the link to her heart's desire! The disappointment was brewing in her heart once more. Some people just wanted to hear the testimonies of the Lord's miracles; she had witnessed continuously for two years when she attended weddings and events where the Lord had been present.

Yesterday at the market where she worked at Amos's bakery, some scribes came to fetch her. She told herself, *this is the visitation!* But it was just to testify to a group of doubters and cynics concerning Lazarus. She confirmed again that she was one of the Lord's followers, following him from town to town and village to village. She had indeed witnessed the miracle of Lazarus transformed from being a corpse for three days to life! She still marvelled at the restoration of life to the dead man. He had been dead for three days!

She narrated the event in tears and excitement as if it had happened at that moment. However, the Scribes and Jewish elders were not excited, and they advised her to keep her 'illusions' to herself!

She did not realise how much her thoughts had taken time. The roosters were crowing. Soon, she got up to bathe, dress, and have breakfast.

Razilla was soon startled by a firm knock on her door, as she was not expecting anyone. She could not make an educated guess. Only very close friends came to her home in the late afternoons, mostly. After her breakfast this morning, she would go to the bakery, where she felt like a queen. She was held in high esteem by all her fellow workers, including Amos, the bakery owner, but he was married. Putting on her veil and eyeing up her humble one-room abode, nothing was out of place. She opened her door and gasped in pleasant surprise before the three people she saw.

'Good morning. Shalom,' she greeted her visitors apprehensively, 'please come in. Make yourselves comfortable and have a helping of the red grapes.'

'Good morning, Razi. We all greet you. Thank you very much,' Elder Benjamin greeted, acting as spokesman and continued, 'Mayada in our household told us you would not have left for the bakery yet. I can see you are getting ready to be on your way. Do you have a couple of minutes to spare?' he asked as they made themselves settled.

'Yes, sir, how can I help?'

'Josef here found his way to our home this morning with a quest. My wife and I thought it wise to get a second opinion on the matter, and Josef humbly agreed with us.' Then, turning to Josef, he said, 'Feel free to mention all your plans concerning you and Eliana.'

'Thank you.'

Josef found himself looking for the appropriate starting point when he realised Razilla was speaking.

'Congratulations, Josef,' she started excitedly. 'I was so happy for you and very proud too when Amina testified how you, yourself, became a believer and led her to faith!' She saw him nod his head and keep his eyes on the ground before replying.

'Oh, did she tell you?' A startled expression was obvious in his eyes.

'Yes!! It was definitely a miracle. You ate the Lord's bread and turned your back completely away from sin. It is amazing! The biggest miracle was how you used that testimony and pulled her away from her sinful life, leading her into the Lord's family. Can you remember that the Lord Jesus said you are already his disciple? I often use the Jocheb's miracle to encourage others as well.'

Josef nodded his head. He was suddenly conscious of something. He was shy, but he was no longer ashamed of his life as a prostitute! Another miracle had just happened to him!

'Razi, is not the Lord amazing!? You and Amina have the same testimony of deliverance,' Mother Tamara added.

'Yes. Not only that, we are both gentiles from the same town, have the same family history, and like me, she was a harlot in the same tavern I had worked!! The way Josef called her out was the same way I was called. The Lord had sent Simeon the Senior to talk to me! That has made Amina and I so close. I will visit her at the end of the month to see how she is getting on. She is the little sister the Lord has blessed me with.'

Josef felt encouraged and bolder.

'Razi. You know the Lord blessed me at Simeon's party as well. He said my desire for a wife and family had already been granted. Eliana is my choice for a wife. This is why I thought Elder Benjamin, a scribe, and his wife here, could be of help in arranging for Eliana to be free of her former marriage.'

'Yes, I heard the Lord ask you what you wanted, but you did not say Eliana's name. Instead, you told the Lord you wanted a wife and family,' Razilla confirmed.

Josef remembered feeling embarrassed at the Lord uttering his privately whispered wish. Why had he said his aloud? What had Eliana asked for? But he could not concentrate. Elder Benjamin was speaking.

'If you go through the third section of the Tanakh, our Hebrew Bible, it says somewhere that if you delight yourself in the Lord, he will give you the desires of your heart. So, if marriage is your desire, put your heart to believe you will get the blessing,' Elder Benjamin advised.

'Yes, nothing is too hard for God,' Mother Tamara backed her husband, 'especially when you give him the first place in your life. Do not make Eliana the reason you think you should believe in the Lord. It is a good thing you want to help her achieve the Lord's plan in her life, and the Lord will help you, Josef. What do you say, Razi?'

'I totally agree with you and your husband. We need faith in Abba, even as small as a mustard seed. It will be enough to move mountains. We need to walk around with spiritual eyes and not carnal eyes. The Lord's word for Eliana is different from yours, Josef. She was asked to stay with her new family. For the Lord to have planted her where she is now means that all her needs and that of her new family will be met there. Abba can use anyone to speak his plans for your life. Try and reflect on this when you get home and talk to God. Let us all pray together for Josef on this issue. Like Johana did, ask Mother Mary whether she approves of...' Josef interrupted.

'I have,' he replied in a broken voice.

'Josef, this is the confidence we have as believers of the Lord. Whatever we ask for in prayer, we will have because God, our Abba, hears us. Then you will get the peace and strength that you need. His gifts bring peace and not sorrow. You said you want to be a disciple, then stay in the words the Lord gave you and not out of it. The answers to all you need are there. Remember, God uses people to talk to us. He sees the bigger picture we don't see. Please, adhere to Mother Mary's counsel.'

When she was not saying anything more, Elder Benjamin spoke,

'We don't want Razi to be late for work. Tamar, please pray a *short* prayer for both Josef and Razi.'

'Abba, You know all the birds of the mountain. You feed and clothe them! How much more Your precious children, Josef and Razilla, whom you know the number of hairs on their heads? Because of them, You sent the Lord Jesus. Now, let the plans You have for each of them be fulfilled and established, so that their faith will not stand in their own wisdom but in the power of God. Amen.'

'Amen,' everyone chorused. They shook hands, and Razi hugged Elder Benjamin and his wife in turns.

Chapter Sixty-Nine

Let us have confidence then and approach God's
throne, where there is grace. There we will receive
mercy and find grace to help us just when we need it
(Hebrews 4:16).

Razi felt the night was warm even after her evening bath. The hot air from the outside, trapped in the room, was warm and tinged with the aroma of the fig trees around their neighbourhood. It was time to pray, but she wanted to first talk to God in her heart. From being at work during the day and at the Bethel Centre in the evening, where young believers gathered to share encouragement through the Lord's disciples, hear testimonies or be updated on events, she had not been able to focus on her own heart. She was glad when she heard that Tobias and Biliah were to be married by the end of the third week. Everyone had cheered so loudly to learn that Biliah had also been blessed with the gift of a father in her life—Uncle Jacob! She believed hers was on the way. *Wait a minute; she was already in a family. Amina was her sister, Nebo, Amina's husband was now her brother, and the new parents of Nebo and Biliah would be like parents to her as well. God had used her to talk to herself as well. When last did she pray for herself? She was busy praying for others and neglecting herself.*

She decided not to fall into the same error as Josef: relying on his human wisdom. Instead, she would stop trying to base her hope on the people who came to her for counselling and hoping secretly that they would link her to her future husband.

'Abba, thank you for the people You sent me this morning. You have spoken to them through me. Let me enjoy Your peace again and help me to always remember that You have plans for me which You will fulfil in time. I like Josef, Abba. Very much. If it is Your will, join us together, and if it is not, show me my husband. I want You to bless me with a husband and family of my own. I will remain at peace in Jerusalem, where You have asked me to stay. Blessed be Your holy name, and may Your will be done. Amen.'

Without any effort, she fell into a deep and blessed sleep.

Chapter Seventy

The Lord will guide you always (Isaiah 58:11a).

Josef was in a mood for reflection as he went through the day's incidents. As soon as he got back home that morning from Razilla's house, he had felt restless. He had not seriously attended to business because he wanted to sort out his love life. He knew he felt very blessed for the visit to Mother Tamar and their eventual visit to Razi's house. It guided him along the right path, and now, he knew exactly what to do. Pray. When did he pray last or talk to God? He had tried it that morning. Finally, he had knelt and spoken to God.

'Good morning, Abba. So sorry I have not been talking to you. I assume You know everything about me and what I have to say and what I don't say. Or before I even think anything. Now, I know better. You prefer that we continually keep close to You since You are our Father. Okay, Abba, please show me who my wife is, if not Eliana. Can You kindly tell me before the end of tomorrow? I will be travelling on a business trip to Sidon in two days' time. Give me success as usual. Thank You, Abba God.'

He got up. There was nothing extraordinary about praying. He remembered thinking that it was yet too early in the day to visit anyone and had decided to go to the town square where he had met Yosey three years ago. He made his way there, and as usual, the rowdiness and heated arguments got to his ears first. As soon as he was within reach of the gathering, someone had called from behind him. Feeling tensed with apprehension, he turned to his left and saw Elder Benjamin reaching out to shake his hands.

'Hello, Josef.'

'Hello, Father Benjamin! Didn't know you were coming straight here.'

'I do every day to pick up news about the plot to arrest the Lord Jesus and send it to Father Silas. He would find a way to get it across to the Lord Jesus and his disciples.'

'Arrest the Lord? Why!!?'

'He has powerful enemies here in Jerusalem. They accused him of starting a new movement that would make him a king. The elders are scared that this new wave of life will make Caesar angry with the elders.'

Josef was silent; he felt horrified and petrified to the bones. This was trouble brewing. But he, like everyone else, secretly believed the Lord Jesus was the King of Jews and his divine powers would be no match for his enemies. The Jewish leaders were jealous of him and felt their power and authority threatened.

'If you are free tomorrow evening, we can go to the Bethel Centre to pray with other believers.' The elder's voice had returned him to the present. 'And Josef,' he drew closer and lowered his voice, 'if you are looking for a good woman to take as a wife, think about Razi before she is taken. Listen, you won't believe this, but someone just asked me if their cousin could ask for her hand. I have told them I would give them an answer tomorrow.'

Lord!!! You are so fast...'Yes, she is indeed a good woman. Thank you for considering me worthy. Please, my father, how do I go about this?' he asked, looking at the 70-year-old with reverence.

'All praise to Abba, who considers us all worthy and for opening your eyes on this matter. We will approach her on your behalf tomorrow evening. As soon as we have spoken to her, we will let you talk with her. Does this please you, Josef?'

'It is an answered prayer. Razi is a lady I have always admired greatly for her wisdom in the things of God and her resourcefulness.'

'Consider yourself taken, Josef, because Razi will never turn down the offer. We will ask her to consider you as husband tomorrow.'

'Thank you, my father.'

'May God's will be done. Ask Amos to find someone to take you to the Bethel Centre. It is a bit tricky to go by just verbal directions. God bless you, my son.'

'Amen.'

Chapter Seventy-One

Without Me, you can do nothing (John 15:5c).

'Please come in!' Timothy responded to the knocker of their humble abode.

'Good evening, Mother Rachel. Shalom,' Mother Adah greeted her friend in a cheerful tone as soon as she stepped in.

'Shalom.'

'Shalom, Mother Rachel,' Timothy greeted as well. 'How is Ariel?'

'He is well, thank you. You can stay with him, next door, if you like. I just want to talk to your mother for a while.' Both women gave a knowing smile as Timothy shot off.

As Rachel settled down, her friend was full of gratitude.

'Thank you so much, Mother Rachel, for all that you and your daughter have been doing for us. Life is so much better. I praise God, and may He bless you both. We will miss you so much, especially Timothy, who is like a twin brother to Ariel.'

'How you exaggerate, Adah!'

'Mother Rachel, you both have taken care of the rent and replaced our lamps and sleeping mats with proper beds! That is no exaggeration!'

'God will continue to sort you out,' Mother Rachel encouraged in a sober tone.'

'Amen.' Adah looked, searching at her friend's face.

'My dear sister, I need your help,' began Mother Rachel.

'You know I cannot deny you any help unless I am unable to. Haven't we been like sisters for six years now?'

'Six years ago! It is just like yesterday. Ariel had just turned four and took an immense liking to your son, Timothy. She shook her head at the memories she only knew in her heart.

'Time goes by so quickly. Adah, I want to travel to Sidon tomorrow. I promised Mother Keturah, my mistress, before I left Sidon, that I would find time to come back and ask after Ariel's mother. I am encouraged to go because the brethren are praying for me. Mother Ahuva is also going with me, and we have enough to pay for our fare and escorts to follow us as well.'

'Praise be to Abba! That is wonderful! Don't worry, Mother Rachel. Ariel will be fine with us. May God bless you greatly for fulfilling your promise to your mistress.'

'Amen and thank you so much. My daughter has not finished with our home in Jerusalem. She has been away for almost two weeks now. But this weekend, she will come back, and we will all go back together. Can you believe that I have not told her my life story yet?'

'There is time enough to bond,' her friend added, secretly amazed at Rachel's change of fortune.

'True. Hold this money to help with caring for yourselves, Adah.'

'Mother Rachel, you spoil us so much! I hope you really have enough for your travel and all other commitments. I still have some money Eliana gave me; you know.'

'Don't worry, Adah. Jehovah, Abba, has already provided more than enough.'

Josef felt very self-conscious and wondered what he would say to Razi, whom he had spoken to so casually the previous morning. He had not been able to take his mind off her. He realised he liked her very much and would cherish the idea of taking her as his wife. Would she feel that way, knowing that his heart and desire had been towards Eliana? Would she secretly loathe him because of his past? He was sometimes so ashamed of his past and overcame with deep regrets for having sunk so low in depravity. If he could loathe himself, how would Razi feel deep down about him? He would ask her for a start on how she truly felt about him. He was thankful for Silas, who led him to the Bethel Centre. It was a maze which he could easily have been lost in!!

At first, when he got to the Centre, he could not locate either Father Benjamin or his wife. He was surprised to see quite some people around. At last, he saw Mother Tamar. She beckoned him to follow her to the outer part of the house, towards the back. There, she waited for him to catch up. As soon as he got there, a door opened at the side, revealing Father Benjamin holding a shy Razi. Taking her hands and placing them in his, Mother Tamara came and tied their hands with a cloth.

He and Razi were secretly betrothed. He was told it would be announced the next day at the Bethel Centre, and they could begin to plan a wedding date.

Chapter Seventy-Two

*Remember me oh Lord when You show favour to Your
people (Psalm 106:4).*

As Rachel realised, it had not been easy locating Father Sosthenes and Mother Keturah's house. Six years was a long time to be away from Sidon. The landscape had changed quite a bit. There were some new roads and more fishing ports, and she noticed a timber log warehouse near the jetty, which was not there six years back. She was relieved to find a helper to locate the part of Sidon where Sosthenes lived. As he took them to Kalal District, she and Mother Ahuva engaged in a conversation.

'So, what brought you to Sidon, Mother Rachel, or had your relatives be living here?' Mother Ahuva asked.

'No! So, you do not know my full story then!'

'No, but I am aware that the Lord Jesus touched your life. I also know that you are separated from your husband, and you fostered Ariel.'

'All that is true, but the real truth is that Asher, my husband, brought me to Sidon to find treatment for my mental illness after finding no luck elsewhere. He left me with the physician treating me, promising him he would get more money and return. He never did. I survived on charity and menial jobs in the markets. Eventually, some good man took me along with his sick mother to meet the Lord Jesus one evening. It so happened that he was Sosthenes, and he was looking for someone to adopt a two-year-old child. By then, I had nowhere to live and had nothing. I, therefore, lived with the family for two years, serving them. There was no news of the child's mother, and his father had rejected him. Two years later, their children had all grown older, and they did not need my services any longer. That was why we came to Capernaum.'

'What a pity, my dear sister. Thank God you are whole now. What was the nature of your ailment before he brought you to Sidon?'

'Hmnnn. Sometimes, I heard voices or saw things, but mostly, my memory was affected. There would be days I would not recognise and remember who I was or my family members. It got so bad that I could not care for myself and our baby daughter.'

'What was she called?'

'Eliana – Mary, but it was the 'Mary' bit of her name that eventually stuck. I believe Asher, my husband, blamed and hated Mary for the ill fortune of losing our sons at that time.'

'Why do you say so?'

'She woke up and started crying, which led the soldiers to where we hid. We were shocked because she usually never cries when she wakes up. Asher had asked, '*Why did she cry to alert the murder of our boys? After all, many other little boys escaped being killed. She is bad luck.*'

Her listener heaved a huge sigh and changed the topic. She herself had lost three nephews and her only brother to that tragic incident. She realised Rachel was still obviously very bitter. 'I think we shall get good news,' Ahuva tried to soothe.

'I hope so, but I don't want to give up, Ariel. He has become like my own son. I don't want to deny another woman her happiness. When I was with Mother Abigail, she told me all about my new daughter, Eliana; how she had gone through different names in her lifetime.'

'What other names did Eliana have?'

'Can't remember them, but she was Miriam for a long, long time and recently is just being called Eliana. She too has become close to Ariel.'

'What if Ariel's mother or the father wants him back?'

'I will give him up, Ahuva. Do you know if it was the sincerity of my heart to return to Ariel someday that God saw and gave me a daughter so that I will not be childless?'

'You are a good woman. May God continue to give you favour and give us favour today.'

'Amen.'

'How old is Ar..'

'That is Sosthenes, the boat maker's house,' their helper interrupted and pointed at a red-stoned house after a while of walking around bends and going through busy lanes.

'Thank you,' both women replied, relieved, as Rachel paid off their escort and helper.

Rachel's knock on the door brought out one of the oldest children, whom she recognised instantly. Both women were ushered in, and after they had been refreshed from their journey, Keturah offered them bread. After their meal, Sosthenes opened up a conversation.

'We are delighted to see you, Rachel. You look very well,' he said, looking at Rachel, who kept a simple smile on her face.

'Thank you,' she replied meekly.

'How is the boy?'

'He is very fine, thank you.'

'There is still no news of his mother, but this last year, Lucas has come twice to ask if we have a word of her.'

Both women shook their heads.

'My cousin has not forgiven himself for letting go of his son,' Keturah said. 'I hope he is really doing well.'

'He is doing well, thank you. It is good news to hear that his father has had a change of heart. How did this come about?'

'When you are ready,' Sosthenes added, 'we could go and see Lucas. But unfortunately, he got into drinking and depression. He is sober now but broken in spirit.'

'What has happened to him?' Rachel asked as they all set off towards Lucas' house. *I can't leave Ariel with an alcoholic father and a failure. He must be mentally ill to have lost his family. I can understand!*

'As you know, the day that his wife left, he rejected their son and denied being his father. Since losing his family, he became a drunkard, gradually lost his business and was completely useless as a person for eight years. Then a relative of his took him to Prophet Jesus a year ago, and he returned sober and started picking up his life. He told us he went to Tyre and other towns to look for his wife, but there was no luck. So, he pleaded with us to let him know as soon as we heard a word of his wife.'

'Here we are,' Sosthenes said. 'This is Lucas's house.'

Chapter Seventy-Three

*If you will keep your mind fixed on me then I will keep
you in perfect peace (Isaiah 26:3).*

A t Lucas' house, Mother Ahuva and Mother Rachel saw a man who was in every way a bigger version of Ariel! He was quiet, withdrawn, and did not show any excitement at seeing his guests after greetings were exchanged. Rachel wondered what kind of man Lucas was!

'Are you relatives of Dinah?' Lucas asked. 'I do not have any hope of ever seeing her. It has been TEN years.'

Mother Rachel saw the way Lucas shook his head hopelessly and the way he had emphasised the years. He looked thin and did not seem interested in life. For a few moments, everyone was quiet, and she was not sure how to open up a conversation. She looked in Mother Ahuva's direction, but just then, Sosthenes took the lead.

'Father Lucas,' began Sosthenes.

'Why honour me with a title I don't deserve? My son, Levi, is gone, and my wife too. All is lost.'

'Levi? Do you mean Ariel?' Mother Ahuva wanted to be clear.

'Ariel is Levi. I changed his name to protect his identity,' Mother Rachel clarified.

'So, all is not lost, Father Lucas. You see, this was why I called you "Father Lucas." You still have your son because Mother Rachel here is in the custody of your son.'

'How is Levi?' he asked, looking in her direction and shocking his listeners at his lack of zeal.

'He is very fine and looks exactly like you. He has always wanted a father in his life. I didn't want to raise his hopes until I knew you had acknowledged him as your son.'

'You have done very well. Abba be praised. Thank you very much for all the years you watched him for me. God bless you. I promise to come and fetch him and introduce myself today. His mother cannot be traced.'

'Don't lose hope, Father Lucas. God will bring her back if we pray. If you come to Capernaum, the Lord will help you if you ask him. But what makes you think you can never trace your son's mother?' Ahuva asked.

Lucas shook his head before answering, 'Before she came here as Dinah, she had been called Safirah. So, how can I know where she lives and with what name she has now?'

Rachel found herself jumping up and screaming as she interrupted Father Lucas. She registered the shock on everyone's face and continued to scream loudly:

'ABBA   GODDD!!!   ABBA!!   ABBA!!   ABBA!!! ABBA...ABBA...ABBA...You are amazing!! You are wonderful. You are mighty, powerful, and great. THIS IS A MIRACLE...'

'Mother Rachel, please calm down and share the mystery and good news,' Mother Ahuva called out as she saw how hope had illuminated the countenance of both Father Lucas and Sosthenes.

'My new daughter, Eliana, is Lucas's wife!'

'What!!?' Father Lucas gasped, looking thoroughly confused as he looked around.

'God, Abba Father, thank you so, so much!' Ahuva praised in a loud voice that gave away her emotion. Soon, she began to cry, embracing Rachel. Ariel's mother had been found, and he had a father who had been introduced to the new life of a believer. This was a miracle taking place in her very presence.

'Can you women calm down and enlighten us, please? What are you thanking God for when Father Lucas has said there is no hope of finding his wife?'

Everyone waited for Rachel to unravel the mystery, but she began to cry and praise God at the same time. At last, Mother Ahuva spoke:

'Your wife, Dinah, is well and alive, Father Lucas. She lives with Mother Rachel and Levi. She does not know yet that Ariel is her own son; her current name is Eliana. Mother Rachel, please explain a bit more. The men are still confused.' She noticed the men patiently wait for Mother Rachel to put her emotions under control. Then finally, she spoke at last, but slowly at first:

'Dinah had begun as Eliana. Then she had gone through using different names, including *Safirah*, which Lucas said he heard. Now, she is called Eliana. For three years, she had been hearing about the Lord Jesus and finally met him last month. Her life has changed around for the best. Then the Lord Jesus blessed me with

Eliana as my new daughter. Oh Abba, I can't believe my ears.' She broke down again and was hugged by her friend.

'Neither me,' Lucas added dreamily. 'People, please, good people, tell me I am not dreaming. You say Dinah is now Eliana?' Lucas got to his knees before Mother Rachel. 'You are now Eliana's mother? Please forgive me for sending away Eliana. She was an excellent wife and mother. She blessed me and the work of my hands with her wisdom and all her earnings. I never gave her the chance to explain. Please, forgive me. I am so sorry. I promise to make it up to her by the power of God.'

'Please, stand up, Father Lucas. You are my son now. The Lord Jesus said we should forgive as his followers and Abba. I forgive you. Eliana will tell you the full story of her life when next you see each other.'

'I will follow you both back to Capernaum,' he replied eagerly as he stood up.

'That is fine, but be prepared to journey to Jerusalem first, where you both will be reconciled properly,' Mother Ahuva advised. 'Also, we will find someone to let Eliana know you have come to seek reconciliation and have her back as your wife.'

'I feel a new strength and hope in me. I knew I had made a terrible mistake and sank into great sorrow and depression. I lost hope completely when I realised that Mother Rachel had moved, taking my son away with her. I began drinking. I couldn't face reality. I should have been able to start over again, but I couldn't. My boat business was affected, and I had to sell off the business. Somehow, I squandered all my savings and relied on being a gravedigger and doing mason jobs. Blessed be Abba, our God!! I couldn't even bear to stay in our former home and moved to this house. Mother Hulda, my oldest sister and Father Joshua, my nephew, invited me to see Prophet Jesus. They told me the miracles they had heard of and witnessed: not only of healing people but restoring people who were mentally ill; people who had lost their minds, or people who had regained their families. That was what gave me hope to follow them. The hope that I might find Dinah. They said they had been praying for me.

I met the Lord Jesus in Bethsaida last year, and he was talking about forgiveness. He prayed for all of us that day as a group. My sister took me to him, and he laid his hands on my head. He said my sins were forgiven and I should receive faith. Since then, the urge to drink ceased. I have been in faith and lived in the hope that one day, my family will come back. I went to Cousin Keturah for word of my family. Though I learnt that Mother Racheal said she would visit, I lost hope of ever seeing Levi. And here she is today with the best news for me!! Abba, thank You!!' he shouted as he raised his hands. 'I give You all praise. Blessed be our Abba Almighty. He is faithful and never fails. I worship You, Abba, for who You are.'

'Amen,' everyone said in jubilation. Then Mother Ahuva spoke:

'God is faithful. He takes care of our future. Father Lucas, this testimony is also your restitution. It is your first step to reconciliation. We are all witnesses to how Abba has restored your health and family. Be prepared to share this with our fellow believers in Jerusalem.'

'I am ready to tell the whole world!' Father Lucas exclaimed as he began to hug everyone around and dance. Soon, he saw everyone join him in dancing and singing songs of praises to Abba God.

Chapter Seventy-Four

I will declare that Your love stands firm forever
(Psalm 89:2a).

liana had just stepped out of the bathroom, feeling gloomy, when she heard the knock. *It has to be Josef.*

They were both going to look for her son this weekend. She would settle her new family first before leaving on her quest with Josef. She realised instinctively that she would let Josef touch her if he wanted to. She felt very needy and in need of solace, but she did not feel like talking to Abba. He had taken Josef from her. Abba, who will want me now?

In this state of mind, she went down the embroidered steps wearing no sash or veil but a slip of a tunic that would leave nothing for Josef to decipher about her real motive. She splashed herself with a bit of heady perfume and gave free rein to the mass of her hair to cascade down her back, hips, and ankles, ready to tease when she tipped her head. She went to open the door. She had made a huge error and hung down her head in utter shame and embarrassment, with tears of humiliation stinging her eyes. Her mass of hair shielded her shame and embarrassment. Standing at the door were Mother Abigail, Mother Rachel, and Mother

Ahuva!!! What would they think? That she had gone back to her life as Miriam? Before she could explain, they all shouted, "Mazel tov," and she knew her fate had changed yet again!

'My Mothers, please excuse my dressing. I have just taken my bath and thought it was Razi,' she lied. 'I didn't want to keep her long at the door. Please, never think I have gone back to the life of Miriam.' *What good news had they brought?*

'Eliana, we came here to rejoice with you! Take your mother up to your room. She is bursting to tell you the best news ever!' Mother Abigail exclaimed. 'Mother Ahuva and I will make ourselves comfortable. Take all the time with your mother and seize the opportunity to bond.'

'And Eliana, I am also a witness to the good news you are going to hear. Congratulations!' Mother Ahuva said.

'Thank you, Mother,' Eliana said quietly, grateful that her hair was hiding her semi-nude body.

'Congratulations, Eliana!!' Mother Abigail said aloud as both she and Mother Ahuva began singing and praising God.

Chapter Seventy-Five

He gives me new strength. He leads me on paths that
are right for the good of His name (Psalm 23:3).

'Marzel tov! Razi and Josef,' Father Benjamin said, taking the lead.

'Marzel tov,' Mother Tamara followed. 'Now, we will leave you both together now. We are sure you both might need to share testimonies,' she said, with mischievous twinkling eyes.

'Thank you, Father Benjamin and Mother Tamara,' Razi said, feeling self-conscious.

'Thank you, Father Benjamin and Mother Tamara,' Josef followed.

As the couple took their leave, Josef looked around and said, 'I never really knew about Bethel Centre, you know. How long have you been coming here?'

'Ah Josef, for about a year now. Shall we start first with testimonies as we were advised, or what do you think?'

'Testimonies?' he asked, looking confused. 'Whose testimonies?'

'Us.'

'Us?'

'Okay, Josef. Please, follow me to somewhere quiet where we can share our testimonies,' Razilla proposed. She wanted to be sure Josef was God's idea and not the pity of the kindly couple playing the role of a matchmaker, matching her to an unwilling Josef!

'Good idea, Razi. Let us go and visit Johana. They have a nice open court where we can have privacy, and we can also chat on the way as well.'

She agreed and went to say her farewells to some people as he waited by the door for her. When she returned, he asked her again about the Centre.

'Lord Jesus came in contact with Jarius when he miraculously brought his dead daughter to life about three years ago!! Jarius owns the room, which he lets people who have been healed to use weekly and share their testimonies. I have been coming since I moved to Jerusalem a year ago.'

'What made you come to Jerusalem?'

'Erm, I used to live in Capernaum, following the Lord and his followers. Then, it was agreed that we had to spread ourselves to help new believers. Some people went to Cana, Dalmanutha, Nain, Gennesaret, Bethsaida, Bethany, Tyre, and Galilee. And even as far as Sidon and Syria. Biliah, Father Benjamin, his wife, a few others and I, came to Jerusalem.'

'You did not find it unsettling to start over in a new town?'

'No. Biliah and I had the Lord's specific backing. He asked us to come here.'

'Okay. I am glad Biliah and Tobias are together,' Josef said.

'Yes, it was a surprise,' agreed Razi.

'Johana will be speechless about us too, Razilla. I want to know how you really feel about me. I know you know about my past through Amina. I do not have doubts about how I feel about you. I know my spirit and soul desire you as my wife. My heart has pure love for you, and I want you to know that our being together is an answer to my prayer. What I had going with Miriam was pure lust. I knew all along but was in denial. When she became Eliana and I became Josef, we thought we could hide from our past in our new identities, but the Lord has said NO. Am I good enough for you, Razi? Are you being forced against your heart and will to follow a man who was once a male prostitute?'

He looked at her as they walked.

'Josef, please don't be so hard on yourself. I can never see you in the shadow of your past—that was Jocheb. I see you in the light of your new image. You are a brand-new person, and Abba will keep you in perfect peace, Josef. I have no regrets about being betrothed to you. I am not doing this against my will. It is an answered prayer, and just like you, my spirit, soul, and heart have pure love for you.'

She felt shy saying all this. She was not used to expressing her feelings. When she looked up to Josef, he was still looking at her, and the way he looked at her quickened something in her. *Surely, he is in love with me! Thank you sooo much, Lord. I am so grateful!!*

303

'There we are! We have arrived, and I can hear my mother's voice. She came to visit Johana.'

'She is definitely excited about something from the sound of her voice.'

'Well, we shall find out, won't we?' he asked light-heartedly.

'Yes. We will and then share our own good news.'

'Yes, my love.' He took her hands in his and briefly embraced her. He liked the strong masculine vibes he felt. Not only did it surprise him, but it added confidence in his complete healing.

'We will tell the family that the wedding will be in the last week of this month. Are you ready, Razi?' His voice had become the voice of a lover, melting her heart and quickening her pulse.

'Yes, my beloved,' she whispered. Then of the month was three and a half weeks away. She couldn't wait.

Josef knocked on the door in a way he knew his sister would definitely know it was him.

Chapter Seventy-Six

Lord, You are my God. I will praise You forever
(Psalm 30:12b)

'Mama, please sit here while I get dressed, then you can tell me this good news,' Eliana suggested, while beckoning her mother to a cosy velvet chair. They could hear the singing of the two women on the lower floor. Then, just as she slipped out of her slip to adorn her nude body with sweet-scented bath oil, her mother gasped and shouted.

'ABBA! ABBA! ABBA! I HAVE FOUND MARY!! I HAVE FOUND MARY!!' She rushed towards her startled daughter, turned Eliana around and examined the birthmark on her lower back more closely. Eliana heard the unbelievable in a very low and soft voice that bespoke volumes of mystery.

'Eliana, this is why I have been so fond of Ariel. He has your birthmark on his lower back as well. It didn't make sense to me, but now it does. You are my birth daughter! The daughter I lost!!! And Ariel is my grandson!! Your father, Asher, has this birthmark as well.'

Eliana could not process this new extraordinary information instantly. It was too overwhelming. All she consciously thought of was that the Lord Jesus had known Mother Rachel was her birth mother, and he had placed her in her true family where she belonged.

She felt Mother Rachel's strong hug while listening to her praising God. It was beginning to dawn on her she did not need Josef's help to find her son. Abba had already answered all her prayers, and she had not even known!! She had her birth parents! This was too much good news for her to handle, so she sat herself down on her dresser stool, her body shaking. She watched her mother stand up and come towards her.

Rachel sat beside her daughter. 'Eliana—Mary, my darling...'

'Yes, Mama. Stop crying, please. I bear no bitterness towards you about whatever happened.'

'Listen. I should have been thankful that Abba had given me a beautiful baby daughter. I should have buried the pain from the loss of your two brothers and invested my time, energy and love in you. I would have been well. You would have been healthy. Asher would not have thrown you away. The evil you have suffered would not have befallen you. It is my entire fault. Please, forgive me with all the new love Abba has given you. I love you so much, and I will always be there for you. Nothing can ever separate you from me again.' She hugged Eliana.

'Mama. There is nothing to forgive. I love you so much, and I am grateful that Abba has preserved us to see this day. When I asked the Lord Jesus why I faced an evil life right from birth, he said that whatever was meant for my harm would turn out to be good. So, let your heart be at peace, Mama. Mine is.'

She felt overcome with an exhilarated feeling. She watched her mother kneel to praise Abba. Then she remembered something.

'Mama! Is this the good news you were bringing for me? Ariel and me? It is a miracle. How did you get Ariel? Mama, what happened? How did you and Papa lose me?'

'You are so full of questions. I will fill you in about the past. First of all, the good news we bring is that we met Lucas two days ago.'

'Lucas!!?'

Eliana stood up with her mouth wide open in apprehension. Her eyes were fixed on her mother with wonder and a sense of mixed emotions. Her ears did not want to miss any information. She had to remind herself that *it was good news!*

'He is a believer and has repented of the evil he did to you. He prays you forgive him. He wants to reconcile with you and Levi. He is ready to meet you this evening if you have forgiven him.'

'This evening!!? Good news, Mama!! I have forgiven him for disbelieving that Levi was his! That is God's will. Lord Jesus said God would give me double blessings for all I have suffered. But Mama, have you forgiven my father?'

'I am a happy woman. I am fulfilled and overflowing with joy. God has made it so easy for me to forgive. I have you back and more!! So yes, I forgive him. I will go and tell him the good news about you this afternoon, and then I will take you to go and meet him tomorrow. Today, we will concentrate on you and Lucas.'

'Mama, I want to hear Lucas's testimony. I can't believe all that God has given me this morning. Anyone looking at me now will never believe that I have just received three miracles in one morning!! I love Abba. I love Him so much. It has all ended well.'

'I am astonished that you are not as excited as I thought you would be when I told you about your husband.'

'I am like that, Mama. I need to process all that I have heard this morning. I planned to settle you and Ariel here this weekend and follow Josef to find Levi.' She shook her head. 'Mama, Abba loves me! Ariel is Levi? Of course, I am excited that overnight, I have my real parents, my husband, and my son back. I am overwhelmed. I feel I am dreaming, Mama!!'

Eliana felt the congratulations were in order then for the 'good fortune' they had expressed when she opened the door. From Mother Rachel, she also heard the unbelievable testimony of Lucas and her mother's life story from Ramah till how she had gotten Ariel.

'Eliana, I hope you are ready to meet Lucas at the Bethel Centre, where you both will be reconciled.'

'I am, Mama,' she replied with a false outward calm, but she alone knew that she felt scared at the same time. Ten years!!! Dinah was a prostitute with a history of 20 years prostitution!!! Was he faking so he could come and punish her for all the suffering, humiliation, and ruin she brought him by her deception? *Abba, give me faith, please!!*

'Very good!' Her mother's face beamed. 'Lucas is so eager. Finish your dressing and let us go downstairs and tell your mothers the next miraculous good news about our true relationship. I still cannot believe how Abba has led me to you.'

Eliana was still awed by her three miracles in one morning!! She dressed hurriedly as she watched and listened to her mother singing and praising Abba about the revelation of her being Eliana's birth mother. Eliana could sense that Mother Rachel's faith was much stronger, and her past pain of loss and brokenness was completely healed. She had just regained a lost daughter, a grandson, a son-in-law and was on the way to being reconciled to her husband! She followed her singing mother downstairs to meet the other women. Her mother had a sweet voice as she found herself getting lost in its sweetness.

'…Somehow, God would fix all that up,' Mother Abigail's voice brought her back from her thoughts of reconciling with Lucas after ten years! And Ariel—her son!

'This evening, Josef and Razi will be officially engaged!! Yesterday, they were secretly betrothed,' Mother Abigail announced.

'What a pleasant surprise!' Eliana responded as she went over to where the woman was seated, and she hugged Mother Abigail.

'I am so happy for Razi and genuinely thankful to God that Josef is finally able to differentiate between lust and love.' Then, turning to her mother, she said, 'Mama, I almost fell into temptation today. Without hearing the news you all brought, I saw myself as a childless woman doomed to no future except to fall back to my life as Miriam with Jocheb!! This news of Josef and Razi is unbelievable!! How did it happen? I wonder!'

'I know!' Mother Abigail confirmed. 'Josef and Razi surprisingly showed up at Johana's house two days ago to visit and shared the good news of their secret betrothal. Their wedding is fixed for the last week of next month.'

'I just praise Abba for making me a witness to the many miracles that are happening to each of you. This will prevent me or anyone from thinking that all these miracles by the Lord Jesus are tales!!' Mother Ahuva nodded her head, with tears brimming in her eyes. She felt emboldened to share a secret at the Bethel Centre during Testimony time. 'Praise the Lord,' she ended quietly.

'Amen,' they all soloed contemplatively.

Today was indeed a special day in her life, Eliana thought as she experienced the same peace that came upon her when the Lord had laid his hand on her head.

Chapter Seventy-Seven

*I am the Lord your God, who directs you in the way
you should go (Isaiah 48:17).*

After leaving her daughter's residence at the Eastern Gate area of Jerusalem that morning, Mother Rachel made her way to the Bethel Centre to hint Apostle Bartholomew of her intentions to meet Asher, her husband. Her two companions would also be witnesses to another miracle of reconciliation. Left to her, she was fulfilling a secret wish for her daughter to meet her father. They met Apostle Bartholomew, who prayed for them and found a worthy saint to accompany them after some final words of counsel and encouragement. She was delighted that Father Benjamin was willing to accompany them to where Asher lived. They were going to let him know the good news about Eliana and that she, herself, no longer bore any grudges against him. She and her companions waited patiently as they saw the Apostle pick up his red-dyed raffia bag, which always held the Torah, give some last minutes instructions and advice to Apostle Simeon, who would hold the fort in his absence. She knew she was a bit tensed, sensing that her life might change significantly if Asher agreed to be reconciled to her. It seemed ages ago since he left her at Sidon. All the same, she still remembered one chance meeting with him, and she sighed under her breath. Finally, the group was ready to depart. As she glanced at their faces, she hoped they could not feel how tensed she was. She felt she was in very good company. She and Abigail had become wonderful friends, and as for Ahuva, their relationship dated as far back as when she first met the Lord Jesus. She wondered again as to how Asher would react to the news of their daughter or their reconciliation. He had not been friendly when they met by chance. She reckoned that was about two years ago. She found her mind reeling back in time while, at the same time, paying divided attention to what her companions were talking about.

Then, she did not have any faith at all, even after a conversation with the Lord Jesus!! She mused to herself at this. She had boldly reached out to him after he had shared Timothy's sandwich lunch with an overwhelming crowd of people. She had noticed that his followers were busy sharing and gathering leftovers, and there was just a lady sitting close by to him, so she had seized her opportunity. Without waiting to finish her meal, she told Timothy's mother to watch Ariel. *She was on a quest for her daughter.* As she approached the Lord, she recognised the lady as Mother Ahuva, a friend of Adah, Timothy's mother. She felt encouraged because she had heard of Ahuva's testimony. Soon, she was with the Master. There had been no restraint from anyone. This was her destiny.

'Rabbi,' she had begun, 'I know you are so discerning. You told Ahuva about the men in her life when You saw her for the first time in Samaria. Please, my Lord, tell me, where is Asher? Please, help me. I want to see my daughter, Mary.' She saw the Lord smile kindly at her and observe her for a few seconds before he spoke.

'All is well, daughter. Forgive Asher in your heart, and you will find your daughter and more. Meet Biliah. She is amongst

312

those women there behind that well to my left. She will encourage you.' He laid his hands on her head, and her bitterness was gone that instant. She remembered that as she was about to make her way back to where she sat, Ahuva had called her.

'Hello! I am Ahuva.'

'Hello. Yes, I know you! You have visited my neighbour occasionally. She told me your testimony, which is why I came to seek help.'

'The Lord has helped you. Don't worry.'

'But I still don't know where my husband is! And to forgive Asher is impossible. You cannot imagine the evil that man did to me! I just want to see my daughter. Her name is Eliana, Mary Zekiah from Bethlehem, but I live here in Capernaum.'

'Then do as the Lord has told you.'

Ahuva had also encouraged her to forgive Asher so that what the Lord had said to her would be fulfilled. 'At least, talk to Biliah for a start! She used to be a whore; a very promiscuous woman, but now, she is a follower of our Lord. In fact, she is betrothed. She is just over there. Shall I call her out for you?'

She remembered how horrified she had felt at the thought. People might think she, too, was a prostitute. She had politely refused the request and found her way back to her seat. One day, she would find Mary, her daughter.

However, she recalled how constantly she had always thought about Biliah's transformation and how Ahuva, herself, had been touched by her encounter with the Lord. She and Ahuva had met miraculously again. It was at the funeral of a woman named Tisha.

She did not know Tisha, but her neighbour, Adah, did and had invited her to tag along. Ahuva was related to the dead woman's family. When she and Adah arrived at the compound of the bereaved, they went to pay their condolences to the bereaved husband. She came face to face with Asher!! Neither of them had spoken to the other, even though he had spoken with Adah. He had looked away from her. When Asher had lowered his head, she greeted him.

'Shalom. I am sorry about your loss. The Lord comfort and blesses you.'

Her husband had not registered any shock or surprise at seeing her, and he had merely nodded his head. That was all that transpired between them. She looked around for Mary then. She eventually got to see Asher's two sons, born to him by Tisha. Each had stood with their wives, and that was when she saw Biliah. Where was Mary? She ought to be here, she wondered. Asher still looked very well, she thought. The years had merely added maturity, which had gifted him charm and comeliness to his person.

She recollected speaking to Biliah at some point:

'I am so sorry, Biliah. Please, accept my condolence. I am Rachel, Asher's first wife.'

'Asher?'

'The bereaved man.'

'Oh, he also goes by the name Uriah.'

'I was his first wife in Ramah.'

'Really! We all had the impression that he was unmarried or if he had been once married, the wife was long dead! Praise be to God,' she whispered. 'Has he seen you?'

'Thanks be to God that I survived. Yes. I have seen him, but I have not seen our daughter, Mary. Where is Mary, my daughter?'

'Mary? He has never mentioned her. You may have to ask him. I am sorry, but you can visit us at Noah's Bay. There's a large sheep pen there. You can't miss the place.'

'Thanks so much, Biliah. I will come tomorrow as I really want to know where Mary is.'

Biliah had welcomed her as a friend and consoled her when she finally discovered what had been done to her Mary by Asher. Biliah had encouraged her then that if the Lord Jesus had said she would 'find Mary and more', she should be hopeful and patient. She remembered her sorrow, bitterness, and betrayal by Asher. After abandoning her in Sidon, he had given away their baby daughter like a give-away trophy. He then took Tisha as a wife and settled in Nain, where he was known by another name—Uriah. He had left no forwarding address at his old house so that she could not trace him.

She sighed inwardly. Could she truly forgive him? Would he be pleased now to hear of that daughter? Such an evil man! Cold-hearted. Callous. Why would she want to be tied together with such a very deceptive and dubious man? She didn't need him in her life! It suddenly occurred to her that had it not been for Biliah, she would never have known that Asher left Nain after Tisha's death in Jerusalem with his family a year ago. As if running away from her discovery of him...

'You are so quiet, Mother Rachel. I hope you are not scared. Don't forget that you are the bearer of exciting news.' *How thoughtful of Father Benjamin! If he knew what thoughts I have had, he would have been shocked.*

Rachel managed a half-smile with some effort. Such a callous-hearted man!! He might have wished that she and their daughter remained dead and non-existent!!

Chapter Seventy-Eight

In Christ, we have the forgiveness of sins
(Ephesians 1:7).

Mother Rachel was surprised that it was Asher himself who opened the door. At first, he had looked startled when he saw Mother Ahuva, Mother Abigail, and Father Benjamin; complete strangers until he saw her.

'Shalom,' Mother Ahuva greeted. 'May we come in? We bring you good news!'

'Shalom. I guess so, but I am not worthy. I have sinned greatly against God.'

'Invite us in first, and the Lord will take control, Father Asher,' Father Benjamin advised.

Rachel saw Asher shrug his shoulders. 'Shalom,' he greeted the other women as he made way for them into his elegant sitting room. He gestured to them to take their seats on wooden chairs that surrounded a spacious table for eight occupants. He deliberately avoided eye contact with Rachel. He then beckoned his family to give him privacy, and Rachel saw them leave the room through a side door.

What does Asher do now? She wondered. He looks very well. He was a boat driver and used to do escort jobs for travellers. Occasionally, he did carpentry jobs. I remember how orderly and precise he was regarding how he kept things. Then she realised Asher was speaking and still deliberately avoiding eye contact with her.

'Please, help yourself with the grapes on the table. They are from my farm…' That had gotten her attention. So, Asher was into farm produce!! She stretched her hands to help herself with fruits. She would not be the first to make eye contact. He should be kneeling to ask for her pardon!

'You are very hardworking. I heard you were into transport business,' Mother Ahuva started up.

'Sometimes, I still do that, but it is more of exporting farm produce.'

'You are blessed to have land, then?'

'Through my late wife's family. They are into husbandry. You say you have good news for me?'

Mother Ahuva took in a deep sigh before responding: 'Yes, but we shall pray first.'

When everyone had bowed their head, Ahuva called upon God.

'Abba Father, how we love you for all the good things you are doing for us through the Lord Jesus. He has made many families unite in peace, joy, and love. Now, we pray your blessings of peace, love, joy, and unity over this home as we testify to your mercy and goodness in the name of our Lord Jesus.'

'Amen,' the gathering chorused.

'Why do you pray in the Prophet's name?' Asher asked.

'There is power in the name of Jesus, Father Asher. He sends out his disciples now and again to heal, cast out demons using his name, and it always does miracles. I am a witness to this. In Galilee, I used his name to open the eyes of two blind men and heal one hunch back. I gave my testimony at the Bethel Centre. The Lord Jesus asks his followers to use his name when we pray to God,' Father Benjamin offered.

'I see,' Asher sounded sarcastic as he watched Mother Ahuva rise from her seat.

'If I may cut in quickly, I also was a witness to seeing the Lord Jesus heal a paralytic, and by his words, I received my own healing at the well in Samaria!' Asher nodded his head but said nothing more.

'Father Asher, I am Ahuva, and she [pointing to Abigail] is Mother Abigail. You already know Mother Rachel. And this is Father Benjamin, one of our elders at the Centre. We are here to tell you that through God's love for you, He has preserved your family and business.'

Asher kept his head down and still said nothing. Mother Ahuva continued. 'Also, Mary, your daughter is alive and has given you a grandson! That is the good news.'

Now, he raised his head, and Rachel saw an immense relief in his facial expressions. It was like witnessing the spirit of guilt physically evaporating from his face.

'Praise God!! Blessed be my God!! Why did she not come? Does she hate me? Where has she been all these years? What does she think of me?' He made eye contact with Rachel this time and saw that she was studying her fingernails. Then he returned his full attention to Mother Ahuva.

'No, she does not hate you! On the contrary, she, too, believes in the Lord Jesus and follows the new way of living life. She is a wonderful young woman and is happy to meet with you and the rest of the family. But are you willing to reconcile with your wife and daughter?'

'I have no objections if they both have truly forgiven my past mistakes. I regret what I did, and I don't deserve their love.' He stood up. 'Rachel, do you truly forgive me with all your heart? If you can't, I will understand.'

'Asher, since the Lord Jesus restored my health and our daughter to me, I have no bitterness, grudge, or anger towards you. The Lord Jesus took it all away from me.'

As she spoke, he took the opportunity to observe her. She looked like one who had suffered lack and some deprivation, but peace and calm radiated from her presence. He was trying to court some young woman he met in the market. Though still in her forties, Rachel was still quite desirable and more beautiful than Leyla. He assessed her: her bosom was still full; her neck still long; her skin was still firm, and her face was still shapely. She was not a stunner and did not possess ravishing beauty, but she had always been comely, decent, humble, and hard-working. He realised she was blushing. He must have given away his thoughts as he gave her a slow, deliberate perusal. He wasn't a man of words. His pride and arrogance also made it difficult to apologise. So, standing up but not leaving his seat, he stretched out his hands towards Rachel. She got up, and going towards him, accepted his embrace.

The words fell out of his mouth like ripe fruits ready to fall at the slightest breeze: 'I am sorry, Rachel. I did you and Mary very great evil. Forgive me.'

'I have. Please, believe. As a follower of the Lord Jesus, I have taken his nature. His nature is love without conditions.' Her entourage clapped and praised God as she went back to her seat.

'Thank you, Abba Father!' Mother Abigail burst out.

'Dan!' Father Asher suddenly called out.

'Yes, Papa!'

'Get your wife and children to come and give their greetings and hear the good news. My first wife and daughter are not dead!!'

'Abba be praised, Papa! Let me get them!'

They came out and shook hands with the guests.

'Marzel tav, Papa. So, I have a sister and a Mother! God be praised.'

'We bless God,' Father Benjamin affirmed. 'Father Asher,' he called out when the gathering was quiet, 'the next step is for you to be officially reconciled before the gathering of fellow believers here. Please, listen and then confirm if this is what you want to do. If you will, do this with Abba as a witness. After your confirmation, we will pray for you and finally, we will arrange for you to meet Mary, her spouse, and Levi, your grandson.'

Rachel heard Asher agree to visit the Bethel Centre with Dan to reconcile to his lost daughter, Mary, of thirty years!!! She also heard him confirm his wish to be reconciled to his wife!! She was sure she didn't hear right.

Presently, she saw Father Benjamin open his bag and bring out the Torah and read some portions from Psalm 51:

HAVE MERCY ON ME, O GOD, ACCORDING TO YOUR UNFAILING LOVE

ACCORDING TO YOUR GREAT COMPASSION, BLOT OUT MY TRANSGRESSIONS

WASH AWAY ALL MY INIQUITY AND CLEANSE ME FROM MY SIN.

FOR I KNOW MY TRANSGRESSIONS AND MY SIN ARE ALWAYS BEFORE ME.

AGAINST YOU I HAVE SINNED AND DONE EVIL IN YOUR SIGHT.

CREATE IN ME A PURE HEART O GOD AND RENEW A STEADFAST SPIRIT WITHIN ME.

DO NOT CAST ME AWAY FROM YOUR PRESENCE.

RESTORE TO ME THE JOY OF YOUR SALVATION AND GRANT ME A WILLING SPIRIT TO SUSTAIN ME....

At that moment, the evil he had done 30 years ago came before him. He had abandoned his wife in a city where no one knew her real name or who she was. He had lied about coming back to fetch his wife. He had lied about his intentions to get more payment and return.

He had lied when he told people he had put their daughter in the care of a childless couple. He remembered she had been an exquisite four-month-old baby. The truth was that he had given the child to a total stranger to put her in an orphanage. He had lied to the stranger when he promised to pay for her upkeep till the mother was well. He had no intention of ever visiting the orphanage, and worst of all, he could not remember the name of the orphanage.

To the shock of Rachel, she saw Asher, a very proud man, break down in front of his son Dan, Keziah his wife, and their three daughters!! She had never seen him cry. Not even when their sons were taken forcefully from them to be slaughtered that fateful black day that could never be erased from her memory. She shuddered and felt humiliation rather than sympathy for Asher. He seemed weak, vulnerable, and not the strong, hard, proud, and very handsome man she had always known him to be. She was so shocked that she stayed put where she sat, wondering whether comforting him would harm his pride.

She was relieved when she saw Father Benjamin promptly come to Asher's aid.

He embraced him and said, 'God is love. He loves you so much and wants you to be free from every guilt. You have made the right move by repenting. As soon as you are ready, you will commit to restitution in your heart. This means telling your wife and daughter what REALLY happened 30 years ago. That confession will complete the healing of your heart and convince God that you are truly sorry. Both your daughter and wife are new creatures in the faith of our Lord Jesus. So, you have nothing to fear as God has sorted their hearts and yours, this very moment.'

He brought out a white strip of khaki cloth material from his bag. Rachel knew what was next. She knew she was merely physically ready in body and not in her heart when Father Benjamin called her, took Asher's hands, and tied them to hers. They were reconciled. *Could she ever trust Asher? Would he poison her?* Father Benjamin said the next words she had been hoping and wishing were never uttered.

'Father Asher, in front of everyone here, I present you your wife, Mother Rachel, who will return to live with you in your home as Abba God has commanded for all who are married under His law. Marriage is lifelong as long as you are both alive, and it should never be broken because it is God-made. Abba will expect that you both honour this divine union.'

'I will.'

'I will,' she confirmed.

Rachel heard everyone cheering, and her tears were seen as tears of joy. Deep in her heart, her tears reflected her shock and disappointment. She never believed Asher would take her back as his wife. She desired to live with her daughter. Was that not what the Lord Jesus wanted? She had come here to tell him his daughter was alive, and that she had forgiven him. She had just told her daughter that nothing would ever separate them again! *Abba had restored her marriage. He must know what He is doing...*

Chapter Seventy-Nine

Teach me Lord what You want me to do and I will
obey you faithfully; Teach me to serve You with
devotion (Psalm 86).

Much later, that same day, as the evening was just deepening to dusk, Eliana was taken to a room to meet Lucas, her estranged husband, for ten years! Her heart was beating fast, and the ten years to her suddenly became like a few days before. *What if Lucas changed his mind as soon as he saw her? What should she do as soon as she saw him? Kneel and beg? Begin to cry and grovel?*

She was so grateful for the seven escorts accompanying her: Father Benjamin and his wife, Mother Tamara, Mother Abigail, Mother Ahuva, Mother Rachel (her mother), and Father Simeon. Their presence gave her confidence. She was too ashamed of her deception in the past and suddenly felt afraid. She did not want to experience rejection in front of all these escorts. So, she stopped.

'Come on, Eliana. Trust Abba. The Lord Jesus has already got it all sorted out. Don't be scared,' Mother Ahuva encouraged.

'He might have come to his senses and changed his mind.'

'No, he has not.'

'Should I kneel as soon...?'

Time stood still for her as she approached and saw Lucas in front of her. Time shifted in three seconds, and the next thing she knew, he had run to embrace her, full of emotions and asking for her forgiveness!! This was totally unexpected. Her carefully rehearsed speech prepared for Lucas was stolen from her brain. She begged her brain, but it seemed to have deserted her and made her seem like a zombie who could not talk. A lifeline was offered to her.

Lord Jesus. Lord Jesus, help me. Still, she found herself speechless. Not only had Lucas stolen her lines, but he had also stolen her actions. She saw him kneel and heard him say,

'Dinah, please forgive me. If I had not thrown you out, you would not have returned to your past. Can you forgive me for my error? Who was I to judge you? I have not prospered since both you and Levi left my house...'

She knew she was too overcome with emotion to hear Lucas. It was her heart rhythm that she kept hearing as it pounded away furiously within her chest. Like one watching events in a dream, she saw her hands put into Lucas's and a white cloth tied around their hands. She was never conscious of when she nodded to signal her forgiving Lucas or consenting to their reconciliation.

She was reconciled to her husband Lucas after ten years!! She hoped it was not a dream...

Even while contemplating what to say or do next, she heard Father Benjamin's voice:

'Eliana. There is someone here from your past who wants to say something to you.'

Eliana looked around as she heard her mother gasp and say, *'Emunah!'* She knew instinctively who the tall, handsome man holding Levi by hand was. He instantly dropped to his knees before her, Levi and Lucas.

'I am Asher, your father. Can you forgive me? I am responsible for the family going apart. I am responsible for the life you led and all the pain and suffering you have gone through for 30 years. I am very sorry, and I have apologised to your mother. Please, forgive me.'

'Papa! Please, stand up. I have forgiven you. You don't know how much I have wanted to say "Papa". I forgive you with all my heart. Razi, a friend, once told me that the gift of Abba brings no sorrow. You are a gift to me, Papa, and I thank God for this reunion. I am overwhelmed with joy.'

She watched as her father stood up and gave Levi and herself a long, warm embrace amidst the cheering of their family. Asher broke his embrace to give Lucas the opportunity to embrace Levi and herself together. She had to remind herself that Ariel was no longer her little brother but Levi, her son! She could feel her heart beating fast, and she prayed her legs would continue to support her. Speech was completely absent, and she was only conscious that her cloudy eyes dripped tears ceaselessly onto her face. *Are my husband and son crying too? The sniffs I hear are they from my parents? Levi? Abba, You love me so, so much. You have drowned 30 years in the joy of one single day!!*

'Blessed be the name of Abba for this miracle,' Mother Ahuva said as Father Asher hugged Lucas in turn and then took his hands and his daughter's hands in his and blessed them in a solemn voice and wet eyes.

'May God, who has done this miracle of reconciliation and reunion, preserve you both from all evil.'

'Amen,' everyone agreed.

'Before the rest of us disperse from here and leave Father Asher and Mother Rachel time to themselves as well as Lucas, Eliana, and Levi to catch up on time, I would like to pray with you all. Please, join your hands together.

Dear Abba, we come boldly before you because we believe You are the Almighty and Everlasting God who loves us so much. You have shown us today that nothing is too hard for You to do. It is your pleasure that we are blessed by your gift of Your Son, Lord Jesus, through whom we are enjoying salvation. We are so unworthy, but You still love us.

Thank You, Abba, for choosing us to be a people for Your own possession out of all the peoples on earth. Help us to always remember this. Thank you for the grace that has enabled us all here to be saved through our faith in the Lord Jesus. Thank you for the grace that has helped us forgive one another. Thank you for Your compassion and presence, which have made it possible for us all to be here today.

By the power of Your Word, through the Lord Jesus, we have been reconciled, restored, redeemed, released, rescued, and reunited with you in hope, love, mercy, and grace for evermore. You have turned the evil from the enemy for our good. We are no longer captives of the devil. Thank you, Abba, for sending the Lord

Jesus to set the captives free. We promise that our children and their generations will learn of Your faithfulness to us this day.

As You have given Asher, Rachel, Lucas, and Eliana a second chance at marital love, we pray for Your mercy and power that they will continue to live in blessed harmony free from all blame, guilt, worry, and accusation that the devil might try to use to destroy their chance of peace and love. And may You, oh God of hope, fill us all with Your Shalom. We pray in the name of Jesus. Amen.'

'Amen,' everyone said with Levi's voice dragging longer.

Chapter Eighty

Jesus did many things as well. If every one of them were written down, I suppose that even the whole world would not have room for the books that were written (John 21:25).

Then some of Abba's angels hovered above the earth in their zillions, communicating the thoughts of the Lord. They knew full well that they were words of life for designated men, women, and children from every city the Lord Jesus visited, was visiting, and would visit.

Courage: For you did not receive a spirit that makes you a slave again to fear, but you received the spirit of sonship. And by him, "we cry, Abba, Father."

Guidance: If you wander off the road to the right or the left, you will hear His voice behind you saying, "Here is the road. Follow it."

Wisdom: Remember Abba in everything you do, and He will show you the right way.

Praise: How awesome is the Lord Most High, the great King over all the earth!

Confidence: We say this because we have confidence in God through Jesus Christ.

Hope: May Abba God, the source of hope, fill you with all joy and peace by means of your faith in Him, so that your hope will continue to grow by the power of the Holy Spirit.

Love: The Lord is good to all; He has compassion on all He has made.

Gratitude: Give thanks to the God of gods; His love endures forever.

Help: Hear O Lord and be merciful to me; O Lord, be my help.

Salvation: He gave us His life to free us from sin and every uncleanliness.

Wisdom: In Him lie all the treasures of wisdom and knowledge.

Salvation: In Him we have redemption through His blood.

Love: Come to Me, all of you who are weary and carry heavy burdens and I will give you rest.

Deliverance: For even the Son of Man did not come to be served, but to serve and give His life as a ransom for many.

Deliverance: But now you have been united with Christ Jesus. Once you were far away from God, but now, you have been brought near to Him through the blood of Christ.

The way Levi's amen had lingered on at the end of Father Benjamin's prayers had registered mused expressions amongst the adults, but it had made both his mother and grandmother exchange quick unspoken conversations with their eyes:

Rachel: *Looks like our marriages are separating us again. Don't be nervous with your husband.*

Eliana: *I know. There we go again, Mama! Please, don't blow it with Papa.*

Her mother smiled back at her as Ahuva took charge of Levi. Then, as others in the room made to leave, she saw her parents go into an enclosed space while she and Lucas were taken to the upper chamber. Razi or Johana had said something about this room, but she could not concentrate clearly. She wanted to look Lucas deep in the eyes and discern if the ten years between them had completely deleted the perfect love they once shared.

'Dinah? Do you mind if I call you by that name?'

The tone of his voice and the piercing looks of love he gave her eroded all her doubts and bridged the ten years between them. Their love for one another was catapulted from the past to the present, and she felt at ease slipping into her Dinah persona.

'Dinah, we are going to start clean as if those ten years are non-existent, as if our deep love has always bound us.' He came nearer her and embraced her. He did not give her a chance to talk, as his mouth found hers in a fierce embrace. She knew then that Dinah was free. *What about the others—Miriam, Safirah, Reubena, and Eliana?*

Were they all free now if the past was just to be buried like that? For now, she felt happy to live in the present and take each day as it comes. Today was love between Dinah and Lucas. After a brief fondling with each other as they trod on the familiar road of their intimacy, she broke off.

'My lord?'

'My love?'

'I never stopped thinking of you and the love we shared. I never forgot it. It was what enabled me to know that love was not the same as lust.'

'Shh, my love. Leave the past where it belongs, even with Levi. He doesn't need to be bothered with details of our past. We were lost, and we found each other again. That will do for a little boy.'

She was back in his arms as they both listened to the throbs of their hearts.

I disagree with you there. It is not wise to drag things under the mat. One day, it will all come out...

But this was Dinah: ever wanting to please, always acquiescing, never disagreeing, very grateful to be a wife and looking to hold on to his love at any cost. There was nothing her Miriam persona could do for now. Still, in his tight embrace, she held on to him as he, too, held her tightly. He held the call card. She waited. He kissed her tenderly again this time and released her.

'Are you happy to move back with me this weekend, in Sidon? You don't have to pack all your things in one go.'

This was a question for Miriam, not Dinah, Reubena, or the other two.

'My lord, Sidon is the past you want us to be far from. We can relinquish one of the properties in Jerusalem here that the Lord has blessed us with. It should be ready for us all within two weeks if we hire workers to start work.'

With a smile that hid his thoughts, her husband simply agreed. 'That is fine, but I want to be with you this night.'

'My lord. My old house has been cleaned out and is perfect for family life. I can stay there temporarily.'

'Dinah, that pleases me. Let us go and get Levi before he thinks we have forgotten him. It will be best he stays with his grandmother this night.'

'Yes, my lord.'

'Thank you, Ahuva. Levi, you be a good boy,' Rachel called out after them as she followed nervously with Asher into an empty enclosed space pointed out for their use. She suddenly felt tongue-tied, but Asher saved her all the trouble.

'How have you been, Rachel? I must say you look great!'

She didn't think so but accepted the compliments. 'Thank you. I can say the same about you as well.'

'Dan thinks so too.'

'Yes. You have done well with raising fine sons. I am sorry about your late wife.'

'Tisha. I never knew I would be able to move on after her death. God is merciful. He has brought you back at a time when there was a void in my life. When will you be coming over?'

'Soon.'

'If I know how soon, I will tell Dan and Tobias to help you with packing stuff.'

'Thank you.'

'Rachel. I want you to know that despite all the evil I did to you and our daughter, you have nevertheless found a way to forgive and accept to return to our home.'

'I have forgiven you. Let the hatchet remain buried, please, so that neither of us gets hurt by it.'

He held her hands.

'You are still beautiful, Rachel. I hope we can both start on a new clean page of peace and love.'

'*Emunah.*'

She did not smile, either in her eyes or her mouth. He released her hands from his.

Asher shook his head faintly. *Emunah*! Faith. It would take only faith in Abba to return to what they shared thirty years ago. Right now, they were like strangers. He looked at his wife, and she looked back but didn't smile. He took a deep breath and remained silent. In times like this, silence was a healer, a rebuilder of broken marital walls, and it paved the way for reflection to set in while bitterness and anger were released out of the body.

As the silence wore on, she remembered something. She decided to test his sincerity.

'Asher?'

'Yes, Rachel.'

'Why did you leave Nain?'

He knew she was testing him. It was a tough question that would expose more of his evil nature of the past. After some painful seconds of doubt, he decided to be honestly open.

'I was still evil in my nature, Rachel. I thought you had died. Your resurfacing at the burial brought all my guilt from my past sins upon me. So, I ran from you, hoping our paths would never cross again. I even changed my name to Uriah.'

'I guessed as much.'

'No one can ever phantom the mind of Abba. His plans for our lives will always be accomplished. In the books of God, it says that whoever forsakes and confesses his sins will have mercy. Abba has been so merciful. But like you said, Rachel, let us bury the hatchet. I would like you to come for dinner with me. Then I could also show you around the house and the family before you fully come over. My room is clean and spacious, with a massive bed. You will be comfortable spending the night with me; you don't need to rush away. It is your home now, and I am your husband. Am I not?' He reclaimed her hand in his again as he watched her with tenderness. Lifting her chin, he could get her to look into his eyes.

That singular action reminded Rachel of the intimacy between a husband and a wife. Her heart softened as she saw the tenderness and intimacy in Asher's eyes. She blushed as a smile lit up her face. His eyes became magnets that drew hers into his, and there they got hypnotised in a lover's lock. She felt the force of his love grip her heart, and its hard crusts melted like candle wax. Warmth flooded her heart until it swelled, swollen with love for her husband. As her eyes shut in shyness, Asher found her lips with his. First, tentatively, his lips teased hers, daring and luring them into an adventure. Then, her lips succumbed and yielded completely into his as she drew her arms around Asher.

Asher would not need an answer to his question. Instead, her actions were loud and clear.

Chapter Eighty-One

It is finished (John 19:30)

*I am the Light of the world. If you follow Me, you
won't have to walk in darkness because you will have
the light that leads to life (John 8:12)*

The New Year was into its first quarter, and Eliana—Mary still marvelled at how the year was moving on as she laid on their bed beside Lucas, her husband. Her mother, Rachel, said she was born in June. That would make her 30 years old!! What had woken her up? She felt it again and put her arm over her tummy, where she had first felt the flutter of life growing in her. She tried to sleep again, but she was overwhelmed with a sickening fear by everything happening in Jerusalem. House fellowships like the Bethel Centre ran secretly so that the Roman authorities and Jews who were not believers of the new faith would not persecute the Lord's followers.

In support of the Jewish elders and scribes, the Roman authorities made plots to arrest the Lord Jesus! So, Amina and Nebo, who had visited them the day before, mentioned. They heard the news from Father Benjamin and his wife, Mother Tamar. Her thoughts briefly touched on the overwhelming ways the Lord's life had affected so many people's lives, including hers, in his three years of ministry. She learnt he had been sent the message not to come into Jerusalem for the Passover; it was not safe. She thanked Abba in her heart for such faithful friends that supported the Lord Jesus. They would ensure he kept away from danger and remained in safety. Then her thoughts shifted back to her own life.

How magical it had felt when she was being reconciled to her husband four months ago. Their lives had continued from where it had stopped, as if there had been no interlude. Their love for each other was purer and fiercer than it had ever been, and each shared their years away from the other in regret. Eliana realised she might never have met her parents or reconciled with her child and husband if she had not known the Lord Jesus!! Lucas, too, had once mentioned to her he now knew he would never have discovered the true personality of his wife and understood the grace and peace of the new faith that the Lord Jesus offered his followers. They both swore that no force on earth would ever come between them till death did them apart. Their son, Levi, was so clever and joyously looked forward to having a sibling. It was a happy ending to a story, Eliana thought, but she discerned that there would be storms ahead as she and Lucas started their journey afresh together.

It had been Lucas's idea for the family to live in a different home. Her mother minded the shop in the daytime. Her father, Asher, had two sons who were married with children. She had met them and their families. Her being very active at the Bethel Centre in the evenings enabled her to know most families and their kids. This had benefitted Levi, too. She felt the fluttering again. She knew she was carrying twins. The Lord had said she would have double blessings. Lucas pampered her so much. As if on cue, he put his arm protectively around her. Soon, her mind became quiet.

Chapter Eighty-Two

I will proclaim His greatness by giving Him thanks
(Psalm 69:30b)

ollowers of the Lord Jesus continued to come once a week to share news of their progress in their faith, testimonies of new converts in their families, and to receive counsel to the problems encountered because of their new faith—the accepted way of life as the Lord Jesus professed as opposed to the hypocritical teachings of religious elders. Also, these days, people mostly wanted to hear how the Lord Jesus was tackling the vehement opposition to his ministry. Followers of the new faith were severely persecuted and considered a threat to the Roman authority and the orthodox Jews.

Amina was glad to see her Jerusalem family every week. She was excited that, like she was, Eliana and Biliah were both pregnant. She prayed others would not have to wait so long that all their children would grow up together as playmates. She was particularly excited that Razi would get married in a fortnight. At the Bethel Centre, she saw that Mother Rachel and Mother Abigail always sat together. She was sure they exchanged information and updated each other about their families. Amina learnt Eliana was particularly glad for Jacob's attachment to their family. Eliana also blessed a lot of poor people with money gifts.

Amina set her mind back to the happenings in Jerusalem. There were so many testimonies of the Lord and what he had done for so many people that it didn't make sense to hear that there were plans afoot to arrest him. What had he done?

During the Passover week, Eliana marvelled that so many people were coming to the Bethel Centre, and many had to stand outside for lack of space. As the Lord Jesus was in Jerusalem, as well, people from Bethany and all the Judea and Jordan regions came to Jerusalem to get blessed. Like everyone else, she prayed that the Lord Jesus would be safe and share bread with his enemies so that their hearts would be changed for good. She was confident of his victory over his enemies because he had shared bread twice before, and many evil hearts had changed for the best. Many others prayed he would be made king and free the Jews from the authority of the Romans. They trusted Abba's favour upon his life and in his powers to do such miracles. His followers were in high expectation. Their prayers had been answered: the Lord Jesus came for the Passover, riding on a donkey but hailed like a king on Jerusalem streets.

Judas, one of his followers, had passed word around that the Lord Jesus would be crowned the king of the Jews. Eliana and her family of believers heard the message. After the fellowship at the Bethel Centre, it was announced that the streets right up from the Northern Gates that led from that end of Jerusalem to the temple would be lined with cloth and flowers for the Lord Jesus. Members were encouraged to adorn their apparel in honour of the Lord Jesus.

To Eliana, everyone, it seemed, who had been touched through the miracle of receiving sight, speech, hearing, or healing in their bodies and their lives were out there. Also, all those who had been freed from demons, mental illness, leprosy, and all manner of ailments were out there. Many others who had been transformed with the renewing of their minds through his sermons, food sharing, counselling, and laying on of hands were all there as well. It was a motley crowd that blessed the sight! They all sang:

"Hosanna! Blessed is he who comes in the name of the Lord; blessed is the coming kingdom of our Father David."

Eliana saw she was among the wealthy others like Johana, Biliah, Mary Magdalene, and Josef that spread out rich silk and velvet cloths and cloaks to give the Lord Jesus a red-carpet entry through the town and into the Jerusalem Temple. The thick throng of people from all over Jerusalem excited many, like Father Sosthenes.

'This is what we Jews have been waiting for! At long last!! Our King! The King of the Jews and the end of all Roman domination!' cheered an excited Father Sosthenes amid joyous and eager brethren.

'Very true,' agreed Father Lucas. 'Lord Jesus is King of the world.'

'Caesar is no equal. He has no divine powers like the Lord Jesus!'

'He hasn't even one miracle to his name!' laughed Lucas.

'We Jews can't wait for our Lord to take over the throne of our Father David!! It is high time,' Jephthah added.

'Oh, what a happy day!' Father Lucas said, 'now, Eliana and Razi will change their opinions about the ministry of the Lord Jesus.'

'How do you mean?' Josef asked out of curiosity.

'They said that the Lord Jesus often claimed that he was not here for any earthly throne. He just wanted to show people the way to God.'

'Oh yes, I heard that,' Josef confirmed. 'We are all going to help him become king. No one else deserves that honour. Lord Jesus is God on earth!'

Chapter Eighty-Three

Do not let your heart be troubled. If you believe in God
also believe in me (John 14:1)

The Lord Jesus' arrest on the following day, early in the morning, took all his friends, helpers, and followers by surprise at the Bethel Centre. Father Benjamin was sure of this as he himself had felt shocked beyond belief. It was so unexpected!! Word went round fast that the Lord had been betrayed by one of his own disciples—Judas! He was one of the selected 12 disciples who went around with him, helping to evangelise Judea about the good news of the Kingdom of Abba God in heaven! It was passed around that Judas Iscariot had led several Roman soldiers to the Garden of Gethsemane, where the Lord Jesus had been praying in earnest with his disciples. Brother James had informed the brethren on the evening of his arrest, mentioning that the Lord Jesus had told them his time on earth was up.

Father Benjamin urged brethren to remain prayerful as they had all been distressed to further learn how his own devoted disciples had fled in fear because they saw many armed soldiers. What was most fearful and unbelieving, which broke the believer's confidence, was that the Lord Jesus was captured without any protest, argument, or a fight from him. He was taken to the various Roman authorities, where he was charged falsely with trying to overthrow the Roman government. Yet, he had remained like one bewitched by some Magi, as he had remained absolutely silent and mute!!!

Brother James had marvelled at what Razi had said, which had given the assembled brethren a ray of hope. She was indeed a woman blessed with the wisdom of Abba:

'My brethren, please remember that the Lord Jesus did not come to reign as an earthly king or start a new religion, but to show us all how to have an intimate relationship with Abba.'

Eventually, the Lord Jesus was crucified on a Friday morning…

Chapter Eighty-Four

You are the people of God. He loved you and chose you for His own. So then you must clothe yourselves with compassion, kindness, humility, gentleness and patience (Colossians 3:12).

Near the cross stood many of the brethren from the Bethel Centre, family members, faithful followers and friends, loyal disciples, and some people whose lives the Lord Jesus had touched in various ways. The Lord Jesus was still alive, and people still expected some sort of miracle to happen that would end the Roman rule in Israel. Instead, from the cross, everyone heard him say, 'Dear mother, John is your son now. John, take my mother to your home. From now on, she is your mother.'

In tears, Levi said to his grandmother, 'Look Grandma, he is still fixing families from the cross.' Mother Rachel squeezed his hands softly.

In his spirit, the Lord smiled at what Levi had said. He looked sadly at all his friends and the people he was leaving behind. He saw the trouble ahead for his disciples. In his spirit, he prayed to Abba:

Dear Abba,

I have obeyed You: sacrificed myself so that all those who believe in You and me will have eternal life. I am coming to You now. Thank you for granting me favour, honour, power, and authority while I was in the world.

Thank you for the helpers You gave me. They were very obedient, courageous, hardworking, and loyal, except Judas, who betrayed me at the end. I taught them everything about You and Your kingdom. Please, protect all my followers, their families, and the new believers who remain in the world after I have gone.

I also pray for anyone who will believe in You through hearing the message about You or testimony.

Let the love You have for me be theirs too. Amen.

Chapter Eighty-Five

I am He that Lives and was dead and buried and now I am alive (Revelation 1:18a).

All the angels in heaven were in wild ecstasy as they sang:

Praise the Lord, you His angels—you mighty ones who do His bidding, who obey His word!

Praise the Lord! Praise the Lord from the heavens: Praise Him in the heights! Praise Him all His angels; Praise Him all His heavenly hosts!

Three days ago, there had been pregnant silence, and His angels were waiting in tension and anticipation of Abba's plans: the enemy had taken the life of Abba's precious son—Lord Jesus. But today, the situation was different! By the power of the Holy Spirit of Abba, the Lord Jesus had conquered the spirit of Death and was resurrected to life. From heaven, they watched Him materialise from the grave in His spirit form and walk out towards Galilee in His human form!! Abba then created an earthquake that shook the earth to accomplish His purpose. As the earthquake clamoured in Judea, Abba sent Angel Harbinger to roll away the big heavy stone that was guarding the empty tomb of the Lord Jesus. As He arrived in His invisible form, He saw eight Roman guards guarding the tomb. They were well-armed, and two of them had a sharp sword in their girth. It wasn't the appointed time to roll the stone and make His presence felt. So, He waited...

That same morning, Eliana found herself suddenly awoken! This was the day that the Lord Jesus was believed by many of His followers to rise from the dead! She could not see the daylight of Sunday yet, but soon, she heard the sound that must have awoken her. *Storms that shook the whole land!* She felt the vibrations in her house. She stood up at once. She was alone. She had come to her old home to sort out some of her stuff. She had moved to join Lucas and Levi in a new home. Lucas was against the family starting in this house where she had been Miriam. She heard the storms again. It was likely to be an earthquake. There was no way she could sleep. She stood up to pray:

Abba Father, You have always answered my prayers. I pray for the Lord Jesus. Help Him rise from the dead as You helped Lazarus rise from the dead. Today is the day, Abba. Let all the people from every nation believe He is the Messiah just as people believed Him when they all heard the testimony of Mother Ahuva in Samaria. The Lord Jesus told her He was the Messiah! Abba, I believe. And Abba, please, I pray that our faiths will never fail no matter what happens.

Let my ears hear the good news that He has risen today!!

Also, please protect all the brethren from the Centre who will be braving this weather and the danger from the Roman guards. Please, send your angels to keep all the Roman guards tame as You tamed the lions in Daniel's den.

Abba, I cannot stop thanking You every day for finding my son and my parents and for resurrecting my life and marriage from the dead. Abba, I thank you for this Sunday because You have resurrected the Lord

Jesus from the grave, and the tomb is empty. Please, keep the earthquake still so that the disciples and brethren will have no difficulty going to the tomb. Thank You, Abba, for the hope You give us all.

Thank You, Abba. It is because of the Lord Jesus that You have already heard and responded to my prayers.

I have prayed in the Lord Jesus's name. Amen.

That same morning, Razi was awake. The sound of some terrible thunder disturbed her sleep, which had sent vibrations that shook her whole house. It might have been from the Dead Sea, which was 13 miles away from Jerusalem. She marvelled at its impact. It reminded her of the fact that though the Lord Jesus had been crucified on Friday morning, there had been darkness all over the land for three hours! It was still very early dawn, and Jerusalem was still asleep, but the thunder would wake everyone up. She heard the strong rumbles of the thunder again and knew that it must have aroused and heightened the curiosity and fear of many followers of the Lord Jesus, especially His disciples. She hoped they were keeping prayerful. She also hoped His followers remembered that the Lord Jesus said He would wake up from the dead three days after He had been buried.

This was the third day, and she felt anxiety mixed with great anticipation. It was a Sunday. May be like what happened on Friday; the earthquake could signify that the Lord has risen from death! She knew she was probably one of the very few who actually believed that the Lord would rise from the dead. She had been a witness to the miracle of Lazarus being raised from the dead after three days!! Another woman who, like herself, would believe was Mary, the sister of Lazarus; not because of the miracle done to her brother, but she possessed a childlike spirit. She hung on every word that the Lord said literally!

Mother Mary Magdalene was also like that. Right now, she knew both Marys were together. Mary Magdalene had not left for Bethany, where she lived. At the Bethel Centre the previous day, where some of them had all met secretly for prayers, Mary Magdalene had let a few people know her plans that she would visit the Lord's tomb this morning. She had been strongly warned because guards were ready to kill any trespassers.

She would not be surprised if Mary Magdalene followed on her word. She was sometimes radical and impulsive in her faith. All the same, Razi found herself getting up; she was going to the Centre. All those who believed that the Lord Jesus would rise would come firstly here for prayers. Father James, the Lord's brother, advised brethren to come to the Centre for prayers. This was one occasion she was grateful she was not yet married and lived alone. A week more, and it would not have been possible! There was no husband or family member to prevent her from stepping out in this stormy weather. She was sure that if she had been already married, Josef would not let her step out. Many guards were purported to be patrolling the streets on the lookout for troublemakers and followers of the Lord Jesus. Within minutes of the waning dawn, she was at the centre and very grateful. It had been so windy, and the earthquake's vibrations could be felt under her feet as she trod her steps carefully on the ground. She was startled by some noise as she got to the Bethel Centre. It was dark, lonely, and no evidence of anyone awake in the upper base where Father Jarius' family lived, who had given up the lower basement of the building for fellowship meetings on Fridays.

Chapter Eighty-Six

So we will not be afraid, even if the earth is shaken
and mountains fall into the ocean depths
(Psalm 46:2).

Two women came out from the shadows.

'Shalom, Razi,' they both greeted in hushed tones.

'Shalom! Thank goodness it is you both,' she whispered. 'I knew you would definitely come out here. You said you would.'

'It is just the two of us for now; Martha said she would wait with the other followers in the upper room to pray. I had to persuade Mary to follow me here instead,' Mary Magdalene spoke.

'Yes, Razi. I thought we should join others in the Upper Room, but you know Mary Mag. Once she has made up her mind, there is no taking a no for an answer. We were just about to start off to Golgotha,' Mary confirmed.

'We have wasted enough time waiting. Let us go,' Mary Magdalene said with an impatient tone. 'I am sure my Lord is out of the grave. Let us hurry before the city stirs,' she urged as she led the way in hurried steps towards Golgotha.

Razi was grateful that the lightning streaks made their paths easier to see. She and her companions walked fast, but quietly. They did not speak to one another. The events that led to the gruesome death by crucifixion, including how the Lord had suffered on Friday, were still foremost in her mind. Like her, she was sure that each of the others wondered what would await them at the tomb. The mere thought of where they were going made her heart beat faster.

Just before they reached the tomb area, Mary halted the group.

'I am surprised that there are no guards here. Where could they be?'

'The earthquake must have scared them,' Mary Magdalene answered. 'Let us wait here. It won't be long now.'

They did. Soon, the cocks had begun to crow, but the sun was still asleep. The air felt crisp and cold, and Razi was grateful for the thick shawl she had on. She became tensed as she and the others heard approaching steps; however, she was glad to recognise some members of the ministerial team she had been part of before moving to Jerusalem.

'Shalom,' the newcomers greeted.

'Shalom,' she replied with others.

Razi realised she was the youngest in the group as she was being embraced quietly by Mother Salome, Mother Johana, and Mother Susanna. She had missed their company. She debated in a second against sharing the news of her secret betrothal. She would testify at the right time. Soon, they were all sober again as they waited apprehensively behind the bush. An hour later of patient waiting, the sun began to peep out, heralded by the melodious singing of early morning birds. Their music filled the air and atmosphere, creating a soothing effect on their moods. To Razi, this was symbolic. The birds were trying to tell them something.

'Let us go now. The birds are already rejoicing,' Mother Mary, the mother of James, said lightly.

'Razi, Johana and Susanna, please wait here and be on the lookout. Even if the guards see Mary or me, they will not want to bother with mature women like us. But young and beautiful women like you lot could bring harm to yourselves. Mary, let us go,' Mary Magdalene urged.

Razi watched them go until they went over the bend, where they could not be seen from their hiding place.

Chapter Eighty-Seven

*You shall walk in all the way that the Lord your God
has commanded you; that it may be well with you
(Deuteronomy 5:33).*

'Do you think our Lord is alive, Mary Mag?'

'We shall see when we get to the tomb.'

'But there is that big stone. Remember?'

'What is that bright light around the stone protecting the tomb?'

'Ssh, we shall see when we get nearer the tomb,' Mary Mag said, quickening her steps.

'Mary Mag, please hold my hands,' she whispered.

Both women first saw the guards swooning in a faint, and they realised why in a split second. The brightness of the light intensified as the stone, effortlessly on its own, shifted aside. An angel suddenly materialised and sat on it.

Razi and her group heard Mother Mary scream, and they rushed out from the bushes to see what was happening.

Immediately, Razi and her group saw the eight guards standing speechless, looking so frightened but making no move to harm or arrest any of them. In the next second, their eyes alighted on the winged human form sitting on the stone. Razi and her troupe screamed at the sight of the angel, not because they were scared but more startled that their Lord had been transformed into what they saw!! Each person experienced the titillating effect of the angel's presence. He radiated goodwill and benevolence, even though his presence created flashes of lightning that seemed to reverberate.

'Shalom, ladies. Please, don't be afraid. As you all can see, the stone has been rolled away, and your Lord is not here.'

'Then where is my Lord? Where has He gone? I know He has risen!' Mary Mag said boldly while the angel remained silent with a smile.

'Please, dear Angel, what have the guards done to the body of our Lord?' Razi asked with a heavy heart. She could hear the hushed sobbing sounds of the other women around her. They were obviously confused.

Angel Harbinger sat on the stone, toying with their minds. Where was their faith? He decided to address Mary Mag.

'Why do you all look so worried and fearful? He told you He would rise today. Did He not? Well, Abba, His Father, has raised Him from the dead and restored His life! Your Lord has risen!!! Go and tell Peter and His disciples.'

Razi and the rest of her companions began to sing, clap, jump up and down, embracing one another in ecstasy while the guards, zombie-liked, watched on helplessly. They heard and understood what had happened and was happening, but they had lost their will to do anything to any of them in the face of the angel before them. Razi and her companions were astonished at this. These Roman guards were also witnesses!

'Where did He go? We want to see Him!!' Razi and Mary Mag said together.

'Go to Galilee. You will see Him.'

'Thank you for this most wonderful news.'

'Now, hurry and go before the guards fully come to their senses.'

Razi and her troupe rushed out of the tomb, all singing their different praises. The angel would ensure the guards did not harm them until they were far away from hurt and danger. Angel Harbinger could hear the host of angels from heaven singing songs that Abba had placed in their thoughts, which would, at the set time, be sung by people on earth. As he joined in the singing, some angels came to join him below:

My soul glorifies the Lord,

And my spirit praises His name,

Even death could not hold Him captive,

Even in the grave,

Jesus is Lord!!

Love: For God so loved the world so much that He gave His only son, so that everyone who believes in Him may not die but have eternal life.

Love: Greater love has no one than this that He lay down His life for His friends - John 15:13.

Salvation: For He has rescued us from the dominion of darkness and brought us into the kingdom of His Son He loves – Colossians 1:13.

Peace: Peace is what I leave with you; it is my own peace that I give you. I do not give it as the world does; do not be worried and upset; do not be afraid – John 14:27.

Love: And being found in appearance as a man, He humbled Himself and became obedient to death on a cross – Philippians 2:8

Before the angels left, they listened to Razi's song as they danced alongside her:

The earthquake woke me up,

My heart said, go to the tomb

My soul lent me strength

My will lent me courage

My spirit carried my flesh

My feet carried me to the tomb

My eyes have seen the empty tomb

My ears have heard the miraculous of all wonders and mysteries:

My Lord is risen!

He has the victory

He has gone before me,

My Lord is Abba!!

Razi's first thought was to get to the Centre and tell everyone, but Mary the Mag took control.

Breathlessly, she said, 'Let us all go and share what we have heard this morning. I will go to Galilee to tell the disciples. Razi, go to the Bethel Centre and tell our brethren there. Salome and Mary, go and tell the Lord's mother and tell her that her son has risen from the dead...'

As Mary Magdalene was going towards Galilee, she thanked God that the earthquake had not discouraged her from visiting the Lord's tomb that early morning. She could feel herself visibly shaken. She remembered their initial worry about who would roll away the big stone from the tomb!! She still held the expensive spices she had brought to anoint His body so that He would smell sweet as He rose from the dead! She had yet witnessed another miracle—the huge stone had been rolled away and the empty tomb. Then an angel of Abba had spoken of the Lord Jesus's victory over death!! None of them had died for seeing that angel who stood before God's face!!! *They even spoke to him!!!* Lord Jesus was Abba!! *The awaited Messiah.* Didn't Ahuva, the Samaritan woman, testify how the Lord Jesus had met her at the well and in love, changed her promiscuous personality? Ahuva had heard Him declare He was the Messiah. Now, she was a follower and a totally new creature!!

And herself? The Lord Jesus had cast out seven demons from her!! And today? She could boast that she was one of His most fervent followers, and she deeply cared and loved Him. She would never understand what had pulled her out that early morning into the earthquake and dangerous Jerusalem, dragging her poor hostess, James's mother! She would and was ready to die for her Lord if His body had been stolen. Someone broke into her thoughts, and she had been startled as she heard her name –

'Mary!'

'Raboni, Raboni!! It is my Abba, my Lord and God!! My Messiah,' she proclaimed in ecstasy as she rushed to embrace the Lord Jesus, but an invisible force stopped her in her tracks.

'Not yet, Mary Mag! Not with this body. I must go before Abba first. Go and tell my brethren to wait for Me in the Passover chamber. I will bless you all with the Holy Spirit. Go now, Mary, and be in peace...'

Three months later, the brethren at the Bethel Centre went into an uproar of joy when seven of the Lord's disciples stood at the front to testify in tears and joy how the Lord Jesus had appeared to them at Lake Tiberias when they had gone fishing with Peter. They testified He had helped them miraculously catch a great harvest of 153 big fish, prepared a fire, and brought bread for their breakfast, and they all had breakfast together. His message to them all was that He wanted them to spread the good news of His resurrection power over death and evil and to preach the hope of His return soon for all who have followed Him in truth as their Lord and Saviour.

The Bethel Centre adopted the sharing of bread and fish at every fellowship.

EPILOGUE -
Victory

I have the keys of hell and of death (Revelation 1:18b).

Deliverance: Abba has delivered and drawn us to Himself out of the control and the dominion of darkness and has transferred us into the kingdom of Abba, through His Son. Now, we have our redemption through His blood, [which means] the forgiveness of our sins and we are born again spiritually.

Courage: Fear not, for Abba has redeemed you; He has called you by your name; you are His.

Salvation: Though we were spiritually dead because of the things we did against God, He gave us new life with Christ. You have been saved by God's grace.

Eliana had a dream, and she remembered it when she woke up. It was her main desire. How Abba was going to bring it to happen, she did not know, but she believed it would happen soon. She recalled her dream as if watching a vision from the future.

The ladies of red had been told that Miriam, now Eliana, wanted to speak to them and offer them gifts. A date had been given, and word had gone round. Many of them had heard of the very wealthy woman who owned the famous 'Miriam's House of Pleasures'. Many came out of curiosity. Many had heard that she had changed her life. Some wanted to know how they could be saved from their present life. Some knew she was living the new life and wanted to see for themselves that she was free from the demons of lust, sexual addiction, and depravity. Others came to learn tricks and be blessed materially wise.

Eliana began by singing. The sight of her fellow colleagues still wallowing in ignorance and darkness and blind to the love, salvation, and deliverance of the Lord Jesus touched her deeply. She understood then how the Lord Jesus was always moved to compassion because He saw humans as people without sight, falling into all manner of pits and becoming helpless in their situations.

She remembered how she had felt all those years ago when there was no other way of survival. There was no hope, family, or friend. She had no future and had lived for what the present day brought. Yet, salvation and deliverance had come knocking on her door through Josef, Johana, and Razi. She had felt doubt, fear, and insecurity. Then she met the Lord Jesus; He delivered her and offered her salvation. He was gone, but He left something in them all to share with others like these...

She began to pray and sing at the same time:

Abba Father, Abba God, Abba my rescuer, Abba my helper; Abba, You are my real love. I have tasted You, and You are so so sweet. You have touched me, and You are a miracle. You saw my hard, cold, empty, and dead heart, making it soft, warm. You filled it with Yourself, and now I live in You.

There is darkness here, Abba; there is pain here, Abba; there is doubt here. Abba, Abba, my deliverer, show Yourself here.

Refrain: *Let there be light; let there be light; let there be light; let there be light...*

The angels in heaven also danced and sang in their rejoicing. Many on earth would be blessed by the song in their hearts and souls.

Eliana: I know God sent the Lord Jesus to find me. His grace has saved me, and I will never be lost again. I have come to let you know how to enjoy the love of our Lord Jesus.

Bibliography

- New Testament and Psalms Bible
- KJV Bible
- God our help in ages past – Isaac Watts [1708]
- Good News Bible
- Scripture Union Choruses – 5 Wigmore Street, London, WIH OAD [1925]

Printed in Great Britain
by Amazon